Rhapsody

Rhapsody

JANINE FRENCH

DOUBLEDAY & COMPANY, INC.

GARDEN CITY, NEW YORK

1986

All of the characters in this book
are fictitious, and any resemblance
to actual persons, living or dead,
is purely coincidental.

Library of Congress Cataloging-in-Publication Data

French, Janine.
Rhapsody.

I. Title.
PS3556.R417R5   1986   813'.54
ISBN 0-385-23565-8
Library of Congress Catalog Card Number 86–4424

First Edition

Rhapsody

CHAPTER 1

Kate Reston normally entered Meade Hall via a rear door accessible to the parking lot, but this April morning she found herself coming in through the entrance. It was closer to the dressmaker's, where Kate had gone after leaving her car. She had needed a final fitting for the navy blue crepe de chine gown she was to wear at Saturday's concert. The dressmaker had assured her that the gown would be finished in time and had gone on to say that though the garment was a veritable jewel, only Kate Reston could make that jewel glow like a sapphire.

Glow indeed, Kate thought wryly. Though other people found her very attractive—long black hair, blue eyes, a tall and slender figure—Kate herself was more objective about her looks. There were flaws aplenty, she knew, though she had rarely given them a thought because music had consumed so much of her time. Now, however, with her elevation to the position of temporary music director of the Whittenburg Symphony Orchestra, she was making an effort to look the part. This morning she was dressed in a tailored white linen suit which the saleswoman at Eisenberg's had assured her contrasted well with her raven hair.

Kate studied the concert hall looming before her. It was as though she were seeing it for the first time. The building was a white stone edifice whose Doric columns gave it an air of majesty. The temporary conductor's position had been Kate's since last month when the symphony's renowned director, Robert Bernini, had become ill. He was recovering now, and rumor had it that he'd be back in two weeks. In the meantime the glory was Kate's, and she was savoring it.

As Kate entered the concert hall, she came face-to-face with a man she had never seen before. He looked as though he was in his late thirties. Tall and lean with blond hair, tanned skin and eyes that seemed either hazel or green, he looked like an alpine skier—except for his suit, which was a conservative gray pinstripe. She wondered why this man was staring at her with such concentration. Whatever his reason, he stood there, his eyes piercing hers, his lips trembling with some unfathomable emotion. Kate lowered her head and when next she looked up he was descending the steps quickly with no glance backward. He strode across the street, indifferent to the traffic careening around him, stepped into a sleek black sports car and maneuvered into the line of vehicles.

Who was he? she wondered. Where was he going? And what had he seen in her face just now?

Still thinking about it, Kate walked through the heavy doors of Meade Hall and up the stairs to the director's office. Soon she was seated at her worn oak desk studying the list of things she had to do this morning. There were three cornet players coming in for a final audition. All were professionals, and quite good, and it would distress her to have to make a choice today. But she'd have to do it and be done with it. After the audition, she would have to decide what to do about the guitar soloist who had called yesterday to tell her that he'd cut his finger badly on some broken glass and would like his protégé to fill in for him. Should she accept the protégé or should she cancel the Rodrigo work, which depended on a solo guitar, and substitute—what?—a Rimsky-Korsakov? a Sibelius? It would have to be something with which the orchestra was familiar because there was only one rehearsal night left.

Harold Rawlins, a brilliant cellist who had wanted this temporary directorship himself, knocked discreetly and then walked into the office. "Kate," he said.

"Good morning."

"I trust I'm not disturbing you," he said.

"No. My audition isn't scheduled until half past ten."

"Good. I was wondering what decision you might have made about the guitarist who was to have played the Rodrigo."

"I was just wondering about that myself." She smiled, and Harold could not help smiling back. He was a short, squat, balding middle-aged man, and though his face was doughy enough to make him look soft and amiable, there was a sharpness in his small eyes and a downward tug to his otherwise shapeless mouth that belied his feigned conviviality.

Kate continued. "Maybe I ought to listen to the protégé. In fact I think I'll telephone him and ask if he can come to the hall today and perform. I want to make certain he can do the job."

Harold nodded and turned to another topic. "They tell me you're thinking about Beethoven's Third Piano Concerto in C Minor for the-second-week-of-May performance."

"Yes, I am."

"But, Kate, Beethoven was still in diapers when he wrote it."

"It's still a great work."

"Couldn't you have chosen the Fifth or the Seventh Symphony?"

"But we're always doing those," she said.

"People prefer music they're familiar with."

"But in order to become familiar with a piece, you have to hear it a first time," she rejoined.

"I'm reluctant to pursue this, Kate, because it might sound suspiciously like insubordination." He paused and took a deep breath. "Kate, you're still something of a college girl even if you are twenty-nine." In this way he was reminding her that though she had obtained a position in the orchestra because the director had considered her a fine pianist, she did not impress those musicians who were less concerned with educating audiences than with giving them what they wanted to hear. Harold continued, "You're not pragmatic enough. I think it was Toscanini who said that when an audience applauds wildly at a concert it's not the musicians they're cheering but themselves—for recognizing the work. If you choose the Fifth or the Seventh, Kate, listeners will be convinced that they are cultured. If you play the obscure C Minor Concerto they'll feel restless and uneducated."

The discussion continued for another fifteen minutes before Kate finally managed to get Harold to leave her office by assuring him that she would think about what he had said. She then telephoned the protégé of the disabled classical guitarist, set up an appointment and returned to her task of choosing the right pieces for the performance during the second week in May. Occasionally she would glance at the program for the Saturday night Pops. "Kate Reston conducting." The words never failed to excite her. How wonderful it would be if this post could be permanent. But Kate didn't ever dwell for long on might-have-beens. Except—

The picture of the man standing on the concert hall stairs this morning came to mind. Those eyes. What color had they been? Hazel? Green? She could not remember.

Harold knocked discreetly again and came back into the office. "I forgot to tell you, Kate, that the symphony's financial problems may have been temporarily alleviated."

"Oh?"

"Just before you came in, Blaine Eddington dropped by for a nostalgic visit to the hall. He hadn't been home to Pennsylvania, except for Christmas, in many years."

Kate nodded. Eddington, as everyone in Whittenburg knew, was a hometown boy who now ran Eddington Motors in Los Angeles. It was a well-known sports-car manufacturing company.

"He's come to build a factory here," Harold said. "To give work to his hometown people, I suppose."

"That's wonderful." Kate hadn't known Blaine Eddington when he'd lived here because he hadn't gone to the public schools and in any case he would be about seven years older than she. "Rather young to have had such success," she remarked. "Thirty-five or so?"

"Just about."

She had heard much about him, knew that he'd been written up in many periodicals, but she had no idea what he looked like and was not curious. She was impatient for Harold to get to the point. How had the symphony's financial problems been "temporarily alleviated" by Blaine Eddington?

Harold continued, as though hearing her thoughts, "Eddington had a grandfather who played the violin years ago when the symphony was young. He—"

Kate nodded. He must mean Sloan Wentworth Eddington, one of the greatest violinists of his time. Kate owned several of his recordings. They never failed to move her.

"Sloan Eddington," she said.

"Yes. And his grandson decided to endow the orchestra with a considerable sum. Wait until Malcolm hears about this." He was referring to the head of the symphony's board of directors.

"Maybe now it'll be possible to staff the orchestra more fully," Kate said.

Harold nodded. "And high time too."

He did not add what Kate was certain he was thinking: that for all to be truly perfect it should be he, not Kate, conducting the orchestra. Kate understood. In a way it was unfair. He'd been with the symphony fifteen years and she only four. It had been explained to Harold that, all other things being equal, directorships generally went to expert pianists who were more conversant with harmonics than single-instrument players tended to be. It had been explained, and Harold had nodded, but the news must have hurt, she thought, though only in his eyes did she ever detect any anger. He'd never betrayed himself in conversation.

And it wasn't as though her promotion were going to be permanent. By next month she'd be back at the piano. And when the director did retire, he might possibly decide on Harold as a successor. Should she explain this to Harold?

But he was talking again about Mr. Eddington.

"The sum he intends to give is staggering. It'll make our fund-raising dinner almost superfluous." He paused. "Mr. Eddington is a remarkable young man. Very dignified, soft-spoken. He didn't flourish his checkbook the way some might have done. He simply said that in memory of his grandfather he wanted to help the symphony. He's a handsome fellow too. Tall, tanned. What with the dark skin and the blond hair he looks rather like a photographic negative."

"Or an alpine skier?" Kate said, suddenly remembering the man on the steps of the hall.

"Yes. That's just what he reminded me of."

"What time did you say he came by?" Kate asked.

"Just before you arrived. Why?"

"I think I met him on the steps outside." She felt her cheeks flame.

Harold grinned. "Would it be presumptuous for me to ask if you were —what's the word?—smitten?"

"I thought he was most respectable-looking," she said archly, looking away.

When she looked up again, Harold was grinning. Or rather, she thought, leering. She shifted in her chair, acutely uncomfortable, resenting his ability to read her so easily. She raised her wrist, glanced at her watch and said, "The auditioning cornet players are due soon, so . . ."

He nodded.

"If you don't mind, Harold—" she began.

"Just one more matter and then I'll—"

The phone rang. Kate picked it up, brushed her thick black hair away from her ear and said, "Hello."

It was Malcolm Merriwether, the head of the board. "Are you sitting down, Kate?"

"With the weight of the Whittenburg sitting on my shoulders," she joked, "what else would I be doing?"

"Kate, Bob Bernini won't be coming back."

"Oh no! Is he worse?"

"No, he's much better, but this month off has given him a new perspective on life. He wants to travel. He wants to compose. He's even thought of writing his memoirs."

"Oh, then he's all right?" She exhaled in relief.

Rhapsody

"Naturally, his recommendation was that you take over permanently but of course not all on the board agreed with that. Some felt that Harold Rawlins, who is older and more experienced, ought to be given the post."

Kate's heart pounded.

"There was a good deal of argument. It went on all morning. But eventually—"

"Yes?" She could barely speak.

"To make the long story short—"

"Malcolm, please!"

"Congratulations, Maestro," he said softly. "Best wishes, my dear."

Kate started to cry. Harold, comprehending all, nodded slowly, murmured something gallant about the best candidate getting the job, and then left the office abruptly.

Over the phone Malcolm was saying, "We'll have a little reception for you Saturday night after the Pops."

"I can't believe it," she murmured. "I can't believe it . . ."

CHAPTER 2

The Pops concert had gone very well, although deep down Kate had known that it would. The new guitarist and the orchestra had meshed perfectly and none of Kate's worries had materialized.

The audience, many of whom knew that this was a special evening for Kate, gave her a standing ovation, and, following the concert, Kate returned to her dressing room. The backstage area of the concert hall was already filling up and though Kate knew she would have to greet people, she hoped they would give her at least a few moments for herself. She needed to change for the reception that Malcolm had planned for this evening, but, more important, she wanted to catch her breath. No matter how many concerts lay ahead of her, she knew that this one, her first as permanent conductor, would always stay with her.

Kate reached for the gown she had prepared, a white cocktail-length dress with a high neck and long sleeves, which accented her firm breasts, trim waist and slim hips. She was just smoothing out her hair when the first knock came at the door.

"Come in," Kate called.

"Kate, that was wonderful!" The chairman of the orchestra's board of directors, Malcolm Merriwether, walked across the small room and gave her a hug. "Some of the other board members might have had a tiny"— he wrinkled his nose to indicate that it was tiny indeed—"bit of doubt about hiring someone so young, but I knew that you were the one for the job."

"Thanks, Malcolm," Kate said. "I appreciate—"

Kate was interrupted by a group of people who walked in through the open dressing room door, among them several close friends.

"Kate, darling, you were wonderful. I always knew you would make it to the top!"

"That goes double for me," a young man echoed.

"Ahem!" Malcolm Merriwether, slowly being pushed out of the room, cleared his throat.

Kate turned to him. "I'm sorry about this crush of people, Malcolm, but . . ." She gestured with her arms, indicating helplessness.

"I know, my dear. And I want you to be able to greet all the people to whom you brought such pleasure this evening. But I want to remind you of the little reception we have planned for you later on. I'll be back to pick you up."

"Thanks. I won't forget." Kate then turned to the people who were crowding around her while Malcolm started to edge his way out the door.

For the next half hour people streamed in and out of Kate's dressing room. Some of them she had grown up with but others she knew only by sight—people who were important citizens of this southern Pennsylvania city. Though she was tired, Kate was buoyed by her enthusiastic reception.

At last the crowd thinned out and only several of Kate's neighbors were left. Malcolm Merriwether found his way back into the dressing room.

"Are you ready, my dear?" he said to Kate.

When the well-wishers had gone, Kate and Malcolm made their way out of the stage door of the old building. "We've taken one of the small dining rooms in the Lincoln Hotel. It's not a fancy affair. Just a way for you to get to know the board members and some of our backers a little bit better. And for them to get to know you."

Some of Kate's earlier nervousness returned. She knew most of the board members, casually perhaps; by name, however, she wasn't certain who all the backers were. She wondered if their support of the orchestra might depend on how a social evening went. As Kate and Malcolm stepped into his Cadillac, he turned to her. "Mrs. Merriwether wanted to be here tonight, but our youngest daughter had the poor sense of timing to have a baby just today. And for some reason, she preferred to spend the evening in the hospital with our daughter and our fourth grandchild." Malcolm tried to suppress a proud grin but failed.

"Congratulations, Malcolm. This is turning out to be a special day for everyone, isn't it?"

The ride to the hotel took only five minutes and Malcolm helped Kate out of the car. "We won't keep you long, my dear," he said. "But it's something of a tradition for the board of directors to have a little do after the first concert by a new conductor."

"It's a nice tradition," she said.

They entered the hotel and walked toward a closed door. Malcolm opened it with a flourish. "Here we are, ladies and gentlemen. I'd like to introduce the new conductor of the Whittenburg Symphony Orchestra—Kate Reston!"

There was applause as Kate stepped into the room. She took a deep breath and plunged into the crowd.

"Such a wonderful performance . . ."

"Your choices tonight were wonderful . . ."

"You certainly are a gifted young woman . . ."

Kate acknowledged the accolades with a smile and an occasional "Thank you very much." But for the most part she was given little chance to actually speak.

"Why don't we get Kate something to eat," Malcolm said, making his way through the crowd to her side.

"Yes, I'd like that," Kate said. "I'm hungry."

Malcolm led Kate to a table that contained tea sandwiches and some pastry. There was an urn of coffee at the end of the table.

"I've already checked this out," Malcolm said in conspiratorial tone. "Over there we have salmon, here are the cheeses and back there it's pâté." He looked directly at her. "And, with your figure, I'm sure you are still allowed to eat pastries. Look at that inviting napoleon." He patted his paunch. "The result of one napoleon too many," he said. "But please help yourself."

Kate looked at the sandwiches. She took an empty plate and was deciding which were the most appealing foods when she felt someone staring at her. She could not ignore the intensity of the gaze. She turned to see who was scrutinizing her so closely and came face-to-face with the man she had seen on the steps of Meade Hall earlier this week—Blaine Eddington.

On his face was the same incredulous look he had had when she had seen him before. She was not sure what she should do. Should she turn back to the sandwiches? Or should she acknowledge this man somehow?

Malcolm said, "Have you met Blaine Eddington yet?"

Blaine's expression changed from one of shock to one of friendly interest. "We have run into each other, yes, but we haven't been formally introduced."

"Well then, allow me to do the honors. Blaine, this is our new and I might add talented and brilliant conductor, Kate Reston. Kate, this is Blaine Eddington, a most generous supporter."

Kate extended her hand and Blaine took it. She felt a thrill shiver through her body at his touch and heat coursed into her cheeks.

Blaine did not seem to notice Kate's sudden lack of composure. "How do you do, Miss Reston?" he said in a deep bass voice.

"Mr. Eddington," Kate nodded. She felt tongue-tied. She was painfully aware of Blaine's overpowering male aftershave. His unforgettable green eyes seemed to be piercing through her.

"I would like to compliment you on a wonderful performance tonight, Miss Reston." He paused, the corners of his mouth turning into a sensuous half smile. "May I call you Kate?"

"Why, uh, of course," Kate responded, totally off balance, her heart thundering in her ears.

"And you must call me Blaine. After all, we shall probably be seeing a lot of each other."

Oh yes, she thought instinctively. Then, surprised at her own reaction, hoped that she hadn't actually mouthed the words. "A lot?" she managed to say.

"Of course. You are the leader of the Whittenburg and, since I help support it, I am one of the men behind the leader. *N'est-ce pas?*"

Kate offered a weak smile in response.

"And now, I'd like to know more about my leader," he said. "You must have had a lot of training to have attained such a position."

"Yes, I'm a graduate of the Boston Conservatory of Music," Kate said, glad to be on firm ground once again. "All during my high school years I studied under Jason Willoughby, who heads the music department at Gettysburg College. And then I—"

"Jason? He works at a college now?"

"Is he a friend of yours?"

"Not really. But he was one of the students Grandfather elected to teach after he retired from his concert tours. And Grandfather was very particular about the students whom he deigned to teach."

"Were you one of them?"

"A student?" Blaine laughed, his resonant voice enveloping Kate. "No, I didn't have the patience Grandfather demanded. But he did play for me all the time. But I'm sorry. I interrupted you while you were telling me about your background."

"Well, I studied with Professor Willoughby and then was accepted into the Boston Conservatory. And when I finished in Boston I found out there was an opening here in Whittenburg."

"And Whittenburg is fortunate that you decided to take that opening."

Kate could feel the heat starting to rise in her cheeks again. "Thank you," she murmured.

"Kate, you still have an empty plate." Malcolm hurried up to her once again. "You have to keep your energy level up."

"I—I—" Kate could not tell Malcolm that her mind was so absorbed with Blaine that she had lost her appetite.

"Here, let me get something for you." Malcolm took Kate's plate and put a couple of delicious tea sandwiches on it. Then he added a piece of French pastry and handed the plate to Kate. "I get vicarious thrills watching people eat the food that I used to enjoy," he said. "Besides, anyone with such a lovely figure has got to enjoy the food that we older folk can no longer eat." He looked up at Blaine, seeking agreement regarding Kate's beauty.

Suddenly, Blaine seemed withdrawn, as though remembering something that had just come to his attention. "It's been a pleasure meeting you, Kate, and if there is anything I can do for you, please let me know." Blaine extended his hand.

Kate took his hand, puzzled by his sudden change of mood. Once again, without warning, she felt a thrill course through her body. What was there about this man that affected her so strangely? And why did he suddenly withdraw?

"You're not eating," Malcolm was saying. "We can't have our new conductor running herself down on her first night!"

Kate took a few bites of the sandwich but then put the plate down. "All of a sudden I feel exhausted. Do you think it would be all right if you took me home now?"

"Certainly," Malcolm said. "Anyone who hasn't met you yet will just have to wait until our next reception."

After saying a few goodbyes, Kate and Malcolm left the hotel and drove to the outskirts of Whittenburg, where Kate lived.

"This night was just the first of many stellar evenings," Malcolm said as he headed the car up the long driveway of the building where Kate had her condo.

"Thanks. I'm glad the chairman of the board has such confidence in me," Kate said, getting out of the car. "Good night and thanks for driving me home."

Kate walked up the remaining portion of the driveway, too tired to be aware of the ivy creeping up the outside of the building, and the turrets balanced on either side of the roof. Normally she was struck by the building's magnificent appearance but tonight, though there was a full moon showing it in clear outline, she noticed nothing.

The building in which Kate lived was an old Whittenburg mansion, now converted into four condos. The last owner, a member of the diplomatic corps, had spent very little time here, and, at his death, his family had sold the mansion to a Whittenburg developer.

In addition to Kate, the other tenants of the house included artists of various disciplines and one socialite pretending to be an actress. Kate was the only musician. Ellie, next door, a painter who taught art in the public school, was her only close friend.

At this time of night the building was quiet except for the click-click of a typewriter. It was a sound the other condo owners tolerated, just as they tolerated Kate's piano practice. Perhaps the reason this house had attracted the types of people it did, she thought, was that it was situated in several acres of parklike surroundings.

Kate let herself into her apartment, a spacious setup which, in the morning, would catch all the rays of the sun. But since Kate preferred well-lit space, even in the dark of night, her apartment seemed to radiate sunshine. She walked into the foyer and put her purse and jacket in the closet nearest the door. It felt good to be home, to be able to relax. She kicked off her shoes and curled up on the luxurious beige velvet sofa that highlighted the living room, gazed absently at her grand piano and thought about this day. She wanted to impress it on her mind so that when journalists in the future asked her about her start as a conductor she would remember every detail.

Her mind swept back to the concert hall, to the musicians playing as though they shared a single heartbeat, and to the audience, who had paid her the greatest compliment an audience can pay. Kate breathed deeply and carried her mind to the reception held especially in her honor. But her picture of the reception seemed to be limited to one image: Blaine Eddington. All she could see now was Blaine standing before her—his commanding height, tanned good looks, those blazing green eyes that seemed to have a vitality all their own and, more disturbingly, the fact that electricity seemed to emanate from him whenever he touched her.

CHAPTER 3

The second-week-of-May performance went off without incident. Kate, hoping to compensate Harold somehow for his having been denied the opportunity to become Whittenburg's music director, had chosen a well-known Beethoven symphony as he had once suggested. But Kate knew that catering to Harold was not exactly professional and she wondered how many more times she would be tempted out of guilt to console him in this manner.

Following the concert, which had been heralded by enthusiastic applause, Kate returned to the dressing room, or greenroom, as it was called, and greeted the well-wishers. She was dressed in a high-necked black surah gown which her artist friend Ellie had said "revealed so little as to suggest so much." She wore no jewelry except a pair of understated silver earrings. The group congratulating Kate consisted mostly of music lovers, though there was one autograph collector who had no opinion whatever about her conducting ability. The young woman told her bluntly that she was here because of Kate's name, which had made front-page headlines in the *Clarion* two weeks before. ("Kate Reston to Head Whittenburg Symphony Orchestra," the paper had proclaimed.) And now she wanted Kate Reston's famous name in her little red autograph book.

Kate had just finished writing her signature when she heard a deep, ironic chuckle rising out of the dressing room's din. It was a laugh so distinctive that she somehow knew whom it came from even before she raised her eyes. When at last she looked up, she was not surprised to find Blaine Eddington smiling down on her.

"I know," he said in a soft but strong bass voice.

"Pardon?" Her heart was racing wildly but she was determined to look composed.

"You're hounded by autograph hunters as soon as your name makes headlines."

In spite of her nervousness, Kate grinned.

"It happened to me," he said, "the year my JC model came out. My engineers and I had spent years working on the concepts, and when the car was finally unveiled all the automotive cognoscenti were on hand to congratulate us. But there were some who did not hesitate to tell me that all they wanted was my autograph. 'A name's a name' was how one man put it."

Kate nodded and smiled. Blaine smiled too, but she could not help noticing that his eyes were surreptitiously moving over her body, missing nothing. What Ellie had said about this black surah gown seemed to be true. Kate blushed.

Other people came in to remark on one or another aspect of the evening's performance and to welcome Blaine back to town. Standing at Blaine's side and receiving guests like this made Kate feel as though she were the Princess and he the Prince of Wales. During the times people talked to Blaine rather than to her, Kate found herself studying him carefully.

She had been struck by those green eyes before but now it was his mouth that drew her attention. It was a proud mouth that rested serenely in a face that was all sharp planes, a strong face but with no hint of the arrogance that is sometimes found in highly successful men. Though he was dressed in an expensive black suit, she still continued to think of him as a skier. With that deeply tanned skin and very blond hair he would fit in so well with a snowy mountain background, she thought.

A man was saying to Blaine, ". . . and so sorry to hear of the death of your wife."

"That was several years ago, dear," the man's wife said, embarrassed.

"Yes, but I never did give my condolences." To Blaine he said, "You were in California at the time."

Blaine nodded shortly but said nothing. His expression did not change but Kate's did. She had not been aware that he'd been married and now she was finding out that he was a widower. How sad, Kate thought, to be widowed so young. She wondered how Blaine's wife had died and whether or not there had been any children. Though the details of his life had been written up many times Kate had not until this moment taken the remotest interest in this legendary Whittenburg multimillionaire. But tonight, when she returned to her condo, she would ask Ellie about him. When she wasn't painting, Ellie devoured every periodical from *The Wall Street Journal* to *People*.

The man who had offered belated condolences to Blaine was now studying Kate's face thoughtfully. He opened his mouth as though to say something, then closed it, looked down and cleared his throat. Blaine glanced from the man to Kate and then he said in an oddly hoarse voice, "If you'll excuse me, Kate, I have an engagement." To the couple standing with him he said, "John, Elena." Then he strode toward the dressing room door and quickly disappeared.

Before Kate could puzzle out this precipitate departure Malcolm walked over with Harold and the two engaged Kate in an analysis of this evening's program. She was having difficulty concentrating on the conversation, however, and soon Malcolm, sensing this, left. In a short while all the others had left the greenroom too. All but Harold, who continued to wonder aloud why Kate had chosen to interpret the first movement of the Brahms in a particular way. He had said nothing about her choice of works for this evening, even though he must have been aware that she'd selected particular pieces in order to make up somehow for his loss. Well, perhaps he was too proud to acknowledge what must surely be perceived by him as a consolation prize.

"Have you chosen the last piece for the next Pops?" he asked.

Kate shook her head. The Whittenburg Symphony alternated the heavier performances with evenings of popular selections. These might include lighter classical works, jazz and show tunes. There was usually an instrumental soloist or a vocal artist featured too, and next week's performance would spotlight the aging but still talented jazz singer Laura Halley. All of the program had been worked out except for the closing orchestral piece. Kate was now trying to decide between an excerpt from Milhaud's *La Création du Monde* and Gershwin's *Rhapsody in Blue*.

"I suppose you know what I'd suggest," Harold said.

"I know. Gershwin. So the audience can applaud itself for recognizing it." She smiled but Harold did not smile back. The downward tug at this mouth indicated that he was not in the mood for levity this evening.

"Well," she said, "I'll have to decide by tomorrow. Maybe I'll just toss a coin." Then, moving deftly to another subject, she asked, "How are Miriam and the children?"

"Fine." His heavy face still would not warm.

"And your students?"

"They're doing well." In addition to playing with the Whittenburg, Harold also taught music at a junior college nearby. The formal training in music that had qualified him for this position made him far better informed than most of the other musicians in the seventy-piece orchestra. His background, however, had not been nearly so thorough as Kate's, which was why she had been chosen as conductor. Harold's teaching did not pay much, and he had a wife and two teenagers to support. Another reason to resent Kate. With her promotion to director had come a nice jump in salary, Kate remembered.

She wished she could help Harold somehow. Maybe he ought to consider conducting in another city, perhaps a city that was just forming its first orchestra. That would necessitate his moving, of course, but maybe such a change would be good for the whole family. Harold's wife, Kate knew, had been itching for a change. "Whittenburg will always be home," she had once told Kate plaintively, "but there's so much more of the world to discover!"

Kate made a mental note to find out who needed music directors and to recommend Harold highly. With Malcolm's help, perhaps Harold's problems as well as his wife's might be solved.

He was saying now, "The outdoor concert we're doing in June—do you have any ideas yet?"

"Yes. I'd like to go modern this year."

Harold frowned. "Who are you considering?"

"Mussorgsky, Copland, Bartók, I haven't quite decided."

He winced at the mention of Bartók, as she had known he would. "Kate, don't you want an *audience* for this performance?"

Oh Lord, she thought. I don't want to get into another argument with him, particularly now when his nerves are still raw from his disappointment. "Well, as I said, I haven't decided. It doesn't necessarily have to be Bartók. And the decision isn't mine alone, you know. The board always has suggestions and they have to review mine as well."

But Harold was still glowering. He seemed to be spoiling for a fight this evening. He plunked his heavy frame onto a burgundy sofa, one of the dressing room's more expensive pieces, and lit a cigarette. He said, "You lean toward extremists, Kate. You always have. Tell me, what are you trying to prove? That atonality is cute? I'll grant you that everyone should be exposed to it once, if only for the experience—which is akin to getting a mild electric shock. But we're talking here about a summer concert under the stars. We're talking about audiences in a romantic mood, people who long for a Tchaikovsky, a Schubert—"

"But the symphony's been selecting romantics for the June concerts ever since I can remember. When I was a little girl and came to listen with my parents it was always Tchaikovsky, Schubert, Chopin, Schumann. It was lovely, I'll admit, but every so often it's good to have a change. And not everyone feels the way you do about the atonals. And besides, Copland's not an atonal and neither is Mussorgsky. They—"

"Mussorgsky! Bah! Glorified folk songs."

"The *Slavonic Dances* are also based on folk songs too, yet you seem to love Dvořák."

"Because he's more disciplined, genteel. Mussorgsky's a ruffian. He should have done the sound track for the Bolshevik Revolution. He has no refinement. The man had very little formal training, and it shows."

Kate wasn't so sure Harold felt as strongly about Mussorgsky as he was suggesting. He was simply feeling cantankerous this evening and nothing she said would please him.

Tired of the arguing, Kate once again changed the subject. "We had a full house tonight. Weren't you pleased?"

He shrugged. "They came to see you, Kate. You're still new, don't forget."

"Meaning that once the novelty's worn off they won't be back?" She was getting angry now.

Again he shrugged.

"I suppose you don't think I have talent enough to draw them?"

"Not true. You have plenty of talent. There's just a dearth of music lovers in Whittenburg."

This subdued her somewhat and she was about to ask him what he thought ought to be done to lure larger audiences when she noticed that he was smiling faintly. It was a particular type of smile that Harold unconsciously exhibited when he was not being entirely sincere. So he *didn't* think she had talent! Kate thought. Or at least not enough of it. Why this should trouble her she did not know. Given the fact that Harold was still harboring a grudge, his attitude should have been understandable. Nevertheless, she felt a bit insecure. She had always respected his judgment.

"I noticed that you were talking to our newest benefactor earlier," Harold said.

"Yes. Blaine Eddington." As she spoke the name Kate's annoyance at Harold evaporated. She remembered again Blaine's departure. It had been so abrupt. And yet he had not been unkind or rude, had not indicated in any way that he was finding her company unpleasant. She tried to remember what had happened just prior to his exit and for the life of her could not recall.

"He's an extraordinary young man," Harold said. To Harold, who was in his mid-forties, anyone less than that age was "young," Kate thought, amused.

"I understand he's widowed," Kate said casually, not meeting Harold's eyes.

"Yes," was all Harold said. She had hoped that he might furnish a few more details on Blaine's life. But Harold was no more interested in celebrity-watching than was Kate herself.

"A man offered Mr. Eddington condolences on the death of his wife," Kate said. "Belated ones, actually. Apparently Mrs. Eddington died a few years ago."

"A millionaire bachelor. If he continues to attend the concerts we won't have to worry about roping in female audiences, will we?"

"I guess not." She tried to smile lightly but she steeled herself for the expected teasing. During the years she had been a member of the orchestra rather than its leader she had endured much good-natured joshing from Harold and other musicians. They considered Kate very attractive, wondered why she wasn't married at twenty-nine, and took every opportunity to send prospects her way. And of course there were eligible men in the orchestra itself. Kate had dated several of them, and whenever this became known by the other members there would be much joking. Harold, in his good moods, would cheerfully join in.

But Harold did not tease her now. Instead he said, "A busy man, this Eddington. The main automotive plant in California plus this new one going up here. Plus his interest in the symphony, and in various other organizations. My wife told me he's joined the Historical Society. He's an expert on the Civil War, you know. Not that this is unusual in a town so close to Gettysburg. It's good to see a hometown boy taking an interest in things."

"Yes." Kate did not know what else to say.

"But in a way it's unfortunate too. A young fellow like that ought to think about remarrying. But I don't imagine he'll consider that for a while."

Kate frowned and Harold noticed this at once. He studied her face for a long moment and then said, "Unless he meets a highly desirable young woman."

Here it comes, she thought. The teasing. But there was no mirth in Harold's eyes now. There was instead a look of—what?—concentration? calculation? He said, "A woman like yourself, perhaps?"

"Really, Harold, I hardly know the man!"

"It's obvious he finds you quite desirable."

"Harold—" Her cheeks were flaming.

But now Harold was talking more to himself than to her. He said, "Wait a minute: someone told me he planned on making Whittenburg home base. He'd still fly to the California plant but he wouldn't live there."

She said nothing, though she thought this was interesting news.

"He'd live here in town and so would his future wife. And if the wife had a career she'd continue in it, wouldn't she?" Harold looked hard at Kate.

"What are you talking about?" Kate said.

"Uh—just speculating on Eddington's future." He shook his head, apparently exasperated. Kate was now totally confused. Sighing, he rose from the couch, stubbing out a cigarette as he did so. "Well, I've got to get going."

"Good night, Harold."

"Good night." In spite of his earlier nastiness, Kate still felt for him. She watched this talented cellist walk dejectedly toward the door, his head looking almost as heavy as his body. She'd have to ask Malcolm to help her locate some city in need of a conductor. If something wasn't done soon Harold would lose his spirit. But it would be done, and the sooner the better. Everything would work out well.

Satisfied, Kate allowed herself to bask in memories of tonight's performance—and of the man who had been with her after her triumph: Blaine Eddington.

CHAPTER 4

It was rare when Kate slept in, because if she wasn't hurrying down to Meade Hall she would practice on the Steinway, which took up a large portion of the living room. Playing the piano was a skill that needed constant honing. And she required it while studying scoring. But things had been running very smoothly and she enjoyed the luxury of sleeping late. She had just slipped into a velour robe and headed toward the kitchen to start some coffee when she was interrupted by a knock at the door.

"Who's there?" Kate called out.

"Ellie. Is something wrong?"

Kate hurried to her door and opened it. Ellie stood before her in a pair of sweat pants and jacket, a band around her head. "Wrong? What do you mean?" Kate said.

"I just got back from running and saw your car still home. You're usually gone by now."

"Oh, I see. No, nothing's wrong. In fact, the concerts have been going well, the orchestra is running smoothly"—Kate furrowed her brow a little, thinking of Harold, but then decided that that, too, was going to work out —"and I have given myself a morning off."

"That's great. How about a cup of coffee?"

"You do have an educated nose. The coffee will be done in a second."

The two women walked from the front door to Kate's utilitarian kitchen. The entire wall was covered with oak cabinets, leaving only enough room for a stove, refrigerator and microwave oven. The glass-topped dining table was in an area adjacent to the kitchen, near the entrance foyer and alongside the living room. Kate went into the kitchen to plug in the coffee while Ellie sat down at the table.

"How's the new painting coming?" Kate asked.

"Not bad, but I've been so busy with the art show my students are putting on that I haven't had much time to work on my own paintings."

"And you're probably too busy reading about the celebrities in *People* when you get home to get to your work."

"Speaking of celebrities," Ellie said in conspiratorial tone, "how about that Blaine Eddington!"

"How about him?" Kate responded, hoping that Ellie could not hear the loud thumping of her heart.

"Come on, Kate. Maybe you usually get turned on by musical scores but you can't have missed that hunk!"

"If you mean that he's an attractive man, I guess I would have to agree with you." Kate turned to the coffeepot so she wouldn't have to face Ellie. She and Ellie had been friends long enough for Ellie to be able to read her eyes, and since she herself could not understand why she reacted so schoolgirlishly every time Blaine was near her, she felt she could not discuss it with Ellie.

"That's generous. The most gorgeous man to float back from California and you call him 'attractive.' There's the understatement! Too bad about his wife, though."

"What about his wife?" Kate didn't want to appear too interested, but she wanted to hear all that Ellie had to say.

"She was a microbiologist, doing experimental things, and I guess she caught one of her own diseases. She was pretty young when she died."

"Were there . . . were there any children?"

"I'm not sure," Ellie said, munching on one of the sweet rolls that Kate had put on the table. "But *People* didn't show any pictures of them and you know how they like to tug at the heartstrings."

"Was she pretty?"

"Oh, yes. Tall, short blond hair. The picture was taken at a distance, but she did seem beautiful."

The two women sipped their coffee, making small talk about the beautiful spring Whittenburg had been enjoying.

"Makes me just want to take a walk and breathe in the spring air," Kate said.

"Why don't you? Or, better yet, jog."

Kate laughed. Ellie had been trying to get her to begin an exercise program for months.

"All you ever exercise are your fingers and your brain," Ellie said for the hundredth time, "and while the rest of you doesn't show it yet, it's bound to, eventually."

But Kate had always resisted, largely because she hadn't had the time to jog or exercise at the local Y or even to do Jane Fonda in her own apartment. Her job took up all her time. "Maybe I'll walk over to the hall, though. It's such a nice day and I'm not in a hurry. I just have a lot of paper work to clean up today and if I start soon I can be in my office by lunchtime."

"Ten miles is a bit much for a start, Kate. Why don't you drive to the hall and just take a long walk around there?"

"Maybe you're right."

Ellie left and Kate showered and dressed. Since today was Saturday and there would be no one in the hall she decided to dress casually. She selected a pair of black wool slacks along with a gray silk blouse and black-and-white plaid jacket. A pair of comfortable black boots, ones in which Kate could walk long distances, completed the outfit.

By early afternoon Kate's desk at the hall was tidy once more and she set out for her walk. Whittenburg was an old town, incorporated long before the Civil War. But it had remained a small town until the 1940s, when several large manufacturing plants were built in the surrounding area. The town began to spread out, going far beyond the region settled by the original planners. But while the outer fringes of the town reflected modern thinking in architectural trends, Whittenburg had been careful to preserve its core. And that was where Meade Hall was located—adjacent to "old" Whittenburg. The newer part of town was attractive with wide tree-lined boulevards, displaying many glass-fronted shops. The streets behind the shopping district contained apartment and office buildings several stories high. But Kate preferred to walk through the older part of town.

The streets of "old" Whittenburg were narrow, with cobblestones peeking up through the asphalt from time to time. The sidewalks, too, were narrow, but they nonetheless seemed inviting. Though most of the shops were modern inside and all the buildings had had their plumbing brought up to code, the outsides looked almost as though it were still the nineteenth century. Signs hung from various shops announcing a bakery or restaurant or tavern within. The windows were hung with red-and-white checkered curtains or white lacy fabric. In one section Kate could see bullet holes dating from the Confederate invasion of Pennsylvania during the Civil War. Kate enjoyed the feeling of being part of a continuum, rather than a separate, isolated unit.

The walk back to the car took less time than Kate had thought, for on her return she walked quickly, without examining any details of the old city. Before long she found herself in the Meade Hall parking lot.

"Kate! Kate! I was looking for you!"

Kate looked up to see Malcolm coming toward her. "Malcolm! Hello."

"Wonderful news, Kate. Come back into your office and listen to what has happened." He took Kate's hand and led her back into the building. Together, in silence, they walked to Kate's office, Malcolm wearing an irrepressible grin and Kate totally bewildered. Finally they got inside Kate's office.

"Now. Sit down," Malcolm said, leading her to the chair behind her desk.

She sat. "Now what are you being so mysterious about?"

"Have you ever heard of Maesterling Recordings?" Malcolm sat back, letting his question sink in.

"Maesterling Recordings? They're the ones who record only classical music, particularly small symphony orches . . ." Her eyes widened. "You mean Maesterling Recordings wants to do a record with the Whittenburg Symphony?"

"I understand that it's under consideration."

"Really?" She leaned forward, breaths coming quickly. "When will we know for certain?"

"I'm not sure. But I just got a call from one of the executives at Maesterling. It seems they want to do a series of recordings by smaller symphonies and we're one of them. One of the executives, William Scott, will be contacting you soon to discuss the matter with you."

"That really would put us on the map, wouldn't it? William Scott, you say? When is he supposed to contact me?"

"I told him that you are usually in your office weekday mornings and I gave him this office number. I think he'll be calling you sometime next week."

"I'll be ready for him." She smiled.

"I trust you're as good with music companies as you are with music, Kate. This will be an exciting event in the history of the Whittenburg Symphony Orchestra."

Kate had gotten a call from William Scott two days before and was now sitting in her office waiting for his arrival. The phone call had been brief and businesslike and Kate did not know how serious Mr. Scott was about the Whittenburg Symphony. He had indicated that he had attended several performances, but the ones he had seen had been performed with the previous conductor. But Kate knew that the quality of the orchestra had not diminished under her leadership so she was certain that they could come to terms. Still, she was nervous.

There was a knock on the door and Kate rose to answer it. A man about Kate's height, with dark curly hair and a smile that lit up his face, stood before her.

"Miss Reston?"

"Yes. Please come in. You must be William Scott." Kate led the man to the overstuffed leather chair opposite her desk. "Won't you have a seat?"

"Why, thank you."

Kate walked around and sat behind the desk. "I'm happy to meet you, Mr. Scott."

"First, please call me Bill. And I hope I may call you Kate."

Kate nodded.

"Fine. Now, Kate, as I told Mr. Merriwether, my company is interested in doing a series of recordings—America Plays the Classics. We think the records would sell well, not only in the small cities where the orchestras are housed, but in the big cities as well. Urban America is beginning to realize that all our talent does not migrate to the major metropolises." Bill paused and smiled. "Nor all the attractive women."

"Thank you, Bill." Kate was somewhat irritated by Bill's remark but she decided it would be best not to antagonize him. "How are you going to select the places that will participate in your series?"

"First, of course, we are interested in quality. While there are many symphony orchestras, some are better than others. And then, of course, we have to be guided by the financial arrangements we can make."

"Financial arrangements?" Kate had spent most of her life with music itself and had no idea of what sort of money arrangements were made with record companies. She was sorry that Malcolm had been unable to attend this meeting.

"Advances and royalties," he said. "We'd have to agree on—"

"This is something that would best be discussed with our chairman of the board. I'd be more comfortable talking to you about the music itself."

"I realize that. And that's exactly what I'd like to discuss now. What we propose to do would be to record one of your concerts live. Maesterling would bring down all the necessary recording equipment. I'm now concerned with the fundamental consideration of the music itself."

Kate felt a tinge of annoyance. "Bill, the music here is as fine as any you'll find anywhere. We hire only the best musicians and the quality of the performance has remained high in spite of Robert Bernini's departure."

Bill laughed. "I'm sure of that, Kate. It's just that we don't want each symphony to be playing the same pieces. We need variety. Otherwise why would anyone want to buy the entire set?"

Kate felt a little foolish. "Oh," she said, then added, "How does the music get selected then?"

"The logistics haven't quite been worked out, but what we think we're going to do is have each finalist submit a program. Then we'll check them over to see if there's any overlap. And if there is, we'll call for a conference and work it out. Does that sound fair?"

"Yes, it does. How soon with you be making your selections?"

"Not for a few months, I don't think. There are three of us traveling around, and after we make our recommendations our boss will make the final choice."

"I see."

"I'd also like to tour your facility. And get a schedule of your symphony concerts."

Kate handed Bill a printed sheet with the season's schedule of dates on it. "Call me when you've decided which performance you want to hear and I'll leave a ticket at the box office for you."

"Thank you. That would be very nice." Bill rose. "And now would you show me the hall?"

"I'd be delighted." Kate stood up and came around the front of her desk.

"Oh, and one more thing, Kate. Would you have dinner with me tonight?"

CHAPTER 5

Ordinarily Kate would not have accepted a date with a man with whom she had had a single business meeting, but Bill Scott was different. Kate considered the dinner to be an extension of their afternoon talk. Nevertheless, when she came home to get ready for the evening she was not certain about how to dress. Should she wear something that would look totally businesslike, something that would be certain to keep the discussion on the same plane as that which had taken place in her office? Or should she wear something a little more frilly to suggest that she'd made a new friend? Finally Kate settled on a pale blue silk shirtwaist dress, something she believed would function in either situation.

Though Bill had told her he would pick her up at seven, he did not ring Kate's doorbell until almost seven-thirty. "I didn't think I would have any trouble finding my way 'round this town," he said as he walked into her apartment, "but you do live a little off the beaten path." He looked at her as though defying her to be angry at his tardiness.

Kate had been annoyed at being kept waiting, especially as she had wanted to use the night for working and had changed her plans specifically for him, but his comment put her on the defensive. "Artists need open spaces in which to create," she said, trying not to let her irritation show, "and a big buffer to keep the tone of the midnight piano from disturbing anyone. That's why my condo is so far from town."

Bill seemed contrite. "This is a very attractive place you have," he said, his eyes sweeping around the living room/dining room area. "Does it have a bedroom too?"

"Of course," Kate said, her tone suspicious.

"No, no," Bill laughed. "All I meant was that I wondered if this was a studio apartment because this room is so spacious."

Bill looked so apologetic that Kate could not help but laugh. "Yes, I do have a bedroom."

"Your apartment really looks comfortable," he said, appearing to be genuinely impressed. "In New York if I were to have a living room this large, it would be bedroom and living room combined."

Kate nodded. "I'm glad this isn't New York. I think I would get claustrophobic in such a small place."

"But I bet you don't spend too much time in here anyway," Bill said, his eyes taking in her black hair and pink cheeks. His dark brown eyes moved down, frankly admiring the lovely figure that stood outlined by the clingy silk dress. "Guys must be breaking down your door to take you to dinner."

"Speaking of which," Kate interrupted in order to change the subject, "would you like some wine before we leave?" Kate walked into her kitchen and Bill followed her. "I have some white wine chilling here and I thought we might have a drink before we left. Or do you have reservations?"

"I might have had reservations about this evening, but, looking at you, they have all disappeared." Bill smiled into Kate's eyes.

Kate felt embarrassed but she reminded herself that this was a handsome, probably sophisticated man paying her a charming compliment. Shouldn't she be flattered? Suddenly she thought of Blaine. Would she have felt differently if it had been Blaine saying this to her? She decided not to dwell on this. She was with Bill tonight and it was obvious from Bill's conversation that he had left his brisk business personality at the hotel and was treating Kate not as though she were a business contact for Maesterling Records but as a woman he found attractive and interesting.

"Thank you," Kate said, "and while I appreciate the compliment, I still don't know if we have time for some wine before dinner."

"With you, my dear," Bill said, twirling an imaginary mustache, "I have time for anything. But seriously, I really don't know this town all that well and I was waiting for you to suggest a nice place for dinner."

"Fine," Kate said, reaching for the wineglasses. "Since we aren't in a rush and probably won't be able to get a table for a little while anyway, why don't we have the wine first? You pour and I'll get some cheese."

When they were both settled in the living room, the cheese and wine having been placed on the glass-topped table that stood in front of the couch, Bill held his glass up to Kate. "Here's to a new relationship—both business and personal."

Kate felt inhibited about drinking to a new relationship, but she knew that she would have a lot of contact with Bill during the next few months if she was going to work with Maesterling Records. There seemed to be no harm in offering her glass and sipping some wine as well.

"Tell me," Bill said, "what brought you to a town of this size when you obviously have the talent for larger cities?"

"Is size the criterion for everything?" Kate said.

"No, but for the recognition artists usually want, it's necessary to be in among large groups of people, not small towns."

"I was born here and I love this town," Kate said, "and besides, you came to me, didn't you?"

"*Touché.*"

"I was wondering, Bill, what made you choose the classical record business as a life's work? Why aren't you involved with pop or rock, where most of the money is these days?"

"And what, may I ask, is wrong with classical music?"

Kate chose to ignore Bill's obvious thrust. "Are you a musician as well?"

Bill smiled at her. "Depends on what you mean by 'musician.' Do I play all the time, studying and working? No. But I do play an instrument."

"What do you play?" Kate was intrigued.

"The trumpet," Bill said, more to himself than to her. He brushed at his curly black hair.

"Why didn't you pursue music?"

Bill looked at Kate. "Probably because I wasn't good enough."

"Who told you that?"

"No one had to tell me. I was a student at the High School of Music and Art in New York City, and while I was good enough to get into the school, I was not as smooth as some of the other trumpeters I worked with. Even I could hear that."

She nodded. "What did you do then?"

"I went to City College and got myself a business degree. That made me a perfect candidate for Maesterling. Music and business. Which is why you see before you a happy man." Bill grinned.

"I like a story with a happy ending," Kate said, smiling. "And now how about heading for that dinner you promised me?"

"I thought perhaps you had forgotten, that we could spend the rest of the evening here, living on love. But if you insist." Bill stood up and took Kate's hand, helping her up. "Where are we off to?"

"I think we should try Christopher's. It's a new place in town and the reports I have gotten from the band members who've eaten there are terrific. French cuisine with a touch of the American."

"Sounds good to me." Bill helped Kate on with her stole and the two of them walked down to the parking lot adjacent to the building.

Bill led Kate to a sleek black Corvette. "Allow me to help you in, madam."

"Thank you, sir," Kate said.

Bill walked around the car and got into the driver's seat. "I'm sorry, but the horses don't know the way to Christopher's. Can you give them some instruction?"

"Easily," Kate said, and directed Bill down the road to Main Street. "Make a left at the next corner and you'll see the sign."

The dining room at Christopher's was beautifully appointed. The room was done in beige and varying shades of brown, the chocolate-brown rug uniting the entire decor. Along the edges hung massive plants held up by elaborate brown macrame ropes. Even the waiters were dressed in beige and brown. The entire room had a soothing effect and Kate felt relaxed as soon as she walked inside.

"If the quality of the food matches the decor then you've picked a wonderful spot for dinner," Bill said, echoing Kate's thoughts. "Träumerei" was playing in the background, not loud enough to intrude on conversation but distinct enough to provide Kate with a feeling of euphoria.

"I'm glad you asked me out to dinner," Kate said unexpectedly, surprising herself as much as Bill.

He looked at her, a pleased smile on his face. "That's one thing we both agree on," he said, reaching across the table to take her hand.

It occurred to Kate that she might be sending out signals that she didn't actually intend. She was just glad to be in this lovely place, sharing dinner with a man who seemed to have similar interests. She hoped that Bill did not misconstrue the comment she had blurted out without thinking. Just then the waiter brought the menus, large brown leather folders, and Kate was able to remove her hand without being obvious.

Bill studied the menu for a while and then looked up. "I'm a steak-and-potatoes person, and this steak looks good. What interests you?"

"I've heard that Christopher's bouillabaisse is wonderful. I think I'll try that."

"Good enough," Bill said signaling the waiter. He gave him their orders and then said, "I think I've been spoiled by all my travels."

"Spoiled? How so?" Kate said, wondering how this open, pleasant man could think of himself as spoiled.

"Well, maybe 'spoiled' isn't the word. Maybe it's fearful. I eat out so much of the time because I'm on the road for Maesterling most of the time. And the only dish that restaurants can't ruin too much is the steak. I've had so many disappointments that I almost always stick to the steak and potatoes now."

"That's too bad. I wish I could say with authority that the bouillabaisse is perfect, but, if it is, perhaps we could eat here again and you can order it instead of steak."

"Even if the bouillabaisse isn't perfect, I'd still like to eat here again with you."

Kate looked down at the table and then reached for the goblet containing the water. She wasn't thirsty but it was something to do, an action that would give her time to think about how to change the direction of the conversation.

"How long does a project like the one you're working on with Maesterling take from start to finish?" Kate said.

Bill made a face. "Do you really want to talk shop?"

"It's not shop for me," Kate said earnestly. "Although I've been in the music business for a long time, I've had no experience with how record companies actually operate. I'm curious as to how a project like this develops."

"Are you sure this won't bore you?"

"No," Kate said, looking as interested as she could, and thinking that as long as she could keep the conversation clear of references to her and Bill as a twosome, she would be interested.

"The idea came from one of our public relations people. He's from a small town, somewhere out in Ohio, and he kept telling us that great music doesn't emanate exclusively from major cities. As a New Yorker I had reason to doubt that—"

"Obviously you're biased and closed-minded," Kate said with a smile, "but go on."

"Anyway, my boss thought it might be an interesting idea and sent me to scout the hinterlands."

Again Kate made a face.

"You asked, and I'm telling you," Bill said, an innocent look on his face. "When I got out to the boonies, I heard such beautiful music I found it hard to return home. It was the song of the Sirens, drawing me to them. After I managed to free myself, several months later, I told my boss that this was a wonderful project."

"Are you ever serious?" Kate said.

"Serious? Of course I'm serious," Bill said. "Haven't you ever been drawn by the song of the Sirens?"

The two of them continued on in their teasing vein until the waiter brought the dinners and the wine that Bill had ordered.

"My good man," Bill said to the waiter, "you have just saved me from a fate worse than death, a serious conversation."

Kate was puzzled by the man with whom she was having dinner. In her office he had been a knowledgeable businessman and here he was a charming clown. Perhaps that was the way to be. Perhaps intensity was proper only when one was actually at work. But Kate couldn't help but be intense about her work regardless of where she was. Her job meant the world to her and she could no sooner turn off her thoughts about music and the orchestra—her orchestra—than she could stop breathing. She thought that perhaps Bill would not have been able to turn away from thoughts of his work as easily if his life's dream had been fulfilled and he had become a working musician, rather than someone who was working on the fringes of the world of music.

"How's the bouillabaisse?" Bill said, interrupting her thoughts. "As good as advertised?"

"Heavenly." Kate said. "I haven't tasted anything as delicious in months." Kate did not add that she had been eating on the run and living on sandwiches ever since she had taken over the Whittenburg.

"Good. That means we have to come here again so that I can try it."

"It certainly is good enough for me to have again," Kate said, but she felt uncertain about having committed herself to another date with Bill Scott. He was a pleasant person but she doubted that there could be anything special between her and Bill.

Kate made no effort to talk business again but she sidestepped any more references to a continuing relationship with Bill. Perhaps when she got to know him better, when she had worked with him some more, she might be able to think about it, but right now, not only did she have no special feeling for him but she had very little time for any real social activities.

Bill did not seem inclined to press the issue and the rest of the dinner went pleasantly. They discussed the choices of background music made by the restaurant and ended up trying to determine which piece of music would go best with which dinner.

He said, *"The Royal Fireworks Music* would be the one to go with the steak, don't you think?"

"Then you'll have to play *La Mer* for the bouillabaisse."

The two of them tried to recall as much of the menu as they could and then assigned pieces to each of the entrees, laughing as they tried to come up with the perfect assignment.

"And *The Nutcracker* goes with the desserts," Kate insisted.

"Speaking of dessert," Bill said, "what would you like?"

"Nothing for me," Kate said. "But you go ahead if you want some."

"No, I'm not a dessert person." Bill smiled broadly. "Everyone tells me I'm sweet enough as it is."

Kate laughed but said nothing. She would not allow the conversation to drift back to where they might discuss a relationship.

"In that case, perhaps it's time to leave." Bill signaled the waiter for the check and, after he had taken care of it, the two of them left.

"That was a lovely dinner, Bill. Thanks so much for inviting me," Kate said as they walked to the car.

"The night is not yet over," Bill said. "Is there anyplace we can go for a nightcap?"

"It's mighty tempting, but I have to get up early tomorrow morning."

"No need to be shy," Bill said, twirling his imaginary mustache again. "There's a wonderful bar in my hotel."

Kate laughed. "I'm sure there is. But I get little enough sleep as it is. And I have a full day tomorrow."

"If you insist," Bill said.

It was a short drive home, but not so short that Kate did not notice how clear the sky was. The full moon shone down on them as they drove and the stars seemed to be set as individual diamonds, all of them twinkling down on her. Instinctively Kate's thoughts turned to Blaine and how much she would have enjoyed sharing a moment like this with him.

"Home again," Bill said as he parked the Corvette near Kate's condo. He got out of the car and walked around to her side; however, Kate did not wait for him and got out by herself. "Let me walk you to your door," Bill said as he took her elbow.

"That's okay, Bill. I can manage."

"I insist," Bill said. "I would never rest tonight knowing I had left you alone in the wilds of Pennsylvania. You must allow me to escort you to your door if only to set my mind at ease."

"All right," Kate said, walking toward the building.

"Seriously, Kate, when can I see you again?"

Kate was caught unprepared by the question. "Uh, uh, my schedule is so erratic, Bill. Even if I checked my calendar now, it's likely that something would come up. Why don't you call me the next time you're in Whittenburg and we can talk about it?"

"Sounds good." By this time they had reached Kate's door and Bill took Kate into his arms. "Conductors turn me on," he said as he kissed her neck.

Kate struggled out of his arms. "This has been a long day for me."

"Not long enough for me, Kate," Bill said. But he did not try to embrace her again. He leaned forward and gave her a gentle kiss on the cheek. "I'll call you as soon as I get back to town."

"Good night, Bill," Kate said as she walked into her condo.

As soon as Kate got in the door she kicked her shoes off. There was something about the action that set her free. What was wrong with her? Why did she want to be "free"? Bill wasn't proposing marriage. All he had suggested was another dinner date. And he was good company. She had to admit that. But all along, nagging at her brain was the picture of Blaine. Blaine, who was so maddeningly elusive that she wasn't sure he cared for her at all. Why did she feel so strongly about not going out with other men? Kate did not understand her feelings, but she was too tired to untangle them. Perhaps another day. She quickly got undressed and went to bed.

CHAPTER 6

As Kate sat in her office the next morning thinking of the previous evening's dinner, she smiled. It had been nice to get away from the problems of conducting a symphony orchestra. Now she could get back to her work with renewed vigor.

Kate checked her calendar to review what had to be done this day and discovered that she had promised to speak to the local Women's Club on the current revival of interest in opera. She remembered that she had planned to outline her talk last night but had forgotten about it because of her dinner date with Bill. Kate checked her watch and found that she had to be at the home of Margaretta Phipps, where the lecture and luncheon was to take place, in an hour.

Quickly Kate began outlining ideas for her talk. Many of the members of the Women's Club were the same ones whose families supported the symphony most generously and she wanted them to know she appreciated them. After half an hour she was satisfied that she would be able to give a cogent, cohesive and entertaining talk.

Kate drove to Mrs. Phipps's house. There were a number of cars in the driveway but Kate left hers out on the street. She did not want to be boxed in by latecomers.

"Kate, dear, we're so glad to see you," Mrs. Phipps greeted her at the door with a hug.

"Take off your jacket, dear," said Malcolm Merriwether's wife.

"Congratulations on the birth of your grandchild," Kate said to Mrs. Merriwether, handing the maid the tan suede blazer she had worn over her soft wool knit dress.

"Thank you. Maybe later I'll show you the pictures we have."

As the two of them walked into the spacious living room, Kate looked around and saw the faces of matrons whose families had long been associated with the Whittenburg Symphony. She did see several new contributors and made a mental note to introduce herself to them when the speech ended.

Mrs. Phipps stood in the center of the room, clapping her hands to get everyone's attention. "And now, ladies, I'm delighted to introduce to you our guest speaker for this afternoon, Kate Reston."

There was some polite applause and Mrs. Phipps pointed to a wing chair that was next to the couch. "Why don't you sit there while you talk to us?"

Kate sat down in the chair. She pulled out her notes and began her talk. "For many years opera was thought of as an art form associated with the rich. True, there were always impoverished music lovers who found their way into the balconies of performances, but this was unusual. Now, however, opera is—to use a current expression—mainstreaming." Kate looked at her audience, all of whom seemed to hang on her every word. Second to creating music, Kate's favorite pastime was to talk about it, and she warmed to her subject. The half-hour talk went quickly and, following the speech, the ladies came up to Kate and spoke with great enthusiasm.

"Luncheon is being served, ladies." Mrs. Phipps stood at the entrance to the dining room. "It's buffet, as usual, so if you will start to line up, you can all have my delicious Mexican fiesta."

Kate got in line, took some food on a plate and ate quickly while making small talk with the ladies who were seated near her. As soon as she finished, however, she rose to leave. "I really do have to get going."

"I understand, my dear. And thank you so much for speaking to us this morning."

"It was my pleasure," Kate said, taking the tan suede blazer that had been brought to her by the maid. "I hope to see all of you soon," she said and made her way back to her car.

Once back at her office Kate began her day's work in earnest. She picked up a printer's proof of the program for the next Pops concert. Though a proofreader at the print shop read it before it was delivered to Meade Hall, Kate had the final responsibility. She carefully corrected minor errors in the program. Suddenly she heard a footstep and looked up, startled.

"I hope I'm not disturbing you." Blaine Eddington looked down on her, a sensual smile on his lips.

Kate, somewhat off balance at the sudden appearance of another person, was even more disconcerted when she discovered that person to be Blaine. Her heart began to race as though seeking to get out of her body, and all her muscles went limp. Kate was glad she was seated and she carefully put her pencil down, for fear it would drop from her grasp.

"No. I'm always glad to see our supporters," she finally managed to say.

"Good," Blaine responded, slipping casually into the chair opposite her desk. "There's something I'd like to discuss with you. I wonder if I might make a suggestion for the symphonic concert you are going to do on May twenty-sixth."

"Certainly." Kate wondered if her voice sounded normal to Blaine because it had a strange ring in her ears. "We always appreciate suggestions from our supporters."

"I'd like you to play Ravel's *Pavane pour une Infante Défunte*. It was a favorite of my grandfather. He'd be one hundred years old on May twenty-sixth."

"I love that piece, too. The parallel ninth chords and the French horn, the flutes—" Kate's heartbeat was beginning to slow down in spite of Blaine's ringing bass voice that played such erotic games with her ears. She was talking about music now and that seemed to calm her considerably. "Maybe we should announce it as a specially dedicated piece."

Blaine reached over and took her hand. "I'd appreciate that." A light shone in Blaine's eyes and Kate forgot that she was just a symphony orchestra conductor talking to a contributor. Fire seemed to emanate at the point where he was touching her. Then he removed his hand and sat back. "But are you sure it would be all right? I don't want to interfere with any plans that you've already made."

"All right? Why it would be wonderful! I think it would add a marvelous touch to the evening!" Kate stood up from her seat and walked around to the front of the desk. She extended her hand for a handshake. "And I want to thank you for letting me know about your grandfather's birthday. Any time you—"

Blaine stood up. He did not shake her hand, though, but took Kate's slender hand in both of his. Blaine's nearness seemed to overpower her. She forgot where she was and who she was and began swaying toward him. Suddenly she caught herself.

"I do thank you for coming in . . . ," she began lamely.

"Kate," came a brusque voice, sounding as though it had been wrenched from Blaine's soul.

Before Kate knew what was happening, she found herself in Blaine Eddington's arms, his lips hard on hers. Kate felt the real world slip away. All she could think of was that she was being surrounded, being consumed, by the most attractive man she had ever seen. Her body seemed to develop a will of its own, clinging to Blaine's hard frame, her lips sending messages of excitement through her body. Nothing seemed to matter except that Kate was one with Blaine.

The clang of one of the outer doors startled Kate, forcing her back into the real world. Kate remembered where she was. The office. Imagine what talk there would be if anyone saw them!

"Blaine. We've got to stop."

Blaine's answer was to draw her more deeply into himself. Forgetting the outside world once more, Kate clung to him. She felt a weakness in her knees and if Blaine hadn't been holding her so tightly she would have sunk to the ground. All Kate knew was that she had to return Blaine's kiss, to match the emotion which he displayed. She didn't care if he noticed how hard her heart was thumping, how sensuous it was to have him stroke her hair. Only she and Blaine existed in the universe.

Once more Kate heard the clanging of the outer doors. This time the sound seemed louder. Kate slowly tried to extricate herself from Blaine's arms. She knew that if she stayed there any longer she would not have the willpower to stop.

"Kate," Blaine's voice whispered, the timbre of his rich bass voice once again enticing her back into the circle of his arms.

But Kate's practical self had been awakened and would not be denied. "We—we shouldn't be doing this," she managed to say.

Blaine slowly released her but held her at arm's length. A cloud came over his face. "Please forgive me. I'm afraid I wasn't thinking." His eyes still had a smoldering brilliance, but he let go of Kate and walked to the other side of the room.

Kate stood where she was, craving more of Blaine's kiss but knowing that this was not the place for it. She wanted to put their relationship back on some firmer business footing.

"Getting back to the dedication, Blaine . . ."

Blaine turned and looked at her, a strange expression coming into his eyes. "I'm pleased that you're going to perform a special piece in memory of my grandfather. And if there's anything else I can do to help promote the evening, please let me know." With that, Blaine turned and left the room.

Kate felt limp. What had happened? Why had Blaine behaved the way he had? And, more than Blaine's strange behavior, what had gotten into her? Kate was usually so reserved, so proper. She was relieved, at least, that no one had seen her. Her arms and legs were still not immediately responsive to her brain, but she managed to get back to the chair behind her

desk. Before her was the program that she had been proofreading before
Blaine had burst in on her. She willed herself back to work.

When Kate had just about finished with the program, the telephone
rang. For a moment Kate held her breath. Was it Blaine, calling to tell her
that he would like to see her again? She picked it up.

"Hi, Kate. This is Bill. Bill Scott."

"Oh yes. How are you?"

"I called to ask if you can accompany me to dinner tonight."

Kate felt torn. She did not want to offend Bill, and she certainly wanted
the contract with Maesterling. But after the episode with Blaine, she did
not feel she wanted to be in the company of another man, pleasant as Bill
was. "Oh, I'd love to, Bill. But I'm afraid I'm busy."

"Can't blame me for trying. I'm leaving tomorrow morning to check
out another orchestra. Say, as long as I'm on the phone, I have a question."

Kate hoped he wasn't going to ask for another date. She said, "Anything, Bill."

"I've been looking over that schedule you gave me, and everything you
have will fit into my schedule. Would you want to recommend a particular
evening?"

"How about May twenty-sixth?" Kate blurted out.

"May twenty-sixth. That's—"

"The program is altered slightly, but I think you'll like it. We've decided to play a selection in memory of Sloan Wentworth Eddington."

"Sounds terrific. Would you put my name on a ticket at the box office?"

"I certainly will."

"I have to be back in town again soon to discuss the money end of the
recording deal with Malcolm Merriwether. Do you think you could save
me an evening then?"

Kate felt obliged to say yes. After all, there was no need to offend Bill
and she had had a lovely time the last time she had had dinner with him.
"Of course, Bill. See you then." And Kate hung up.

She tried to return to work but her mind kept drifting back to Blaine.
She could still feel the strength of his arms, the emotion generated by his
kiss. Surely that was not an act. No one could pretend feelings like those.
But what had caused his sudden departure?

There was no point in dwelling on the man, Kate told herself. It was
apparent that while he might have found her attractive, he did not want

to develop any ongoing relationship with her. And she had her own life to live, involved right now as she was with proving to herself and to the world that she was a good musician and a good symphony orchestra conductor. For the moment, that would have to be the limit of her life.

CHAPTER 7

In the end there were two pieces chosen for the special salute to Blaine's late grandfather: Maurice Ravel's *Pavane pour une Infante Défunte* and Samuel Barber's *Adagio for Strings*. During rehearsal one evening Malcolm came in with some questions about Maesterling Recordings and Kate had to ask Harold to take over. It was a passage in which the music was supposed to swell in such a way that it engulfed the audience and swept them into a place that seemed all light. It was difficult interpreting that particular passage, but even as Kate and Malcolm continued to talk, Harold was managing it. The strings sounded like a unit now, where before only two of the violinists had seemed to comprehend the effect they were supposed to be achieving.

"Harold's good," Malcolm said to Kate. "And considering that he's never been crazy about Barber, he's downright amazing."

"Yes." Kate nodded, a little uncomfortable. Yes, he was good—and he deserved to be a conductor too. She and Malcolm had made recent inquiries about possible directorships for Harold but had come up with nothing. An opening in Hartford, Connecticut, which had sounded promising, had been filled the very day Malcolm had phoned an influential friend in that city. Even if they had been successsful, Kate thought, what would they have said to Harold? Would they have said, "Why don't you go up there to be interviewed? Then, if they like you, you can pack up the family and leave"? Would they ever be able to say that? Kate looked at Malcolm, sighed, and decided not to think about it tonight.

But Malcolm would not let the subject drop. "I know what you're thinking," he said. "You're wondering if perhaps Harold should have been given charge of the Whittenburg. I'll be honest, Kate, and tell you that several board members did prefer him and the rest of us felt that if you didn't want the post then no one but Harold would have served. But we chose you finally because you're a tad more open-minded about music, willing to experiment a little and get us attention. Maesterling wouldn't have been so quick to seek out the Whittenburg if Harold had been at the

helm. And you're also much gentler on the musicians. You're both perfectionists, but you're much more the diplomat. Listen to him: he's shouting
'*Dolce! dolce!*' and getting all red in the face. The word means 'Sweet,
delicate,' and Harold's bellowing as though it meant 'Get this right, you
idiots, before I kill you.' "

Kate smiled. "True," she said ruefully, "but even though he bellows he
gets a good performance out of them. Or maybe it's *because* he bellows."

"Yes," Malcolm agreed. "One of the great mysteries of life is how
musicians can play *dolce* while they're being shouted at or *vivace* when
they're ready to drop from exhaustion. And yet they do it. The show must
go on." He sighed. "You'd better get the baton back from Harold before
he starts battering that new viola player. I just stopped by to tell you that I
sent the revised program on to Maesterling and William Scott phoned to
say it sounded good. This Barber *Adagio* happens to be his favorite American piece and he wanted to know how you'd guessed that."

"I didn't guess. I chose it because it's also Sloan Eddington's favorite
American piece." Kate grinned. "One of the older violinists remembered
that. I had nothing to do with the selection."

"It hardly matters," said Malcolm. "What matters is how it's played.
And Scott is also crazy about Ravel. He says the *Pavane* isn't played nearly
often enough." Malcolm sighed. "This is true. When someone took the
theme and turned it into a horror called 'The Lamp Is Low' the *Pavane*
just sputtered and died."

"Well, we're resurrecting it," Kate said. "It was the one piece Blaine
specifically requested. Odd, because it isn't a violin showcase at all. But
apparently Sloan Eddington was too much the consummate musician ever
to let his own discipline affect his judgment of orchestral works."

"Blaine's a very important man," Malcolm said as Harold walked toward them clenching the baton tightly. "Let's make sure this memorial
section of the Pops is flawless."

"I'll do my best," Kate said, feeling her heart begin to race. She'd rarely
been nervous during performances before, but she knew with a sinking
heart that Saturday evening would be different. With Blaine and Malcolm
both out there, both expecting perfection, and with Bill Scott of Maesterling judging her too, she'd be lucky if she didn't drop the baton.

Harold had come up to them now. Malcolm said, "You do fine work,
Harold. That Barber is very delicate. Has to be handled just right."

"Thank you. I'm sure Kate will do well with it." He did not add, "Now
that I've shown the musicians how to play it." But he did look at Kate

briefly, unable to suppress the triumph in his eyes. Then he said, "Blaine's already quite taken with you, Kate. If the performance goes well, he'll be enraptured beyond all reasoning."

"For heaven's sake, Harold!" Kate blushed crimson. Malcolm chuckled.

"Don't pretend you haven't noticed," Harold said. His tone was warm and teasing, as it had been in the old noncompetitive days, and Kate could not quite understand why. Had he at last resigned himself to the fact that he was not going to be the director of the Whittenburg? Or was he being nice to her because he honestly appreciated Kate's acceptance of his advice? He did not know of her plans to find him a directorship, but whatever the reasons for the change in Harold, Kate was happy about it.

"Admit it," Harold said, "you're smitten." He had reverted to his old big-brother stance—hands on hips, small mirthful eyes boring into hers, the trace of a smile lightening his heavy face.

"All right." She smiled. "Blaine is—interesting."

"Yes, and you're nervous because this concert will be partly for him."

"Well, maybe a little, but—"

At this Malcolm started. "But I've never known you to have stage fright, Kate."

"Of course I don't!" she said with feigned disdain. She knew that Malcolm could tolerate a lot of things in this orchestra, but never stage fright. Though there had been many imperfect performances under the direction of Robert Bernini, the man had always been confident, always given the impression that he'd known exactly what he was doing, and he'd demanded this attitude from the musicians. Even music critics had been fooled. One had mistaken a poor performance for a "bizarre but exciting interpretation."

To Malcolm she said, "I don't get nervous. You know me better than that." She winked at Harold. "I'm just playing along with this tease over here so he'll leave me alone. Oh, when *will* you people get it through your heads that I can survive quite nicely without a man?" She forced enough chuckles to placate Malcolm and to get him started on another subject: the courtship of his wife. Then she sighed in relief and vowed that, no matter what, she would not let herself get rattled.

On Saturday night Kate stood in the greenroom ordering herself to be calm. The final rehearsal last night had gone off perfectly and now the memorial section of the concert was virtually flawless. She could not say the same about the rest of the pieces, but they were for the most part popular light classics with which the orchestra had long been familiar. Not perfect, perhaps, but far better than average. Bill Scott would be satisfied, she was sure.

Harold came into the greenroom along with Nancy MacFarland, a forty-year-old mother of six who would be soloing in the opening bars of Ravel's *Pavane pour une Infante Défunte*.

"I've never understood," Harold said to Nancy, "how such a petite little lady could master the French horn. I shouldn't think your lungs would be big enough."

They all laughed at this, which had the effect of allaying Kate's nervousness even more. That could only help the performance.

"I peeked out at the audience," Nancy said. "Quite a crowd."

"This show had plenty of publicity," Harold said. "Blaine Eddington made sure of that."

"I saw him coming in," Nancy said.

"Yes, so did I," Harold nodded. Then he frowned, glanced at Kate and glanced quickly away again. "He came in with Gloria Hutchinson, but I'm sure it's not true what they're saying."

"What're they saying?" asked Nancy eagerly. She could never resist gossip.

Harold shook his head and sighed. "That she's *the* woman in his life. But I doubt that." He winked at Kate. "I have a feeling there's someone else who interests him too."

Nancy, who knew nothing of Kate's feelings for Blaine, asked innocently, "Why don't you think it's true? Gloria's a beautiful woman— young, wealthy, unattached."

Kate bit her lip and said, forcing her voice to be calm, "Did you say she's here with Blaine tonight?"

"Yes," Harold said. Then he chuckled. "I'm sure it's an arranged thing though. The Hutchinsons and the Eddingtons were always very close. All that money in common, don'tcha know."

"And after all he's only just recently got back to town," Nancy said. "He hasn't had time to find anyone else, but I'm sure there'll be eager maidens waiting. Oh, but he's handsome, isn't he? If I were twenty years younger and didn't have a husband . . . And to think he's going to be watching me play the opening to his grandfather's favorite piece. I'll have to make it special, so special that he'll remember it till his dying day . . ." She was still murmuring dreamily as she made her way from the greenroom to the stage. Kate and Harold were now alone.

"What's the matter, Kate?" Harold asked.

"Nothing." She bit her lip.

"Me and my big mouth. I shouldn't have mentioned Gloria."

"They why did you?" she said irritably.

He looked disconcerted, as though he hadn't expected this question. "Because—because—I thought you might have heard some of the gossip about them and I wanted to tell you how foolish it was so you wouldn't be nervous tonight."

"But I hadn't heard any gossip about them. Not a shred."

"Really? Well, I'm surprised." He shrugged.

A voice called into the room, "Ready, Miss Reston."

She took a deep breath and walked out to the stage.

Midway through the performance Kate came perilously close to tears. The only thing that was saving her, she thought, was the fact that the orchestra was so well acquainted with these light classics that they could have done them well enough with or without the aid of her baton. For her baton certainly hadn't guided them, as it had in past performances. In fact, it had become a positive hindrance in the Pachelbel *Canon* when she'd blundered by starting off in a tempo much slower than the version they'd rehearsed. The harpist had looked at Kate, confused, frantically fingering an interlude to cover the error. But too late. The extra notes, based on a faster tempo, had already been played, and connoisseurs in the audience would certainly hear the mistake. Kate had remembered that Bill Scott was in the audience and she'd groaned inwardly.

The other problems hadn't been so fatal, but they'd been serious enough so that Maesterling would surely take notice. And Malcolm! What would he be thinking? And Blaine! Good heavens, if the tribute to his grandfather was as lackluster as the rest of the concert was proving to be he'd be so disappointed.

She had seen him as soon as she'd come onto the stage. He was there, front row center, with the lovely Gloria Hutchinson beside him. Kate had wanted to believe that Blaine's only interest in this enchanting blond Whittenburg socialite had to do with the fact that their parents were friends. But Harold had said there'd been talk about them, and surely there must be if it had reached *his* ears. Harold normally took little interest in gossip. "Why should I clutter up my mind with that stuff," he was forever saying, "when it's cluttered enough already with everything from the rules of the road to income tax regulations? There'd be no room left in my brain cells for music."

So it *had* to be true, Kate thought. There must be more between Blaine and Gloria than friendship. She had just come to this conclusion when she'd made that fatal timing mistake in the *Canon*.

Now the memorial tribute was coming up. Kate swallowed hard, walked over to the microphone and said softly, trying to keep her voice even, "We conclude the evening with a tribute to Sloan Wentworth Eddington, who, as many of you know, was a violinist in this orchestra for several years before going on to achieve worldwide fame." This was all she said. Blaine had asked her to keep it brief. And she needn't have worried about her delivery because the moment she spoke the name "Sloan" people had been unable to resist applauding, thus helping to drown out her faltering voice. Grateful to them, she thought, So far, so good, as she turned and raised her baton in Nancy MacFarland's direction.

To Kate's astonishment and delight this portion of the program was flawless. Part of the reason was that they had rehearsed it so often. Afterward, in the greenroom, many people also came over dutifully to congratulate Kate, who was standing next to Malcolm but still had not been able to meet his eyes. She was grateful for people's politeness, but she wished they had not come. She'd been awful, and she didn't want them to patronize her.

"Well?" Malcolm said at last, his mouth tight. "What happened out there?"

"I don't know what you mean."

"Come on, Kate, what was it? Having Eddington in the audience?"

She thought fast and then said, "Oh, you mean you didn't think I was up to par?" She forced a laugh. "I *thought* you might misinterpret what I was doing." She took a deep breath. "This is going to sound a bit unconventional, but what I was trying to do tonight was spotlight Sloan's special music by deliberately seeing to it that the regularly scheduled pieces were —uh—more low-key."

"What?" His expression was incredulous.

"I know, I should have discussed this with you before. But it only occurred to me at the last minute. I thought if the rest of the performance was adequate but not *too* good, then the memorial pieces would be set in starker relief. And they were, weren't they? We got a standing ovation." Kate smiled eagerly.

"Yes, but that's not the way you're supposed to—"

Malcolm didn't have a chance to finish. Blaine Eddington was now striding toward her, his hand already extended. "Kate, you have done great honor to this family. I'll never forget it. We thank you so much."

At the touch of his fingers Kate's hand trembled involuntarily and her throat constricted with joy—and with longing. "You're quite welcome, Mr. Eddington. The pleasure was ours." She stole a glance at Malcolm, who was now smiling broadly. Had he swallowed her lies, she wondered, or was he just being charming to the Whittenburg's most generous supporter?

"I'd like you to meet Gloria Hutchinson," Blaine said. And he introduced the two women, who really did not require the formalities. They had both grown up in Whittenburg and had met before. Kate wished she could dislike Gloria. At least that would be a healthy response to a rival. But Gloria was a genuinely kind person as well as a beautiful one. She was also disarmingly honest, as when she said, "I don't understand everything you did, Kate. Music is such a complicated subject. All I know is that it sounded so beautiful. The second piece made me cry."

"Barber's *Adagio?*"

"Oh, it was so pretty. I wish Blake had been here to hear it."

"Blake?"

"Blake Aldrich. The man I'm engaged to. Don't you read the papers?" She laughed self-consciously.

It was as though a heavy weight had been lifted from Kate's shoulders. She exhaled so audibly that Blaine and Gloria could not help noticing. As other Eddington family members came forward to greet Kate, gently forcing Blaine into the background, Kate found herself smiling with genuine happiness. And when Harold came up to her she whispered, "Gloria is engaged. And not to Blaine."

"Oh?"

"Where did you get the idea that she and Blaine were an item?"

"I—I—didn't know she was engaged." He looked disconcerted, as though one of his performances had gone awry. She was puzzled by this. "You must have confused the first names. They sound alike."

"Yes," he said. "Yes. Yes, that's what I did." Now he looked a little relieved and she couldn't understand this either.

And to think she'd come near to losing her job tonight because of him. Kate shook her head. "Stick with music, will you please, and leave the gossip department to Nancy. She never gets names confused."

He nodded and walked off, though he turned twice and looked back at her, his expression again puzzled. As Kate turned to greet Blaine's uncle, she brushed a drop of perspiration from her brow. Everything had turned out well after all, but oh, what a close call! And it must never happen again!

CHAPTER 8

It took days for Kate to convince Malcolm that the poor performance of Saturday night had not been owing to her nervousness. But eventually Kate managed it by explaining the episode as former conductor Bernini might have explained it. "I don't care if you believe me or not, Malcolm. I knew exactly what I was doing." She rose from her office desk, strode over to the window and leveled an imperious Bernini-style stare at Malcolm. "And I didn't 'mess up,' as you put it. I did a low-key performance. I'd planned it that way."

"You can't deny that the Pachelbel was messed up."

This much Kate had to concede. "Malcolm, there are so many versions of that piece that they've made a whole record of its endless variations. And that night there was—uh—some confusion, I'll admit, but the new harpist covered nicely, and it was only three or four notes that—"

"All right, all right. But please, Kate, don't ever again conduct badly in order to set special pieces in 'starker relief.' It's downright insane."

"Yes, I suppose it is."

He softened, smiled and gave her a fatherly kiss on the cheek. "End of lecture. Now for some good news. Bill Scott of Maesterling was so impressed with that memorial tribute that he forgave us the rest of the concert. He wants to record us."

"Does he? Oh, that's wonderful!"

"So all's well, after all. How about a truce lunch with my wife and me?"

"I can't, Malcolm. I've got to work on the scoring for the first of the summer outdoor performances. June's almost here, you know."

"So it is. Well, see you Saturday then." Malcolm picked up a briefcase and left with a cheerful wave.

Kate went down to the stage, sat at the piano and began making notations in the scoring for Copland's *Appalachian Spring*. She was deeply absorbed in her work when a bass voice from behind said "Busy?" and so startled Kate as to cause her to drop both the score and the pencil.

"Blaine!" she gasped.

"I frightened you. I'm sorry."

Heat coursed into her face as her blue eyes met his green ones. "It's all right," she said with a faint smile.

"I wanted to thank you again for my grandfather's memorial concert." She nodded. "I received the note from your family. It was beautifully written." She went on to tell him that Maesterling had selected the Whittenburg for a phonograph record. "They'll be coming in to record us— live! Everyone's very excited."

They chatted for a while about the record offer and about the Copland Kate was now reviewing. Of Copland Blaine said, "He's our most American composer, I think. I particularly like his *Lincoln Portrait.*"

"Yes, we do that often in our Pops concerts. Malcolm likes to do the narrative portions." She smiled. "He's a bit of a ham."

"I don't blame him. It's not every man who gets to read Lincoln's lines for an audience."

She said, "You're a Lincoln expert, I understand."

"Only insofar as I'm a Civil War buff, and Lincoln was a part of the period. Which reminds me," he said more to himself than to her, "the Historical Society wants me to lecture on Pickett next month and I'll have to be gathering my research soon."

"Pickett?" She knit her brow. "I studied him, but I don't remember . . . Which side was he on?"

"You live twenty miles from Gettysburg, and you don't—" He broke off and began to laugh.

"Oh, I know, I know," she said, sighing. "Anyone from Whittenburg is supposed to know more about the Pennsylvania invasion than Bruce Catton. Well, I don't. I never could get all the names and regiments and battle sites straight. All I know about the Civil War is the music, and I did do a good job at last year's pageant if I do say so myself."

"I missed that," he said.

"You were out in California making sports cars and didn't care enough about Eastern history to make the trip home. Shame on you!" She laughed. He touched her arm lightly and began to laugh too, warm soft chuckles that caused her to shiver with emotions she could not understand.

"Are you busy right now?" he asked.

"I'm working on the Copland score."

"Don't you think it's time you went to Gettysburg and learned about Pickett?"

"I've *been* there, Blaine. In school they had field trips every other year. And I still don't know which general fought in which—" She broke off as she realized that what he was doing was asking her for a date. Then she smiled. Often she had imagined this moment, had wondered whether her acceptance ought to be enthusiastic or civil or a little cool. The smile had come to her lips, however, before she could consider the options again. In a way she was glad. She'd never enjoyed playing coy games. She said, "I really shouldn't leave. I just finished telling Malcolm how busy I was going to be this afternoon. But of course that was before I remembered that I'd lived for twenty-nine years without ever learning about Pickett. Suddenly I knew that no concert, no Copland could possibly be more important than this. And so," she said, rising, "I must hasten to Gettysburg and commence my education. Would you care to come with me, sir?"

He laughed again and took her arm.

Blaine gave Kate a guided tour of Gettysburg that finally clarified and put into perspective all the jumbled facts she had dutifully memorized during her school years. She was especially moved when he took her up to Cemetery Ridge, site of a dramatic Confederate offensive which had involved thousands of men marching across an open field to assault the entrenched Union Army. It was here that the Southern invasion of the North had finally been stopped. His impassioned description of the legendary Pickett's Charge gave Kate chills. And by the end of the afternoon, Kate not only understood Gettysburg but had begun to take an interest in the Civil War itself. "It's hard to believe that they went on to fight for another two years," she said.

He nodded and went on to talk about Grant's thrust into Virginia. He continued to talk as they got into his sleek black sports car and began driving out of town. And he was describing the siege of Petersburg when he pulled up at a Pennsylvania Dutch restaurant and said, "I'm hungry. Are you?"

"Yes. It must be all that vicarious fighting."

He smiled. "This is a fine place. The house itself dates from before the Civil War and the food is much like that which the soldiers might have eaten if they'd been invited into an Amish house for supper. Come on."

When they were seated with drinks in a cozy corner, looking forward to the food they'd just ordered, Blaine said, "When Lee invaded Pennsylvania he forbade his men to forage or take meals without paying. It was late June, and the land was lush, and his men must have been sorely tempted to disobey him. But Lee was a gentleman, even in the worst days of the war. Of course, that was a very gentlemanly age. Wars were fought by the book; chivalry was prized. A far cry from later wars, particularly Vietnam."

"You know so much about those days one might almost think you were reincarnated. And the way you tell the stories—I almost feel I was there."

"That's the only way to understand history, Kate. To put yourself into the skins of the people who were there. For example, you can read from now till doomsday about the battle of Gettysburg taking place on July first to third, 1863. But what do those numbers mean? What does the name of the town mean, for that matter? Nothing. Nothing at all—unless you take some time and try to imagine what the people must have felt—what it looked like, what the weather was like, how the attack might have appeared to a soldier who'd never seen battle before. It's—"

He was interrupted by the plump waitress, who was setting the first course in front of them. Kate had chosen *gruumbier suppe*, a potato soup nicely enhanced by parsley. For an entree she had sauerbraten but Blaine insisted she have a bite of his *boova shenkel*—beef-and-potato tarts served with a creamy sauce. There were also red cabbage, parsnip patties and cucumber salad, and for dessert a sour cherry pie plus bites of Blaine's walnut gingerbread. Over coffee they discussed the décor of the restaurant and then Blaine described having come here once with an account executive from a New York advertising agency which represented Eddington Motors. "He thought Pennsylvania Dutch meant just that—Dutchmen who had settled in Pennsylvania. He was surprised when I told him that 'Dutch' was a corruption of Deutsch, or German. Most of the settlers were German-speaking."

This was something Kate already knew. The Mennonites and Amish were well represented in Whittenburg. But Blaine had, during the day, fallen into the role of lecturing professor and was enjoying it so much that, to humor him, Kate continued to play student. After all, her turn would come. If ever he meant to learn about the intricacies of music, then *she* would be the one to enlighten *him*. And she'd be sure to laugh heartily if he couldn't tell the differences among the Brandenburg Concertos or if he confused a term like *pesante* with the name of an Italian composer. Oh yes, she would get back at Blaine for his teasing! But not right now. Right now she just wanted to gaze into those riveting eyes which seemed to grow even greener and more hypnotic as he expounded on his various subjects.

In time he drove her home to her condo but did not ask to come in. Instead, he walked her to her door and took both her hands in his. "Your homework is to explore the end of town where our civilians shot at Jeb Stuart's cavalrymen."

"Where the bullet holes are, you mean? And wasn't Stuart a cavalry general?"

"Yes. He got separated from Lee, came too far north, and was probably in this area when Lee called him down to Gettysburg. Bullets flew here, yes, but no one was killed." He paused. "Go to the library and read about Jeb in the microfilmed Harrisburg papers. I'll quiz you Saturday after the concert."

"What is this, a college without walls?" she laughed.

"I hope without walls." He said softly, leaning forward to brush his lips against hers, "Yes, I definitely prefer us without walls, Katherine. That is your name—Katherine?"

"Of course." He had stepped back now but her lips still burned where his lips had touched them. In a quavering voice she said, "But Kate is simpler, I guess. Only one—uh—syllable . . ." She trailed off as their eyes met and he bent toward her again, this time taking her into his arms. His tongue probed at her closed lips until it found entrance. By this time her heart was hammering wildly and she began to moan softly. Her body loosened and she yielded to his attempts to hold her closer, harder. But just as she could discern his low moans too he stepped back suddenly, as though confused. He studied her eyes once more, and then his own eyes slowly glazed over. She sensed he was no longer with her. Slowly he stepped back and said unsteadily, "We shouldn't go too fast too soon. I know you must feel that way."

She didn't feel that way. Or, more accurately, hadn't had a chance to think about how she felt. But she said, "I guess you're right."

"Good night, Kate." And before she could say goodbye, he had turned and left. Kate stood watching him for a long time wondering why he always left her in so abrupt a fashion. Was he simply afraid to get involved? Or was he promised to another woman and consumed with guilt whenever tempted to betray her? The latter seemed the most logical. But Kate did not know what to do about it. Should she come right out and ask him? Should she say nothing and wait patiently for Blaine to explain? For the time being, she thought, she would do nothing. Nothing except to remember what a fascinating, challenging and puzzling day this had been.

CHAPTER 9

The memory of the day at Gettysburg flashed in and out of Kate's mind. She hoped that the expedition was just the start of things to come. But in the meantime, Kate had to get her mind back on her job. And her job this Friday morning was to meet with Bill Scott to discuss the recording for Maesterling. Malcolm and Bill Scott had settled on the financial arrangements and now all that was left was for Kate and Bill to settle on the details of the performance itself.

"Hi, Kate. How's my favorite symphony orchestra conductor this morning?" Bill Scott knocked on the open door of Kate's office and walked into the room. He plunked himself down into the leather chair facing the desk.

"Good morning, Bill. It's nice to see you again. Would you like a cup of coffee?"

"That sounds good."

Kate got up and walked to the corner of the room. There she poured coffee for herself and Bill. "It's always easier to talk over coffee."

"And easier still over dinner. How about we postpone this discussion till tonight, while you and I are enjoying a candlelight dinner at the Lincoln Hotel?"

Kate smiled. "But if we do our work this evening, what's left to talk about this morning?"

"This morning we can run over to Gettysburg and you can be my guide. I've passed by Gettysburg many times, but somehow I've never managed to visit the battlefield. How about it?"

Startled, Kate realized that Bill was serious. Maybe someday she might visit Gettysburg with someone else, but right now she considered it the special place for her and Blaine. She wanted no one else to intrude. "Gettysburg? That's for history buffs, Bill. Not for us musicians." She spoke in a tone of mock derision.

"I guess Gettysburg is out. Then how about dinner anyway?"

Kate thought for a moment. She had to work on the scoring for a concert that the orchestra was going to perform in the armory for the

Founders' Day celebration in mid-June. But she supposed she could spare a few hours for dinner. After all, this was business. "Sure," she said, trying to look as interested as she could. "But right now we'd better get down to work."

"All right. But let's settle the most important detail right now. Shall I pick you up at seven, seven-thirty or eight?"

Kate laughed. "You really are a nut. Seven-thirty will be fine."

"Now that that's settled, how about taking me down to the concert hall?"

"I'd be glad to, but you've seen that already." Kate was puzzled.

"Oh, I know that acoustically Meade Hall will be perfect for the recording, but I have to see where we'll put our equipment."

"All right." Kate stood up and walked toward the door.

As they left Kate's office, Bill draped his arm around her shoulder. It was a possessive gesture and Kate was very uncomfortable with it. She did not want to simply shrug it off but on the other hand she did not want to be seen by anyone in this intimate fashion. "I think I'll need my jacket," Kate said, slipping out from Bill's arm and heading back into her office. "I'll just be a minute."

Kate returned carrying the beige suede blazer that she had worn to work in the morning. As she walked she slipped her arms into the sleeves, thus preventing Bill from getting too close to her. "There," she said, the jacket finally on.

"I would have been delighted to keep you warm," Bill commented, but he made no further move to touch her.

The two of them walked through the corridors to the concert hall itself, talking now of the music that other symphony orchestras were planning to perform for the series of records. Kate led Bill to the proscenium of Meade Hall.

"This is a nice big stage," Bill said, walking around it. "Exactly how much room is left after the entire orchestra is seated?"

"I'm not sure. Our stage manager could probably be more helpful to you with that than I could." Kate stepped off to the side. "Eddie?" she called out. Then she turned to Bill. "I'm not sure if he's here today, but I'll check."

Kate walked off, and returned shortly with a thin, gray-haired middle-aged man. "This is Eddie Barnes," she said to Bill. "Eddie, this is Bill Scott, who is laying the groundwork for a recording we're going to do for Maesterling."

"Glad to meet you," Eddie said, extending his hand.

"Same here, Eddie. Now if you could tell me—"

"If you don't need me right now, I'd like to get back to my office, Bill. Eddie will show you how to get back when you're done."

"Very good, Kate. I'll see you later."

Kate walked back to her office. Along the way she thought about Bill. He was a nice person, an interesting man. And he was obviously attracted to her. They shared the common interest of music. Why didn't his touch set her on fire?

When Kate returned to her office she found the program for the armory concert on her desk, left there by the delivery boy from the print shop. She picked it up, noting some minor problems and correcting them. She put the program aside, planning to drop it off at the print shop after lunch. Then she went back to the score she had been studying.

"I guess he gave me the right instructions."

Kate looked up to see Bill standing at her door. "Instructions?"

"Eddie. Instructions to your office. It seemed so easy when I was walking with you, but this place sure has a lot of back alleys and corridors. But I'm here at last." Bill gave Kate a broad grin and sat down in the chair facing the desk.

"Did you get all the information you need?" Kate asked.

"Pretty much," Bill said, his voice somber. "And now, if you'll sign this agreement." He held out a printed sheet.

Kate looked up, puzzled. "What agreement?"

"Oh, you know. The one dealing with quality."

"Quality? You mean decision over the sound track itself?"

"Yes. The technicians on our staff really know their business and they are the ones who make final decision on how the record is completed."

"Your technicians?" Kate looked horrified. "Technicians make final decisions on symphony orchestras?"

"Perhaps 'technicians' is the wrong term, although that's what we call them. Maybe 'studio musicians' might be a better term. But I assure you they are all qualified—"

"Qualified! If they're qualified, why aren't they heading their own symphony orchestras?" She could not contain her outrage.

Bill looked upset. "This is a standard form, Kate," he said, waving the paper which she had refused to take. "It doesn't say that you won't listen to the master and make whatever changes you deem necessary."

"But your technicians"—Kate turned her nose up at the term—"have the final say."

"Sort of." Bill looked as though he wanted to end the discussion.

"Sort of? Either they do or they don't." Kate was making a serious effort to control her temper but she felt she was losing.

"Well . . ." Bill hesitated. "They do. But that's only after you have heard the recording and have made all your suggestions—"

"Suggestions, are they? I don't make 'suggestions' when I lead this orchestra. I decide what plays and what doesn't play. And I decide how this orchestra will sound."

"You will. You will." Bill seemed anxious to placate Kate.

"I will what? Make final decision over the sound that gets labeled the Whittenburg Symphony Orchestra? Not if I sign that paper I won't."

"It's not exactly what you think, Kate. Some of this has to do with the technical end of music reproduction. Our studio musicians know how to get the best possible sound out of an orchestra."

Kate gave Bill a cold look. "And just what do you think my job is?"

"I'm sorry I've upset you, Kate, over what is actually a formality. Why don't I give you time to think this over?"

"Think about turning my responsibilities over to some studio"—she said the last word with distaste—"musicians?"

"There is a solution to this, believe me. But I think you need to cool down first."

Kate looked up at Bill. "Perhaps you're right. But cool or not, there's no way I'll allow anyone to determine the ultimate sound of the Whittenburg Symphony Orchestra."

"We'll discuss this at dinner. Okay?"

"Okay." Kate was grudging with her acceptance, but resolved that she would give him no peace until this thing was settled.

"Seven-thirty. Right?" Bill was smiling as though nothing had happened.

"Yes. And now if you'll excuse me, I have to get back to work."

"Righto, Madam Conductor. See you later." And Bill left the room.

Kate returned to the score she had been studying but could not bring her mind to absorb any of the music. She was distressed. On the one hand, she was very anxious to do the recording. Although she was not interested in leaving the Whittenburg for a more prestigious position, if the recording went well she might be asked to perform as guest conductor for other symphony orchestras. People might travel from great distances to see the orchestra perform. That would even be good business for the town. But there was no way that Kate would allow strangers to have the final say over her orchestra. The dilemma caused her head to ache.

Kate was tempted to call Malcolm, but she put the thought aside. There was always time to call him and for now she wanted to work the problem out by herself. She was, after all, the head of this symphony orchestra and she should be able to solve the more sticky managerial problems by herself. She decided, though, that it would be best if she left the office. She wanted to go home and relax by playing the piano. During times of stress, even when she was a child, she would seek the solace of the piano. The act of touching the keys, of concentrating on what her fingers were doing, kept her mind busy, and the music itself lulled her into tranquillity. Yes, that was what she would do. She would go home and practice for a while.

Kate left her office quickly, leaving behind the score she was supposed to be working on and forgetting the program she was supposed to drop off. Her only thought was to get home.

When she arrived at her apartment the muted beiges and browns in her living room soothed her and she dropped her jacket on the overstuffed club chair, kicking her shoes off at the same time. She sat down at the Steinway that took up the entire corner near the windows and began to play.

Instinctively she began with Chopin's *Polonaise Militaire*, which had been a favorite of hers since childhood. She associated it with all the momentous occasions in her life: when she had been accepted at the Boston Conservatory, when she had gotten a job with the Whittenburg, even the night she had found out she had been appointed director. She played it during the small moments of triumph and when things went badly. The music cheered her. She could probably say that had she written down all the times she had come to this piece without thinking, she would have a record of her life.

And now the melody did not fail her. She played until she felt sufficiently calmed down so she could really practice.

Kate looked through the music that was lying on the top of the piano. She hadn't performed since she had become conductor, but she liked to make certain that she would still be able to perform. Today she thought she would do the first section of a Bach concerto, a difficult piece with nuances that were hard to achieve without sufficient practice. But Kate felt up to trying. Here was something she could get lost in.

Kate had forgotten about time. A knock at the door brought her back to Whittenburg. "Come in," Kate called, unwilling to leave the piano. "It's open."

"Hi! Hope I'm not interrupting you." Ellie walked into the room, still carrying the briefcase she used for her school papers. "It's so seldom you're home anymore I thought I'd grab the chance to say hello."

"Glad you did, Ellie. Come on, sit down."

"Just for a minute. The school art show is being held tonight, and I just have time to shower, change and go back. I have to make sure everything is displayed properly. What's new?" Ellie headed toward the couch and was sitting down when there was another knock at the door.

Kate walked over to open it and saw her neighbor Marissa, the socialite who wanted everyone to think she was an actress, standing at her door. Marissa never condescended to socialize with the other condo owners and Kate was surprised to see her. Nevertheless, Kate invited her in.

"Just for a minute, darling. I met that gorgeous Blaine Eddington last night and he mentioned that you two had met. I was just wondering how much you knew about him."

"Know about him?" Kate was wary. She did not like Marissa, a beautiful, platinum-haired woman who considered her condo an amusing retreat from her parents' lavish estate.

"You two dating?" Marissa asked.

"We have a business relationship," Kate said sweetly. "Is that what you came over to discuss?"

"Just wanted to check. I'm interested in him myself. See you." Marissa gave a little wink and flounced out of the room.

"What do you suppose that was all about?" Ellie said, still in something of a stupor.

"I haven't a clue." Kate looked perturbed.

"She probably came to flaunt a new conquest. She does sort of look like Blaine's former wife."

Kate was puzzled. "I thought you didn't know what Blaine's wife looked like."

"I don't really. All I could tell was that she was blond. And Marissa's blond. Maybe he thinks blondes are more fun."

Kate's mood turned even blacker than it had been when she had come home.

"I gotta go now, Kate," Ellie said, rising from the couch, seemingly unaware of Kate's depression. "Got to display the next generation's artists." She headed toward the door. "Maybe some evening when you're free we can have dinner together."

"Sure," Kate said, wondering how she was going to get through the evening with Bill. She had no solution to the problem Bill had raised regarding artistic control, and now this! She hurried back to the piano, once again hoping to get lost in the music. But this time it did not work. Blaine's face kept coming into her mind, stirring her passions. In the background there was always Marissa's face.

Kate decided she had better shower and change for her dinner date with Bill. Perhaps she could somehow convince him that the studio musicians could make their suggestions first. After her shower, Kate changed into a dusty rose silk dress, embellishing it with a strand of pearls. She combed her long black hair back and then pinned it up. She applied some light makeup and was finishing just as the doorbell rang.

"Come in, Bill," Kate said in as cheerful a voice as she could muster. "Care for a cocktail before dinner?"

"Actually I'd probably use any excuse to get you alone but I'm afraid we have reservations at the Lincoln Hotel." He kissed her cheek. "But maybe we can be alone after dinner."

Kate smiled and let Bill help her with her jacket. "In that case, let's go."

As they drove toward the hotel Kate and Bill made the kind of small talk that most friends make. But gradually the conversation turned to the problem with the recording.

"I've thought and I've thought of a way out of this mess," Kate said, hoping that Bill would hear the earnest plea in her voice, "and I think I have a solution."

Bill looked wary.

Kate continued, pretending not to notice his expression. "Why don't the studio musicians make their suggestions first and then I'll decide if it's in keeping with the standards of the Whittenburg?"

"You don't seem to understand, Kate. Our technicians have to consider quality of recording as well as quality of music. And while I defer to you in determining how a piece should sound, I believe you know very little about the technical end of the record business."

For one moment Kate thought she might have lost the battle. But she recovered instantly. "Am I to understand that Maesterling is more interested in the technical mastery of the record business than in the music itself?"

Bill turned from the steering wheel and assumed the expression one uses for a recalcitrant child. "Not at all. But there are aspects of recording that can cause difficulties that live concerts don't present. That is why we hire our technicians. They know the technical end of the business as well as the music."

Kate looked unconvinced and was starting to get a headache. "I don't think this is getting us anywhere."

"Maybe not. Maybe I'm not explaining all this properly. Why don't we leave the subject for later."

"Good idea."

As he was assisting her from the car, her eye was caught by a sleek automobile that could only be a product of Eddington Motors. In fact, it looked like Blaine's own car, the one he'd used on the trip to Gettysburg. Was it his? She had not looked at his license number that day, and she couldn't very well peer in through the windows now. But if the car was his, then Blaine was here at the hotel. Doing what? she wondered.

But she hoped she'd never have to know.

CHAPTER 10

The Lincoln Hotel was a typically Victorian structure. It had been built in the 1880s, at a time when many were honoring the slain sixteenth President by perpetuating his name. In those days the modern new hotel had been the talk of Whittenburg. And even now it still attracted many visitors because of its nineteenth-century charm. Its dining room appealed to those residents of Whittenburg who liked hearty meals. The chef eschewed nouvelle cuisine in favor of succulent meats and rich French sauces, heavy foods that might have delighted the original Victorian patrons.

"I heard they have excellent steaks here," Bill said. "And my mouth's watering."

Kate, remembering that he had once said steaks were the only dish restaurants could not ruin, nodded and smiled.

But Bill was forced to postpone his culinary transport. Because the leisurely ambience of the Lincoln was so much appreciated, people sometimes lingered over coffee longer than would have been the case in newer hotels and restaurants. Thus even those with reservations were often asked to wait in the cocktail lounge until a table was ready. Such was the case with Kate and Bill.

They sat at a small table near the window from which the beautiful old Federal-style courthouse could be seen, now illuminated by streetlights. Bill ordered scotch on the rocks and Kate chose white wine. At first she kept her eyes either on Bill or on the table. Since she thought she had seen Blaine's car outside, she feared that if she looked around she might see him seated somewhere with a beautiful woman. But a man passing by in an outlandish plaid suit caught Kate's attention, and as she followed his progress across the smoky room she noted that Blaine was neither at the bar nor at any of the tables. She found herself sighing in relief. The wine soon relaxed her more, and finally she was able to turn her full attention to Bill.

They made a handsome couple. Kate looked elegant. And Bill, normally a man who would not be considered outstanding, was wearing a beige suit the shade of which complemented his brown eyes. His dark curly hair, slightly tousled because he had driven with his window open, gave him an almost rakish aspect.

Recorded music played in the background. It was of a genre called "easy listening," though rare was the person who actually listened. But Kate and Bill, ever the musicians, and having decided not to discuss their business disagreements this evening, commented on the songs as they had done during their last dinner date.

"That's Harry James," Bill said, cocking an ear in the direction of one of the music speakers near the bar.

"I know," Kate said. "I'd recognize the style anywhere. 'Sleepy Time Gal,' isn't it?"

Bill nodded.

"You look wistful," she said.

"I wish I'd had his talent." Bill looked down. "Not that trumpeters or swing music itself would have been in much demand during our rock era. But still . . ."

"It's not solely a question of talent," she said. "I mean, practice is a big part of it, and if you'd really been determined to be a good jazz trumpeter—"

"Yes, I know, I know. I never put forth enough effort. These guys, in order to be good, have to practice passages over and over again. As you must know," he added, smiling wryly.

"Oh, how I know!"

"I could never do it, Kate."

Kate remembered the years when she'd studied piano. Hour after hour trying to get one passage right. It hadn't simply been a question of the correct notes and timing. It was what to dramatize and how to dramatize. It was deciding whether to make the notes crisp or whether to allow a microsecond's worth of resonance. Practice and more practice. There had been an element of tedium, true, but her need to get it just right had so consumed her that she could never say she'd been bored.

"I know what you're thinking," he said. "You're thinking that if I'd cared enough about my work none of the repetition would have bothered me. And you're right. I have dreams but not enough patience to pursue them. So I ended up a listener rather than a performer."

"But why the classical end of it? Why not jazz, if you like it so much?"

"I tried recording jazz. And one day when I was doing one of the revivalist swing bands I had this enormous longing to be up there playing with the group. They were doing 'In the Mood' and I wanted so much to be a part of it that I almost cried." He was silent for a while; then he said, "Anyway, I couldn't record jazz. It hurt too much. And to do rock would have meant practically getting a master's degree in acoustical implementation. So I settled on classical music. I've always liked it, although I'm not open-minded enough to appreciate every period. I don't like most chamber music. Too studied, too stuffy. I'm always put off by the thought of drawing rooms and tight corsets." He grinned, sat up stiffly in his chair and tilted his chin upward, apparently mimicking the posture of eighteenth-century ladies in drawing rooms listening to Bach concertos. Playing the clown again, Kate thought. Perhaps it was because he sometimes didn't want to face himself.

But he said, more seriously, "I do like a lot of classical material, though. I'm particularly interested in Romantics and the moderns."

"Then you're going to make a career of recording classical music?"

"I guess so."

"When what you'd really like to do is play the trumpet in a jazz band?"

He shrugged.

"Oh, Bill." She sighed. Then she shook her head and said, "I'll just have to take you in hand; that's all. We can't have you abandoning your dreams."

"You sound like my sister."

"Pretend that I am."

He studied her face, dropped his eyes a little and said with a grin, "You've got to be kidding."

"Never mind that," she admonished, shaking her finger and continuing her lecture. "It all comes down to practice, Bill. Ninety percent perspiration, ten percent inspiration. Sometimes you've got to force yourself to practice. That's something you just have to accept. Like studying in school or brushing your teeth or anything you know you have to do no matter what." She paused. "Let's say you get up at nine in the morning and you just can't face rehearsing that flourish in 'You Made Me Love You' or whatever the song is. Okay. Just promise yourself you'll spend five minutes at it. That's all; five minutes. So you get out your trumpet and pretty soon you get all involved, and then you find that the five minutes have turned into three hours." She paused, eyes bright with the hope that at last he understood. Then she said, "Once you've started, you see, you usually can't stop."

"I can always stop," he said.

Kate sighed. She had expected him to be propelled to action by her sermon. She said, "I don't believe you. But if it's true, then music isn't really your passion at all. Maybe there's something else you want more and you just don't know what it is. I know someone who freely admits that though he loves music he never had the patience to pursue it as a career. But so what? He's enormously successful in his own field."

"What's that?" Bill asked idly.

"Automotive engineering."

"He's devoted his life to perfecting the piston?" Bill mocked.

"To perfecting the entire sports car. I'm talking about Blaine Eddington."

"Blaine Eddington? You *know* him?" Bill looked stunned.

"He's a contributor to the orchestra."

"That's right. Someone told me this was his hometown. Blaine Eddington, huh? I've been saving for years to get the Eddington JT4." He paused. "The guy's a genius; no doubt about it. And yes, he must have a passion for his work in order to turn out a product that good. But to return to the subject of myself, Kate, it's not that I prefer another field. It's that I can't apply myself to this one. I've never . . ."

But Kate was no longer listening. When Bill had said "passion for his work," Kate had remembered Blaine displaying another kind of passion, remembered Blaine's lips coming down hard on hers on the night of the Gettysburg tour.

". . . and you can't dismiss talent as a factor, Kate," Bill was saying. "I've never been sure I had the talent."

"Oh. I see."

And then Blaine had stepped away, she thought. He had said, "We shouldn't go too fast too soon." What had he meant? Would he have preferred someone more reserved? Had she been too forward, too eager?

"Kate?" Bill was saying.

"Hm?"

"Did you hear me?"

"What? Oh." She blinked hard as though removing a film from her eyes. "I was just—just thinking of what we should do. To help you, I mean. Uh, help you overcome your reluctance to practice."

"But that's what I've been trying to tell you. I don't think the problem's as simple as that. There's the question of talent, you know. And I'm not sure I have—"

They were interrupted by a gray-haired, very dignified maître d' who informed them that their table was now ready. And as they passed tables filled with formally dressed, cheerful men and women, Kate saw Blaine. She caught her breath. He was seated not with a lovely woman but with two men who might have been business associates. She exhaled in relief. While she was passing his table, Bill stopped to have a word with the maître d' behind him. Thus Blaine, assuming Kate was alone, quickly rose and said, "Kate. Have you just finished dinner here? Why not join us for a while."

Blushing slightly, she said, "I haven't even started dinner. And before I sit down, I'd have to ask my escort—"

Blaine apparently hadn't heard her, for he interrupted, gesturing toward the men at his table, "There are two of my vice-presidents. They flew in from L.A. on the redeye last night and slept all day. I guess you could say the *boeuf bourguignonne* here is their breakfast." He smiled, indicated a chair for Kate and formally introduced her to the men. Then he described for them the nature of her career and the ways in which she had already distinguished herself.

Kate was basking in Blaine's praise when Bill appeared. Kate smiled and made introductions all around. At Blaine's signal a waiter soon fetched some extra chairs, and then Bill and Kate were seated and given menus. Bill had been very impressed by the fact that Kate knew Blaine Eddington, so now she attempted to engage the two men in conversation. But Blaine answered questions about his JT4 in monosyllables. At first Kate could not understand why but in time she decided that Blaine was being reticent because the answers to Bill's questions might involve company secrets. Conversation between the two sputtered out, and Bill found himself conversing exclusively with Blaine's two vice-presidents. Kate and Blaine, seated next to one another, tried to talk. But Blaine's sentences were still perfunctory, and it was Kate who had to initiate the halting conversation.

"Are your vice-presidents impressed with Whittenburg?" she asked.

"They haven't had a chance to explore it."

"I'm sure they'll find it charming," she said.

"Doubtless," he grunted.

"I suppose you'll take them to the historic areas and to Gettysburg."

"They're here to work."

She wondered what was wrong with him. Just a few minutes before, when he'd asked her to sit down, he had seemed so cheerful.

For a while they sat in total silence while Bill and the two vice-presidents chatted animatedly about car design. Appetizers arrived for the two visitors to the table. Kate, leaving her onion soup untouched, studied her napkin. Blaine, who had already eaten, sipped at his brandy. His brow was furrowed.

The seconds ticked on. Now and then she would cautiously glance his way, taking note of his very blond hair and his strong, chiseled features. She decided to make one more attempt at conversation. If he did not respond, she thought, then she would announce to Bill firmly and haughtily that she would prefer to be served at another table where the atmosphere might be more congenial. But first she would try one more time, out of consideration for the fact that Blaine had been so cordial earlier.

"People still talk about your grandfather's memorial concert," she said.

"Oh?"

"Although some were disappointed that we didn't do the music Sloan Eddington was best known for."

"Popular stuff," Blaine said, a note of contempt in his voice.

"That doesn't make them unworthy works." Her temper got the best of her sooner than she had intended. "You sound like those tourists who, after they go to Paris, try to convince everyone that Paris is for the callow and that the in place is Sumatra or Helsinki."

He looked directly at her, his expression unfathomable. Finally he said, "I'm not dismissing popular works as substandard. I simply observed that there were certain pieces Grandfather had to play ad nauseam."

"Yes! And I wish I'd thought of doing them at your grandfather's memorial."

"You've already said that."

"Well, pardon me for my redundancy!"

Kate's strident tone caught the attention of Bill and the two vice-presidents. They turned almost in unison and looked at Kate and Blaine inquiringly. Kate opened her mouth to explain, decided that she could not explain and bit her lip. Blaine looked over at the three puzzled men, his gaze direct, his expression self-possessed. "A difference of opinion regarding the contest for congressman," he said smoothly, alluding to two hopefuls who were convinced that they had already sewn up their parties' nominations long in advance of the official campaign season.

"I didn't know you were political, Blaine," remarked one of the vice-presidents.

"When have you had time to consider the issues, Blaine?" the other asked. And then he said, "Oh, I get it. One of the parties is more favorable to an Eddington factory than the other is. Enlightened self-interest, eh?"

Blaine raised an eyebrow. Kate noted that this was all it took for Blaine to remind the men that he was their superior and that the boundaries of business etiquette had been crossed. The subordinates lapsed into silence and Kate thought contemptuously, "Well doesn't *he* think he's lord of the manor!" But she was forced to concede that she too had had problems when members of the orchestra had undermined her authority by means of inappropriate jokes.

For a long time no one at the table spoke. Kate was about to announce that it would be best if she and Bill were moved to another table, but before she could suggest this, Bill, looking acutely uncomfortable, made an attempt to start a conversation.

"This is a lovely hotel," he said. "When they sent me to listen to the Whittenburg, I had visions of staying at some sterile chain-motel on the outskirts of town. But this place is so—"

Blaine interrupted. "What do you mean 'listen to the Whittenburg'?"

Bill glanced at Kate. "Didn't our lovely conductor tell you? I'm going to record the symphony's music."

Kate, who had been petulant up until now, decided suddenly to provide the details. Her anger at Blaine had nothing to do with Bill, after all. Bill was a good man who, whatever their differences, deserved a plug. She said to Blaine and his men, "Bill is from Maesterling Recordings. He's helping to do a series of albums called 'America Plays the Classics.' He heard the memorial to Sloan Eddington and decided to include the Whittenburg in an album. Now we're discussing exactly how to record our work and I'm proud that Maesterling has chosen us. They're very selective." She smiled at Bill and at the vice-presidents. She did not look at Blaine.

"Is that who you are?" Blaine blurted at Bill. "A representative from Maesterling?"

"Well, yes, sir. Who did you think I was?"

Blaine said quickly, "I didn't know. You were introduced only by name." Kate now expected Blaine to give her a critical look as though to say that she too had violated a code of etiquette. But astonishingly Blaine now seemed to relax. He actually asked her with a smile how she liked the sole amandine. And presently he was discussing with Bill the design of the JT4. His demeanor was friendly, enthusiastic. She could not account for the sudden change in him.

After a while he said in a low voice, "I apologize for that little altercation."

She shrugged. "Apology accepted. And I'm sorry I lost my temper too. But what I don't understand is why it happened. You seemed so warm at first and then, all of a sudden—"

"I was out of sorts. I've been working long hours."

She didn't believe this. Blaine was the type who thrived on work. And he was too self-possessed ever to risk offending a woman he liked simply because he was tired. She considered for a moment. Possibly he might have been jealous of Bill. But she soon dismissed the thought. A man like Blaine was too sure of himself ever to be jealous. Unless he was so conceited that he expected all women to want him exclusively. But no, she thought. Whatever his faults, she doubted that Blaine was that arrogant. His sullen behavior had been just a personality quirk, possibly akin to the sudden reserve that caused him to pull away from her after they had kissed. Blaine was such a puzzle. She wasn't sure she wanted another puzzle in her life; there were enough challenges to contend with already. And yet, looking into his mesmerizing eyes, she wasn't sure she wanted to avoid this particular problem either.

No, she definitely did not want to avoid it.

CHAPTER 11

Bill returned to Maesterling headquarters in New York and Kate went back to work. By Saturday following the dinner at the Lincoln, she had rebounded from her setback of the week before. Tonight's performance, which included a Brahms and a Mozart, was so faultlessly and enthusiastically rendered that one music critic would later write, "Katherine Reston, perhaps because of her youth, brings a freshness and vitality to these hardy perennials. One cannot help but be reminded of Ozawa's first appearance on the scene."

In the greenroom, Malcolm was overflowing with praise, and several longtime subscribers, conspicuously absent the week before, made sure to stop by now. Their presence reminded Kate of the potential problems with the Maesterling recording setup, but she willed herself not to think about it this night. One reason the performance had been so good was that the rehearsals had gone smoothly. No one had been absent. No one had even been tardy. The brass had applauded her patience with certain passages, the guest piano soloist from Denver had admired Kate's interpretation of the score, and Harold had given her the ultimate compliment by telling her that the strings had never been better.

On the drive back from Gettysburg, Blaine had told Kate that this Saturday he was planning to give her a quiz on Jeb Stuart. She hadn't known whether or not to take him seriously, but yesterday morning she'd dropped in at the library and asked to look through the newspaper microfilms dating from late June and early July, 1863. Now she knew quite a bit about the dashing Confederate cavalryman and was looking forward to telling Blaine. But where was he? He had said after Gettysburg that he'd meet her Saturday after the concert but so far he hadn't arrived. Had he been put off by their acid exchange at the Lincoln? She wasn't sure.

A part of her brooded on Blaine's absence even as she smiled and accepted compliments. Had he been in the audience tonight? She hadn't seen him in the front rows. Perhaps off to the side far back where darkness would obscure even Blaine's arresting face?

". . . in the park," Malcolm was saying.

"He's in the park?" she said, brow knit.

"What?" Malcolm looked confused.

"I thought— Never mind. What about the park?"

"I was just telling this gentleman that your outdoor performance next Saturday will be in Hancock Park."

"Um." She nodded, only half listening.

Then a deep familiar voice was saying, "Kate." She turned. Blaine had sounded so odd—weary, almost. His face too seemed different—eyes cloudy, mouth tight, the hint of a furrow in his brow. "Kate," he repeated, "I promised you I'd be here."

"Yes. Thank you for coming, Blaine."

"Did you hear the concert?" Malcolm asked, beaming.

"Not all of it, I'm afraid." He looked away, and Kate was certain she understood now. There was something else he had wanted to do tonight, but he'd made a promise to her and obviously he'd felt obligated to honor it. It was some time before the room cleared enough for Kate to have a word with Blaine. He was looking a little less preoccupied now, but Kate's mind was fixed on the expression he'd worn on coming in tonight. "Is something wrong, Blaine?"

"What would be wrong?" He looked annoyed.

"Was there something you had to do?"

"Pardon?"

She had no chance to continue. An older man had walked up to her and, not realizing that she was speaking to Blaine, had begun to tell Kate how outstanding her performance had been. He turned out to be a music critic and Kate could not help basking in his profusions of praise. When at last she turned back to Blaine she found that he was nowhere to be seen. Swallowing hard, she tried again to concentrate on her well-wishers.

Fifteen minutes later Kate had changed into street wear—a silk print blouse paired with white linen pants and a matching blazer. Ellie had said it was a "smashing outfit." The trousers accented Kate's height, her long legs and her slim hips. Sighing because she had chosen the outfit with Blaine in mind and he hadn't even seen it, she picked up her attaché case crammed with scores for Saturday's outdoor concert and walked into the hall and down the back steps to the parking lot. She didn't know what she ought to have expected of Blaine. After all, he'd said only that he'd planned to quiz her after the concert. But somehow she'd pictured going to Jennifer's supper club for a drink and then—well, at the dark table she had hoped that the conversation would eventually move from the Civil War to something more personal.

In the parking lot she saw Blaine under the light of a lamp. He was leaning against his low-slung sports car, smoking a pipe. As she walked out into the lot, he straightened up and came toward her. "Kate," he said. His voice was hoarse.

"Blaine, what happened to you? One minute you were standing in the greenroom and the next minute—"

"I hate crowds; can't imagine how you tolerate them night after night."

"Yes, it is wearying hearing yourself praised endlessly, but I endure it somehow." She smiled, even though she was not feeling mirthful at the moment. The least he could have done would have been to tell her he was leaving. But she was rather pleased to see that he had waited after all, and she decided not to question him further.

"You look lovely," he said.

She nodded. "And you look very well." It was too dark to see the color of his suit, but she had seen it earlier. Dark blue. She already knew that he favored dark suits, conservative ties and shirts. He'd even been in a navy suit on the day they'd gone to Gettysburg, though he'd mentioned having come from a meeting that morning. Never, in the few weeks she'd known him, had she seen him in casual attire. She had a fantasy of skiing with him at Lake Placid. He'd be wearing—what?—a red-and-green sweater? A yellow parka that matched his hair? No. It would be a pure white cable-knit turtleneck that would look spectacular against Blaine's tanned weathered skin . . .

". . . perhaps to Jennifer's?"

She had not heard what he was saying. "Pardon me?"

"Would you like to go to Jennifer's for a drink?"

It was on her lips to say, "I'd love to!" but she did not. She hadn't appreciated his behavior this evening. He hadn't commented on her performance. She wasn't even sure he had seen it. And then he'd left the greenroom without a word of explanation. And now here he was, taking it for granted that she'd be slavering at the thought of Jennifer's. She supposed good-looking millionaires took a lot for granted, especially when it came to women, and she supposed she'd risk losing him if she turned him down now. Nevertheless, it had to be done. She said, "I've got a lot of work to do tonight, Blaine."

"Even now? Saturday night? After a bravura performance?"

Vanity overcame resolution. "Bravura?" She could not resist a smile.

"So they tell me," he said. "I—didn't hear all of the concert myself."

Her smile was gone. Why hadn't he? But she would not ask him, would not give him the satisfaction of knowing she cared.

"You didn't answer my question," he said. "Why do you have to work on a Saturday night?"

"I've got three scores to go over," she said. "The Copland I was doing the other day plus a Mussorgsky and a Debussy."

"For Saturday? Which Debussy?"

"*La Mer.*"

"Ah. My favorite," he said.

"I like it too. I have a Daniel Barenboim recording of it that I—"

"Daniel who?"

"Barenboim."

He looked puzzled.

Suddenly she saw a chance to get back at Blaine for all the taunts she'd endured at Gettysburg. "Don't tell me you've never heard of Barenboim." She feigned a disbelieving laugh. With a little effort she managed to work it into a series of hearty guffaws. "Surely you're joking, Blaine."

"He's not exactly a household name. Is he a composer?"

"A composer! Of course not; he's a conductor. I thought *everyone* knew that. He's one of the greatest—the most important—well, actually you could call him the General Pickett of the Orchestre de Paris."

Blaine slowly smiled. "All right," he said. "*Touché.*"

"Yes. And your homework is to write a learned thesis comparing Daniel Barenboim with Edo de Waart."

"The latter is Dutch, I presume?"

"Yes, but not Pennsylvania Dutch. Did you know that in Pennsylvania the word 'Dutch' is a corruption of 'Deutsch'? Bet you didn't know that, Blaine."

"Was I that obnoxious?" he said, laughing.

"Pretty close," she said.

"Did you ever do your own homework on the Pennsylvania invasion?"

"Of course not," she lied. "Though one of these days I may get around to it."

"Well, if you don't," he said, becoming serious again, "I won't be able to say I blame you. Your music must take up most of your time. I noticed that the other day, glancing at that Copland score. The music lines for everything from flute to trombone are listed one under the other, and you have to keep track of all of them simultaneously." He paused. "How do you do that?"

"It takes a while to learn," she said.

"And you have to understand every instrument, what key it's tuned to, its range, what effect it's supposed to achieve. Then you've got to make sure the orchestra's balanced properly. If two extra violinists are hired don't you have to bring in a trumpet or a horn or some other—"

"Yes, the proportions have to be maintained," she said.

"All this plus knowing music, the various composers, the various schools. Don't you generally group baroques with other baroques in a concert, impressionists with other impressionists?"

"Generally. Not always. And usually not in a Pops."

"Conducting takes a lifetime to master, doesn't it?"

"A lifetime's not enough. But isn't that also true of automotive engineering?"

He did not comment on his own field but went on to ask, "How do you choose the pieces you're going to play?"

"Some pieces are old favorites, done again and again at regular intervals. And some are chosen to fit in with a theme. For example, the Pops we're doing in the park next month for the Fourth of July—"

"Don't tell me—The *1812?*"

"Of course. And 'Stars and Stripes Forever.' Everyone expects them. But just the other day I had another idea. Morton Gould's *American Salute.* We've never played it before."

"I don't think I'm familiar—"

"For shame! You've heard of the Round Tops in Gettysburg but you've never heard of *American Salute?*" Before he could reply that she was overdoing the teasing she went on to say, "It was my trip to Gettysburg that inspired me, actually. This work is an orchestral piece that uses the tune 'When Johnny Comes Marching Home' in many different styles and tempos."

"Oh, yes, I have heard that."

"So I thought I'd include it. I got the idea while I was standing on Cemetery Ridge wondering how many of those Johnny Rebs and Johnny Yanks actually did go marching home."

They were both leaning against his car, their backs touching the windows. Blaine had finished smoking his pipe and had set it down on the car roof. His right hand was now free, and he casually touched her forearm as though to say that he was glad the experience at Gettysburg had moved her so deeply. Though it was a light touch, Kate felt as though it had reached the center of her nervous system. For a long time they were quiet. She half expected him to renew his invitation to go to Jennifer's but he did not. Instead he said, almost to himself, "So many things the same; yet there are differences too."

"What did you say?"

"The sense of humor. You do like to tease, don't you?"

"Oh yes, especially when it's deserved," she said. "But who or what are you contrasting me with?"

"My—uh—sister Louise. She's a—music aficionado too. But much more serious about other things than you are."

"Louise, yes. I met her on the night of your grandfather's tribute. She loved the performance."

"Um." He had a distracted look in his eyes.

"Blaine?"

"I'm sorry. What did you say?"

Why are you always going away from me? she wondered. What private world are you forever retreating into? Aloud she said, "I was just commenting on how your sister liked our dedication concert, particularly the Barber. She loves string ensembles, especially cellos, she said."

Blaine said, "Harold Rawlins is a cellist. He was the first man I met at Meade Hall when I came back to town."

"Yes."

"I see him often these days. His house is very close to the site of the plant we're opening. The noise from the excavating must bother him a good deal, though I try to tell myself that he's accustomed to dissonance and decibels."

"Is that how you describe my orchestra?" she said.

"Only when it's tuning up." He smiled. "Last week he walked over to the site, stood beside me listening to the blasting and the steam shovels and the general pandemonium, and then he said, 'Bartók?' "

"Sounds just like Harold," she said, grinning.

"I felt responsible for the pain he was enduring and took him down the street for a drink. Very interesting man. Strong opinions on many subjects and that's a novelty in our indecisive age. He has a hollow leg too. He drank me under the table."

Kate was surprised. In the past Harold had been fairly abstemious even at the post-*Messiah* Christmas parties when, in an annual ritual established early in director Bernini's tenure, orchestra and chorus piled into a local pub for Christmas cheer. Harold had rarely had more than a sip of champagne and he'd always left early. Now Kate frowned. Harold was changing. But she did not think it appropriate to speculate with Blaine as to why.

Kate could not help noticing that Blaine seemed much more relaxed now where earlier in the evening he had been tense and distracted. What could possibly have been the trouble? An argument with a girlfriend? Had he had dinner with someone and then remembered at the last minute the promise he'd made to see Kate? If that had been the case, then he must have had to make some excuse to the woman and this might have annoyed him. But now, obviously, his irritation had worn off. He seemed to be enjoying the evening, such as it was. Though a parking lot hardly had the atmosphere of Jennifer's supper club, it had a special ambience of its own. The June evening was warm, clear and starry, and the scent of fresh-mown grass and honeysuckle drifting in from the lawns and yards of the houses in the city's historic area stirred Kate's senses and her imagination.

"Well," he said, "I don't want to take up any more of your time. I'll be in touch again when your schedule isn't so hectic."

She wanted to say, "I've changed my mind. Let's go to Jennifer's." Instead she said, "By Tuesday I should have gotten the most difficult parts out of the way."

"Good. How about Tuesday evening for dinner? Or do you have a rehearsal that night?"

"No. Tuesday would be fine."

He walked her to her car and waited until she had started the engine. The *largo* of a Bach violin concerto drifted from the tape deck, further enriching the gentle, sweet-scented evening. As she rolled down the window to let in some air and to say a final goodnight to Blaine, he leaned in and kissed her chastely on the lips. His were firm lips but warm, warmer than the evening, and she was flooded with sensations that set her nerves on fire. The feel of his mouth! Ah, what pleasure it gave her! It was a tactile representation of all that was glorious on this piece of earth she occupied. It was the glow of the moon overhead, the scent of the grass and the honeysuckle, the poignant sound of the violins—his kiss was everything.

"Good night, Katherine," he said—and now his voice too became part of her special world.

"Good night, Blaine." She started the engine and drove away. But it was some time before she knew where she was going.

On Tuesday evening she spent two hours getting dressed. She wore a new earth-toned silk print Rovetti dress with a scooped neck, full sleeves and a full, flowing calf-length skirt. Complementing the dress were delicate beige open-toed shoes of fine Italian leather. Small gold hoop earrings and a beige clutch bag completed the outfit. He was to pick her up at eight o'clock. She poured herself a glass of iced tea, sat down at the piano, and waited. Eight-thirty—and he did not come. Perhaps she'd gotten the time wrong. Nine o'clock, and still no doorbell, no phone call. Nine-thirty . . . Could he have forgotten? Ten . . . ten-thirty . . .

At eleven o'clock she removed the lovely dress, the expensive shoes and earrings. Maybe she'd got the date wrong. Maybe . . . but in her heart she knew. She'd known since that first time on the Meade Hall steps when he'd looked hard at her, then turned away and bolted for his car. He'd been attracted—perhaps mildly, perhaps strongly. But there was someone else. There had to be. And whoever she was had prevailed.

CHAPTER 12

As a musician, Kate had to understand the emotion in a work in addition to the technical specifications and on the morning after Blaine stood her up, Kate found herself at the piano playing an excerpt from Puccini's *Madama Butterfly* with a passion she had never felt before. In the middle of a very poignant passage, she suddenly stopped and said aloud, "What are you doing, you fool? Comparing Butterfly's predicament to your own? Oh, you idiot! Blaine's not worth it. He's an ill-mannered boor, and you're well rid of him." She took a gasping breath and went on, still speaking aloud, "Puccini indeed! As though he were that important. If I play any music at all it ought to be something that suits Blaine. I wish I had the sheet music for 'Hit the Road, Jack'!"

In the kitchen, the microwave buzzer went off, announcing that the frozen French toast was now edible. Upon waking up this morning, after a restless night, Kate had determined not to let last night's disappointment affect her. She had poured her orange juice, lined up her vitamins and popped the French toast in the microwave. She had decided that Blaine's insult would not destroy her appetite. And she wasn't going to let herself go either. But what had she ended up doing? Here she was in her nightgown, orange juice unpoured, vitamins unswallowed. Here she was in utter dishabille, all but weeping over Puccini.

Disgusting.

She had intended to get to the office by ten to go over the score of Mussorgsky's *Pictures at an Exhibition*. Rehearsals started tonight. By Saturday the orchestra was expected to be playing the first of the summer concerts in the park. She had studied the scores of the Copland and the Debussy but hadn't looked at *Pictures at an Exhibition* in years. Not since she herself had played it as a pianist. So she'd better get dressed pronto and get to the office.

Yes, she'd better, Kate thought. But at nine o'clock she was still in her nightgown, her French toast untouched. She was, in spite of all the admonitions of her brain, still thinking of Blaine Eddington and wondering why he had not appeared last night. If he had called with an excuse, any excuse, she would have forgiven him. But he hadn't. And he hadn't been killed in an automobile accident either. She had already checked the papers and listened to the morning news. Could he have died of a stroke? She considered the idea but soon dismissed it. Unlikely. If it had happened, surely someone would have told her. Unless he was lying unconscious somewhere and hadn't been discovered.

Oh, ridiculous! Why not just face the facts? He had changed his mind about wanting to see her and, being too cowardly to tell her to her face, had opted out of their date. So that was the end of that, she thought, getting up from the table and walking into her bedroom. Blaine was history and she, Kate, had a performance to do. She showered, put on some lipstick and slipped into a tan gabardine pants-and-vest outfit. As an afterthought, she added a bright red neckerchief. Good, she decided. She looked perky and full of energy. No one would ever guess that she'd spent the night staring at the ceiling asking herself "Why?"

Who cared why? Certainly she didn't. She strode purposefully into the kitchen and poured herself a cup of coffee.

At nine-fifteen the doorbell rang. It was, to her dismay, Bill Scott.

"Sorry I dropped in without phoning first," he said.

"I thought you were in New York."

"I was. And now I'm driving into the South to hear several more orchestras. The highway passes right by Whittenburg, and since you're not far from the exit—I mean, I suppose I should have found a phone booth first, but there weren't any between here and the highway."

"No need to apologize," Kate said politely. "I was just about to have a cup of coffee. Why don't you join me?" She gestured in the direction of the kitchen, and as he walked in she wondered if he was here to ask her again about whether she would agree to giving Maesterling quality-control rights. Distressing as that topic was, Kate actually hoped that Bill was here for business reasons only. It had been obvious after that dinner at the Lincoln that given any encouragement he would pursue a personal relationship as well. And she didn't want that. She didn't want to get involved with any man. Maybe not ever.

As it turned out, Bill was here for both reasons. He wondered if she'd made a decision on the quality-control dilemma and he wondered if she'd be free for breakfast.

"I haven't decided about the quality control," she said.

"I just thought, before I drove South, that it might be nice to know whether or not you and your orchestra will be on our record."

"I'm sorry, Bill. Could you give me more time?"

He sipped at his coffee and shrugged.

"Bill?"

"I guess I'll have to," he said.

"Now, about breakfast," she said, "it's nine-thirty and I'm on my way to the hall. I've got to work on a Mussorgsky score."

"Can't you go in late?"

"Not too late. I've got so much to do. And then there's rehearsal tonight. So I don't have time to go out for breakfast, but if you're hungry I can fix you something here."

"Do you have any eggs?"

"Plenty. How do you like them?"

"Over easy."

"Fine." She opened the refrigerator door. "Bacon?"

"No, thanks. I'm watching my weight."

"Toast?"

"Only one slice, please."

She went over to the stove and began to heat the frying pan. Bill, at the table, poured himself another cup of coffee and asked, "Which Mussorgsky are you doing?"

"Pictures at an Exhibition," she said as she cracked the eggs into the pan.

"Ah, yes. That was the one Ravel had to interpret and orchestrate."

"Do you like the work?"

He nodded. "But not as much as *Night on Bald Mountain.* That's a wild thing, isn't it?"

"I love it," she said. "I'm going to do it next year in one of the Pops concerts." She smiled. "Harold Rawlins, one of our cellists, says it could have been the sound track for the Russian Revolution."

"I understand the Soviets are very fond of Mussorgsky," Bill said.

She nodded. "Even though the man died before anyone had ever heard of Lenin."

"I like Mussorgsky," Bill said. "He's passion unbounded. Has the Whittenburg ever done *Bald Mountain?*"

"Not while I've been a member. Our former director thought it was too passionate for staid old Whittenburg."

Bill smiled. "It wasn't too frenzied for the staid Queen of England. Did you read about Roger Thulin's performance in London?"

Kate nodded. Conductor Thulin, who was currently America's favorite, had last week overwhelmed the British and their monarch as well. Sometimes Kate wondered if she would ever attain fame of that magnitude. She did want it, not so much for the adulation as for the freedom to do daring things. But it would never be possible, she reminded herself, if she did not take advantage of opportunities like Maesterling Recordings. She wished she and Bill could come to an agreement. But what if his sound men amplified the wrong instruments and the record was ruined? The Whittenburg would be dead before it started.

"What's the matter?" Bill asked.

"I wish I could sign that contract of yours but I'm so afraid that the technicians won't act responsibly."

"Well, there's still time to decide. I don't want to pressure you. I'll be in the South for a while, too busy to worry much about this particular dilemma. Why don't I check with you when I get back?"

"That's a good idea," she said.

He had finished his eggs. She expected him to rise and say goodbye. But he chose instead to pour himself more coffee. Kate glanced surreptitiously at the clock. She'd better be leaving soon if she was going to get all her work done. But Bill had embarked on the subject of his problems with his trumpet-playing career and she did not have the heart to break in. Finally he said, "I did take your advice, Kate. When I was home in New York I forced myself to practice."

"Did you?" She nodded. She was always delighted when people were inspired by her words.

"It worked well two mornings in a row. Then on the third day I kept procrastinating until it was time to go to work." He paused and said, grinning, "What I need is for someone to nag me. Can you phone me every morning and do that? Oh, and be sure to call collect."

She laughed and was surprised at herself. Never would she have believed that she could laugh so soon after an ordeal like last night's. The human psyche, she thought, was very resilient.

Bill said, "I was just joking, of course. I couldn't intrude on your time by asking you to phone me every day. But I may ask my sister to do it. Yes, I'll definitely give the job to her, although she could never motivate me like you can. There's something about you." He thought a moment. "I'm not surprised they made you music director."

Kate affected maidenly modesty but she was so pleased by the praise that she coyly encouraged embellishment by saying, "What do you mean?"

"Well, for all your mastery of the nuts-and-bolts aspects of orchestration, when you're actually on stage it's passion that drives you, I think. I could see that during the Sloan Eddington tribute. That *Adagio for Strings*. The expression on your face during the crescendo near the end. You were inside the music. You were feeling every nuance."

Kate nodded. It was true. How perceptive of Bill to have known that, though she was glad he hadn't been around to watch her playing *Madama Butterfly*. He probably would have guessed what was going through her mind.

"So what I'm saying," Bill went on, "is that it's not enough to have my sister call me and nag me to practice. I also need someone to remind me of why I have to discipline myself, someone who'll remind me of how all this work may lead to my being a Harry James. And you, with all your fire and enthusiasm, would be the one to do that."

"Well, maybe a couple of phone calls a month," she said lightly. But flattered as she was that he seemed to need her so much, she was faintly irritated that he could not function without such prodding. A man who loved swing music as much as Bill allegedly did should not need people hounding him to keep at it. He ought to take charge of himself.

Bill pushed his chair back from the table and stood up. "Well, enough of my problems. I appreciated the breakfast, Kate. I was very hungry and the meal was delicious. Thank you."

"You're most welcome." She rummaged through her shoulder bag and said, "I can never find my keys. I think I ought to chain them around my neck."

He smiled. "You're late for work. I'm sorry I kept you so long." Glancing at his dishes on the table he added, "Shall I put these in the sink? Run water over them at least?"

"Good idea." It was a rare man who thought of the consequences of eggs crusting on a dish. Bill would make some woman a very good husband, she thought.

They cleaned off the table and then prepared to leave. Bill waited for Kate to lock up, then walked with her to her car. "This is hilly country," he remarked as his eyes swung over the land to the west. "Very picturesque."

"We're close to the mountains here," she said.

"Yes. The Alleghenies, South Mountain. And down in Virginia it become Blue Ridge. All part of the Great Appalachian Chain. I realized that when I was boning up on the Civil War last night."

"Why were you studying the war?"

"I've been through the Pennsylvania–Maryland corridor at least five times in the past couple of months. And everywhere I look there's some sort of monument. So I'm going to stop at Gettysburg before I go South. I've never been there." He paused. "I guess that must sound strange to you. I bet you grew up knowing the names of the generals better than the names of your own uncles."

She smiled. "Not really. I knew that Meade Hall was named after General Meade, who commanded the Union Army. And I knew that Hancock Park was named after the man who stopped the Confederates on the third day. But I never did take much interest in the details until—" She broke off.

"Until?"

"Well, just recently I decided to read about it." She forced a light chuckle. "When I become as famous as Roger Thulin and Johnny Carson has me on his shows and asks me about the history of southern Pennsylvania, I've got to be able to tell him something, don't I?"

"Why would Carson want to know about the history of this area? Seems to me he'd want to know about your music."

"I was kidding," Kate said. But she did not go on to explain why she'd suddenly taken an interest in the War Between the States. Her thoughts had turned to Blaine. She remembered him standing on Cemetery Ridge at Gettysburg describing the Confederate offensive that had later been called Pickett's Charge. "One of the most outstanding feats of daring in the history of warfare," he had said. And he had made the scene come alive for Kate. For the first time she could picture those brave Confederates, could hear the Union canoneers shouting, "Number one—fire!," could feel the heat all around her, could smell the acrid sulfur.

Blaine had pointed out the "high-water mark," where the last of the battle had been fought, hand to hand. Unconsciously he had acted out that struggle, his teeth clenched, eyes blazing, blond hair tossing in the wind. For one long suspended moment he had been the ultimate soldier who epitomized everything that the war had meant. He had been neither Union nor Confederate but both sides simultaneously. She remembered how chills had consumed her body as she had gone back in time to the last battle fought on that most legendary of battlefields. Watching Blaine, she had at last been able to understand what the struggle had meant.

"It's coming over you again," Bill said.

"What?"

"Passion. You're feeling passion, aren't you? I can see it in your eyes."

Kate was astonished. How could he tell? She blushed deeply and turned away.

"And it's not for me," Bill sighed. "It's for that Mussorgsky score you're going to work on, right?"

"Right," she lied.

"What do I have to do to make you feel passion for me?"

After struggling awhile to regain her composure she was able to say airily, "You have to practice."

"Until I'm Harry James or Bobby Hackett?"

"At least Bobby Hackett."

"And only then can I stir your soul? Oh, woman, you do drive a hard bargain."

"Don't I?" Oh, she hoped he wasn't taking her seriously. What if he did go home and turn himself into Hackett and then came back and laid his accomplishment at her feet? What would she tell him? That it wasn't enough?

But she was getting ahead of herself. Surely if Bill became that accomplished he would not be seeking out Kate Reston alone. He'd have a world of women to choose from. And what made her think, in any case, that his prattle about needing her and wanting to stir her soul was serious? He liked playing the clown. He had almost admitted as much. So it was possible that all his talk this morning meant little.

But she knew intuitively that this was not true. There had been something very domestic in that breakfast scene and Bill had liked it. So had she. It was good to discuss music, their mutual interest, over morning coffee. It was good to be with a male companion who was not above putting dishes in the sink. And it was especially good to know a man so open that he did not shy away from sharing his troubles or from admitting that he needed her. There was no mystery in Bill, no remoteness. He laid himself before her and said, "Here I am." It was touching and very flattering, and yes, she had liked it.

Now, where would they go from here? This was something that she knew she could not think about. Mixing business with pleasure was anathema to Kate, and until the quality-control impasse was settled neither one of them ought to pursue a more serious relationship. But once it was settled? Well, if he was still talking the way he'd talked this morning then it would be good to have him as a friend, or possibly more.

Yes, it would be very good.

Why, then, wasn't she happier?

CHAPTER 13

At the office later that day, Kate tried to keep everything in perspective. So much had happened but she must not let it affect her. She had to concentrate on that Mussorgsky score and nothing else.

But it was hopeless. Thoughts of Blaine kept intruding. And Bill. What would happen with him? What did she want to happen? Thoroughly agitated, she decided that a walk in the fresh air would help to clear her mind, give her a chance to talk to herself. If things continued this way, she was in danger of making a mess of the one job she had dreamed of all her life. Kate pushed the score that she had been studying to the middle of the desk and stood up. A half hour's walk in old Whittenburg might be just the tonic she needed. She grabbed her jacket and was about to step out the door.

"Good morning, Kate." Harold Rawlins stepped inside the office before Kate had a chance to leave.

"Good morning, Harold."

"Going somewhere? I thought you'd be knee-deep in the scores for tonight's rehearsal."

Kate pointed to the music on her desk. "I am. But I need to think something out and I thought a walk would help."

"I hope there's no problem."

"Oh, uh, no," Kate stammered. "It's just that I've been working for hours and I think some fresh air will do me good."

Harold wore a knowing smile. "Can't hurt," he said. Then, "By the way, isn't Marissa Avalon your neighbor?"

Kate turned sharply. "Yes. Why?"

"Nothing. I thought I saw her with Blaine recently. She's a beauty, isn't she?"

"Perhaps to some people."

"But you're more attractive," he said. "More depth. If I were you, I'd give the lady a good fight."

Marissa had said something about Blaine. Kate wondered if Marissa and

Blaine were really dating. Aloud she said, "I think I'd better go for my walk now." Kate hurried out of the office, leaving Harold to stare at her back.

That was probably it, Kate thought. Blaine had been out with Marissa last night and hadn't even had the courage to call Kate and cancel their date. Probably he had made the appointment with Marissa after he had spoken to Kate. Perhaps he had even forgotten about his date with Kate. The more Kate thought about it, the angrier she became. There was such a thing as good manners. Being handsome and rich did not excuse anyone from behaving in the proper way. Kate's walk became brisker. This was good, she thought. The more angry she became, the less likely she would be to daydream about the eligible Mr. Eddington. In fact, Harold's bit of news might have been just the thing to get Blaine out of her system.

By the time Kate got back to her office she was feeling much better, more in control. She worked on the Mussorgsky and Debussy scores for the rest of the day. A small personal problem was not going to interfere with her professional life the way it had done on the evening of the dedication to Blaine's grandfather. Kate had worked hard to get where she was and she was going to stay there.

Kate sent out for a sandwich for supper and by the time the musicians assembled in the hall for their rehearsal she felt that she knew what she wanted and how to achieve it.

Most of the musicians were at their places when Kate entered the hall. She walked in, stepped onto the podium and rapped for attention.

"Good evening. Tonight we're going to run through the pieces we're scheduled to do for Saturday." Kate looked around quickly. Being in the concert hall brought back visions of Blaine. She had trouble thinking about the task at hand but did her best to bring her mind back to the present. "All right, let's start with *La Mer.*" After the musicians had located the work, Kate raised her baton. Before she could bring it down she heard a noise at the side of the auditorium.

"I'm sorry, Kate, but my car broke down." Ted Merskin came hurrying into the room, carrying his trombone in front of him and trying to look as inconspicuous as possible.

With a start, Kate realized that she had been about to start the rehearsal without the full complement of orchestra members. She glanced at Harold and could see a smirk on his face. She tried to ignore him.

"We were about to start without you, Ted. I didn't want to hold up the entire rehearsal because of your tardiness. We're starting with the Debussy. I'd appreciate it if you'd get settled as quickly as possible."

Kate tried to look stern. She hoped that no one realized she hadn't even known that Ted was missing. Kate could not forgive herself for being so lax. Imagine not even knowing that the first trombonist was missing! She didn't know whether or not the other musicians had bought her excuse for starting prematurely, but when she glanced over at Harold he was looking down at the music and she could not see the expression on his face.

"Now that we're finally all here"—Kate gave Ted a scathing glance—"let's begin."

The musicians began playing. Kate interrupted repeatedly, asking the strings to play alone, then the brass, then both together, and finally she was able to continue with the ensemble.

"That sounds good," she finally said. "Now let's start again."

During the next try, the brasses came in early.

"No! No!" Kate shouted. "What're you doing?"

"You cued us in," the first trumpet called out. "We wondered about it, but we thought that's what you wanted."

"Sorry," Kate mumbled. "Let's go over that again."

The orchestra began playing and Kate's mind began to wander back to Blaine once again. Although she knew the seats behind her were empty, somehow she could feel Blaine's presence. And, sitting right next to him, was the spirit of Marissa. She had stopped thinking about the music and forgotten where she was. She cued in the brass without thinking and realized that once again she had cued them in too early.

"Sorry," she said before anyone could comment. "There's so much we have to get done tonight that my mind seems to be jumping ahead. Let's get back to that *andante* measure." Kate could see Harold smirking, but she pretended not to notice.

This time Kate did remember to cue in the brass properly, but she cued the strings in a beat too soon. All she seemed to be able to feel was Blaine's scrutiny burning her back. And Marissa's disdainful grin. Kate was tempted to cancel rehearsal and go home to her piano, but she knew that it would be an unprofessional way to behave.

Kate finally finished the rehearsal of *La Mer* but it had taken at least an hour and a half longer than necessary because of Kate's inability to pay attention to what she was doing. She got through the Mussorgsky with great difficulty and by the time she got to the Copland she was exhausted from the constant strain of reining in her wandering mind.

"Perhaps we should adjourn till tomorrow night," Kate announced. The thought of Blaine kept eating away at her, the frequent errors she had made during rehearsal upset her and the combination served to make her feel genuinely ill. "We'll meet here tomorrow night. Seven-thirty sharp." Kate was tempted to look directly at the tardy trombone player as she said this, but she had made so many errors during the evening that she felt she could not criticize anyone else.

Kate hurried out of the concert hall making an effort not to meet anyone. She just wanted to be left alone to deal with her own confused thoughts.

Kate returned home and tried to relax by playing the *Polonaise Militaire*. Not only did it not help, but she could hear that she was playing badly. She decided instead to take a hot shower and get into bed. But this did not help either. Kate tossed and turned all night, visions of Blaine coming toward her and then suddenly receding, visions of Marissa taking Blaine's hand and visions of Harold smirking at her, reaching out for her baton. By the time morning came Kate felt as though she had been tortured in some prison camp.

She took her temperature and discovered to her dismay that she was not ill. Which meant she had to go to work this morning. Kate dressed in bright colors, a lavender dress complemented by an ice-green scarf. She had been sitting at her desk only a few minutes, trying to decide which job to tackle first, when Malcolm knocked at her door.

"Mind if I come in?"

"Not at all." Kate smiled, hoping that the turmoil that raged within her would not show. "What brings you here so early in the day?"

"Kate! You look awful! Do you feel all right?"

"Is that what you came here to tell me? That I look awful?" Kate tried to make a joke of Malcolm's concern but he refused to rise to the bait.

"No, it's not, and we'll get to that in a minute. Are you sure you're not ill?"

"I'm fine, Malcolm, but I appreciate your concern. I would love to be a ravishing beauty every day, but some days I miss." Kate gave Malcolm a genuinely warm smile, glad that he cared. "Now, what can I do for you?"

"I heard that you have an extra rehearsal scheduled for this evening."

Kate wondered how Malcolm had heard of the newly scheduled rehearsal so quicky and what he had learned of the previous night. "Yes. We couldn't finish all the work we were supposed to do, so I asked the orchestra members to come in tonight."

"But, Kate, the cost of an extra rehearsal is not in our budget. You know that."

"Yes, I know. And I've never asked for this before. You know that."

"I don't mean to act like Scrooge, Kate, but this orchestra runs on a very tight budget. And paying all those people an extra night's salary—"

"But we do have to maintain the integrity of the orchestra, Malcolm, and sometimes that means an extra rehearsal."

"May I ask why you couldn't finish the rehearsal for the Pops last night?" Malcolm's voice was kind, sympathetic, but Kate could tell by the look in his eye that he knew the reason very well.

"What did Harold tell you was the reason?" Kate wasn't certain it had been Harold who had told Malcolm, but since the rehearsal had taken place only last night, she knew it had to have been one of the members of the orchestra.

"Actually, he told me very little. He called me this morning because he wanted to send a baby gift to my daughter—they knew one another in school—and he mentioned that there would be an extra rehearsal this evening. When I asked him why, he hedged. Just said that you couldn't finish last night. Kate, why couldn't you finish last night?"

"First the trombonist came late. Said it was his car." Kate looked up at Malcolm. "That happens sometimes, you know."

"I know."

"And that seemed to start the night off badly. Everything went wrong" —Kate did not say that she'd been the one at fault—"and nothing seemed to flow." Kate looked up at Malcolm once again. "It was just one of those off nights." She paused. "But you know what they say. Better the problem in rehearsal than during the concert." Kate gave Malcolm what she thought was a confident Bernini smile. "And I think the concert itself will go wonderfully well."

"It had better go wonderfully well to a full house, to cover the cost of the extra rehearsal," Malcolm grumbled.

"Don't tell me that Bob Bernini never had a rehearsal fall apart on him."

"Well, yes, but never at the end of our financial year. He always seemed to need the extra time right after fund-raising when we were flush with money."

"I guess I'll just have to time it so that I only goof up when you're getting funds in."

Malcolm had to smile. "Sorry if I sounded like an old curmudgeon, but it is work to keep this orchestra in the black. You understand."

"I do, Malcolm, and I'm sorry about the extra rehearsal. But we really do need the time."

"I hope the pressure of being in charge of an orchestra isn't getting to be too much for you, Kate."

Kate looked up in shock. Did this mean Malcolm didn't trust her any longer to act as conductor? "What makes you say that?"

"You do look awful, you know. Almost as though you hadn't slept at all last night. If the weight of acting as director is too great, you can always take your old spot in the orchestra."

Kate looked down at her desk. What was happening to her? Even Malcolm was beginning to worry about her ability. Malcolm, the one staunch supporter she had always had. Kate looked up at Malcolm, peering directly into his eyes. "No, this job isn't too much for me. The job is wonderful. I've never been as happy in my work as I am now. It's just that —just that"—Kate couldn't bring herself to tell Malcolm what she could hardly admit to herself, that she was in love with Blaine Eddington but that the feeling was not reciprocated—"it's just that a friend came to visit and was telling me about her problems. I just got to thinking about it and I guess I didn't sleep well last night. But it's only a temporary situation." Kate hated to lie outright to Malcolm but how could she admit her true feelings? Malcolm would feel sorry for her or, worse yet, laugh at her. But one thing that she had told Malcolm was not a lie. This was only a temporary situation. She considered herself a strong woman and she would get Blaine Eddington out of her mind.

"I hate to see you looking this way, Kate. I like you too much. Why, you remind me of my daughter, and I hate to see you burdened down at a time in your life when everything should be wonderful."

Kate looked at Malcolm, feeling gratitude for the kindly man. "I am very grateful for your friendship, Malcolm, and I appreciate the trust you've placed in me." She stood up and walked around her desk to take his arm. "And I won't fail you. The Whittenburg Symphony Orchestra will be the best there is."

Malcolm smiled, looking relieved. "I'm sure it will be." He started to leave the office when he suddenly turned. "Have you spoken to Bill Scott lately?"

Kate thought back to yesterday's breakfast, when she could not bring herself to discuss the matter of artistic control. "We're in touch," she said.

"He called the other day and said the signing of the contract had to be delayed a little bit because of some differences he was having with you. He said he was confident that the differences would resolve themselves, but he did postpone the signing. Anything I should know about?"

"Just the matter of who has the last word on how the master sounds. I think I should have it and Bill thinks Maesterling should have it. But, as Bill said, it will resolve itself."

"Good, because I think it would be wonderful for us to have a recording of our orchestra's performance sold nationally."

"I think so, too. And I'm meeting with Bill as soon as he comes up from the South. He's working with another orchestra down there as part of the series." Kate may have sounded confident but she was worried. She hoped she wouldn't blow the record the way she had blown last night's rehearsal. Ever since Blaine Eddington had come into her life, things had gone steadily downhill.

CHAPTER 14

On the night before her first outdoor concert Kate tossed on her bed, worrying. There still hadn't been enough rehearsal time, and if tonight's performance went badly she would be in real trouble with Malcolm and the board. Compounding the problem was the Maesterling dilemma. What should she do—accede to Bill's wishes and let technicians make decisions that were properly the province of the music director? All well and good if the technicians did the right thing, but what if their decisions were unwise? Record critics all over the nation would have their fun at the Whittenburg's expense. And if Malcolm didn't fire her for a bad performance then he'd certainly fire her for becoming the laughingstock of the music world.

Maybe she ought to phone Malcolm now and tell him how serious the impasse with Maesterling was. But it was three in the morning, and even if it were midday he'd have little respect for a director who couldn't handle these problems on her own. What would he think if she went crying to him with "Malcolm, Bill Scott and I can't come to terms. Do you think you could talk to him for me?" Surely he'd think she was a child.

She got out of bed and padded into the kitchen for a glass of warm milk. As the evening was warm enough to begin with, she questioned whether or not this old wives' remedy for insomnia might really help. But she heated some milk in the microwave and dutifully downed it, fighting nausea with every gulp. Then she went back to bed and waited for sleep to come.

Her eyes closed, finally, at five in the morning. At seven a trombone player called to say he was down with a summer cold and was coughing too much to play tonight. She groaned, saw that it was too early to call the union for a replacement and went back to bed. At nine the dry cleaner called to say that her navy gown had been inadvertently torn. Did Miss Reston have something else to wear this evening? Of course Miss Reston did, Kate thought angrily. Miss Reston had a black linen suit that she'd worn the past five summers. She'd been so looking forward to wearing the silk gown tonight. She'd thought that having an impressive-looking garment might somehow make her performance impressive. And now the gown was ruined.

"We'll compensate you at once," said the woman. "Can you come in and—"

"I'll come on Monday." Kate sighed. Too angry to say goodbye, she hung up and went back to sleep.

At ten-thirty the new violinist called to tell Kate that the bandstand in Hancock Park was too small for the orchestra.

"Of course it's too small!" Kate was angry over having been awakened yet again. "It's always *been* too small, Doris, but unless you can drum up the money to have a larger one built—"

"Kate, you said we'd have to double up on music stands. That's easy enough for most everyone but I've told you about the problem with my left eye. You know I can't see well if I have to—"

"Yes, and I told them to bring an extra stand for you."

"Oh, did you?"

"Yes. If they forget it you'll just have to tape your music to Joe Romano's back."

"What?"

"A joke, Doris. Goodbye." Kate hung up, remembered that the phone would surely ring again and decided to take it off the hook. She went back to bed but this time, hard as she tried, she could not make herself sleep. Oh, wonderful, she thought. Her premiere performance in the park and she'd be too tired to hold the baton. Marvelous! Maybe Malcolm would dismiss her right there on the stage. A Whittenburg first. Drama in real life . . .

Sleep continued to elude her. She stretched toward her nightstand and turned on the radio for the weather report. She was hoping fervently that the forecast would be rain. No, not just rain. A downpour. A torrent, maybe even a tornado that would sweep away the bandstand and spare them all the agony of tomorrow's reviews. But the radio announcer, a chatty fellow who edited his own news and weather copy and gave unsolicited advice to listeners, was exulting, "Another perfect weekend, folks! Warm and clear tonight with dry air moving in and humidity skulking out. A great night to stroll with your sweethearts, so be sure to . . ."

Oh, no! thought Kate. Half of Whittenburg might turn out tonight and probably Channel 4 News as well. Her drooping eyes and canyon yawns would be beamed all over southern Pennsylvania!

The announcer continued, "So you and your sweetheart make sure to leave those air-conditioned houses and . . ."

She heard the word "sweetheart" and suddenly the image of Blaine Eddington was before her. She and Blaine, that night in the parking lot. The warm honeysuckle-scented air, Blaine's head bending toward hers . . .

Yet on Tuesday he hadn't come. Where had he been? Where?

Marissa Avalon. The name popped into Kate's brain. Harold had said that Blaine had mentioned Marissa Avalon to him. Kate hadn't wanted to appear to be too interested so she had not asked Harold anything else. But she wondered again if Blaine had been with Marissa Tuesday evening. If so, he would have had to come here to the condo to pick her up. Unless she'd spent the night with her parents—and she often did that. They had room enough in their mansion to accommodate not only their daughter but twenty of her friends.

All right then, Blaine might have picked up Marissa at her parents' house. And then they would have gone—where?

The radio announcer was saying cheerily, "And you people planning on going for a drive tonight be sure to stop off at Whittenburg and check out the Hancock Park Concert. A new, young, very talented and very lovely conductor named Kate Reston will be making her summer debut . . ."

Oh, Lord! she thought. Oh, if only it were a normal day she'd be thrilled to be hearing this announcer plugging the concert. But not now. Not when she was so tired and dejected that she was ready to sell her soul for a good rainstorm. Kate shook her head and groaned. It was going to go badly tonight. She knew it.

Kate left for the park well in advance of the concert. She had to see that everything on the bandstand was arranged properly. Only a few musicians had arrived and these were complaining, as they did every year, about the lack of space. Kate gritted her teeth, told them to bear up as best they could and looked over the music stands. They had brought down Doris's. At least one thing was going right tonight . . .

"Channel 4 News is going to be here," one of the oboe players remarked, unconsciously straightening his tie. "The June opener always makes news."

"Yes," Kate said tightly.

"They'll probably excerpt the *Appalachian Spring.* That's what everyone likes best."

And it's what we play worst, Kate thought, shaking her head. But she was suddenly conscious of her appearance. How would she look on camera? Sighing, she brushed at the arm of her suit. The outfit was five years old and had a street-length skirt, and the jacket lapels were too narrow. Kate had been planning to donate it to a charity. She had decided to buy several new summer gowns suitable for conducting. But so far she'd bought only that beautiful navy blue—and the dry cleaners had destroyed it!

Calm down! she ordered herself. Calm down *now!* Nuts to Channel 4 News and the outfit and all the rest! Your job is to make music. Now, concentrate on that and only that! Do you hear me, Kate? Are you listening, Kate?

Other musicians were coming up to the bandstand now and each new wave brought a new flood of complaints about the lack of space. Kate, unable to bear it, stomped down the stairs to the grassy park and paced rapidly, taking deep breaths and chanting, "Calm down . . . Right now . . . That's an order."

"Kate?" came a familiar bass voice.

She looked up to see Blaine looming over her. He was dressed in a white open-necked short-sleeved shirt and dark brown trousers. So awed was Kate by the spectacle of seeing him in something other than a suit that she forgot for a second how angry she was. "Blaine," she murmured, unable to take her eyes off the powerful muscles in his arms.

"What's wrong?" he asked. "You seem very upset."

"I—" Now she remembered Tuesday night. She stared at him, her expression savage, but she said nothing.

"Is it something I've done?"

She remained mute. Didn't he even remember?

He studied her for a while and then, in what was obviously an attempt to fill the silence with some sort of conversation, he said, "Well, the trip was eventful."

"What?"

"My trip. To Los Angeles. Harold gave you the message, didn't he?"

"What message?"

"There was a problem at the plant. I had to fly to the coast Tuesday night. I was going to call you from the airport to tell you I'd have to cancel our date but I saw Harold when I was turning onto Maple Street and I asked him to call you and explain."

"He didn't," she murmured skeptically, not sure that Blaine was telling the truth.

"You mean you waited for me all evening?"

She was about to say yes but she caught herself in time. She would not give him the satisfaction of knowing. "I waited half an hour. I figured something had detained you, so I went out." She let the word "out" hang there between them. Let him wonder where she'd gone and with whom. Though she knew she ought to be more angry with Harold than with Blaine, she was not satisfied with Blaine's explanation. All right, maybe he hadn't actually stood her up, but he might have tried a bit harder to make amends. He might have wired flowers and an apology or at the very least phoned her from Los Angeles. Conveying a message through Harold was hardly chivalrous conduct, no matter what Blaine's excuse might be. And hadn't Blaine considered the possibility that Harold might forget? Kate thought about that briefly, wondering why the normally punctilious Harold would forget a message, but Blaine's eyes were riveted on hers and the question fled her mind.

He said, "You waited for me half an hour? Is that what you're angry about?"

"No," she lied. She wished she could go on to add, You're darn right I'm angry. Mostly at myself for caring so much that I fouled up a rehearsal, lost several nights' sleep, and may yet lose my job. I'm very mad at myself, Blaine, for being so caught up in you when it's obvious you don't think enough of me even to deliver a message personally. But of course she said none of these things.

"You haven't told me what's wrong, Kate."

She straightened up and said in as steady a voice as she could manage, "I'm preoccupied with tonight's performance."

"There's something else bothering you."

"No, there is not. Although . . ." She deliberately let her voice trail off.

"Although?" he prompted.

"I'm troubled by your attitude. Now, mind you, I appreciate your concern for me, Blaine, but I think that perhaps you take me a bit more seriously than circumstances warrant."

"Circumstances?" His eyes were boring into hers.

"All this worrying about how I feel, what you might have done to put me in a mood. What makes you think your actions are so important? And as to what I feel—well, what I feel, I'm afraid, is nothing. I'm sorry if you misinterpreted my friendliness to be something more, but—"

"What did you say?" His mouth had fallen open. Good, she thought. Let him think that there was at least one woman in town who could not care less about his comings and goings.

"Kate, I want you to look me in the eye and tell me again that you feel nothing."

The concert mistress was leaning over the rim of the bandstand hissing, "Kate! Kate! It's three minutes of."

"Coming!" Kate turned and hurried toward the stairs shouting over her shoulder to Blaine, "We're on, Blaine. Sorry." And she smiled sweetly into his outraged face.

The concert was a sensation. Propelled by her delight in having had the last word with Blaine, Kate conducted as she had never conducted before. The musicians were quick to pick up on her ebullient mood and after the first few measures their discomfort was forgotten. Never before had the strings sounded so lyrical, the brass and the winds so spirited, the timpani so definitive. Never before had the ovations from the park been so clamorous. The concluding Mussorgsky set off cheers that seemed to rebound off the trees. And Kate, taking bow after bow, nearly cheered too. Though she didn't have a mirror, she knew how she'd look on Channel 4 News later tonight. She'd look flushed and buoyant and more than capable of handling an orchestra. Never again would she have to see that doubting look in Malcolm's eyes!

After the performance many of the musicians and their friends went over to Tony's Pub. They begged Kate to go with them and she did. After watching themselves on the television set behind the bar, everyone cheered the success of the concert, blew kisses at one another and then settled down with frothy beers. Kate, who had slept little the night before and was more fatigued than she realized, soon grew so dizzy and giddy that she almost forgot about Blaine. But not entirely. When Harold and his wife came over to the booth at which Kate was sitting, Kate said to him, "Harold, Blaine Eddington said he gave you a message the other night."

"Message?" Harold glanced at Kate, then at his wife Miriam and then at the floor. "Oh, yes. Something about not being able to see you. Didn't I tell you about it?" He cleared his throat.

"No, you never did," she snapped.

"I must have forgotten." He coughed.

"But, Harold, you never forget messages. You're very conscientious about that." Kate looked at Miriam as though for confirmation. Miriam nodded.

"I forgot that message, apparently. I don't know why. I hope I didn't ruin your—what was it, a date he had to cancel?"

"It was—sort of—well, yes. A date." She hadn't wanted Harold to know too much about her association with Blaine for fear that he'd tease her.

"Kate, I'm so sorry." He gulped his drink down. Then, as someone called out to him, he walked on, his movements jerky.

Kate frowned at Miriam and said, "Have I upset him? I didn't mean to. It's just that I've never known him to be so forgetful."

"Nor have I," Miriam said, genuinely puzzled.

"Sit down," Kate patted the seat beside her.

Miriam complied and then said, "I guess it's that we've been under pressure lately. Problems with the kids."

"Anything I can help with?"

Miriam shook her head and laughed dryly. "Teenagers. They're an incurable illness. Still, it's not like Harold to forget something so important. He must have been very distracted that day. Part of it might have been the noise from Blaine Eddington's construction site. But that's over, thank heaven, so . . ." She trailed off and said to Kate, with a grin, "So you're dating Blaine Eddington? Very interesting."

"Not 'dating.' He'd asked me to dinner that night."

"A nice catch, Kate."

Kate shrugged. "I'm not interested."

"No?" Miriam looked skeptical. "Why not?"

Kate shrugged. "My career takes up all my time."

Miriam nodded. "You must be so happy about being director."

"Yes." Kate felt guilty. How Miriam must wish it had been Harold. They could certainly use the money, Kate knew. But one of these days Harold's turn would come. Just yesterday she had heard that a directorship might be opening up in Ohio. Kate wished she could tell Miriam about it, but it would be foolish to say anything so soon. Instead she patted Miriam's hand and said, "I'm sorry for snapping at Harold that way. I know he must be very tired what with the teaching job and the symphony, the house, the kids . . ." Kate was exhausted just thinking about Harold's responsibilities. What must it be like for him to endure them? And she had gotten angry because he'd forgotten one silly message. How terribly thoughtless of her.

As Miriam began to chat about her children, Kate's mind drifted back to Blaine, to the sight of his face as she'd mounted the bandstand. He'd looked so outraged—and she'd been glad of it. She'd wanted to make him pay somehow for having unwittingly caused her so much misery. Now, relaxing over a beer, the performance behind her, Kate wondered if perhaps she had been a little unfair. Well, yes, she had been, and under ordinary circumstances she might have apologized. But this situation was not ordinary. An apology would mean seeing his melting smile again, his hypnotic eyes. Not even over the phone could she make amends, for his deep sensuous voice would also unnerve her. And she must not risk being under his spell. Emotionally she just could not handle it. One more week like this one might finish her career forever.

CHAPTER 15

That night Kate slept soundly, but though she felt wide awake in the morning, something was missing. Her life seemed empty. She tried to tell herself that it was just the expected let-down after all the excitement of the past few months—her sudden appointment as symphony conductor, her emergence into the limelight, limited though it was to Whittenburg and her meeting with the first man who could ever take her mind off music.

Kate thought about the problem with Blaine as she drove to her office. It was a lovely spring day, flowering plants spreading their color all over the lawns and the sides of the road, the purples of the irises and peonies mixing with the reds and whites of the azaleas. They signified a new beginning and Kate determined that that was just what she would have. She would concentrate on the one thing in her life that was always there and would never let her down—the one thing that always brought her happiness, soothed her when life got difficult and gave her a feeling of accomplishment and self-worth—her music. Everything else would now be secondary. And that included Blaine. She determined to treat him the way she would treat any other man with whom she had dealings as part of her responsibilities as symphony conductor.

Kate felt a surge of determination as she drove into the parking lot. Today was going to start a whole new life for her, one where she was in total control. Feeling much more spirited than she had felt when she left her condo, Kate got out of the car and walked in a determined fashion to her office. This was the new Kate.

When she got to her office there was a note on her desk in Harold's handwriting. "Bill Scott called and said he would like to come in to the office at two. If that is not convenient, please call him at the Lincoln Hotel."

Kate looked at her watch. It was eleven o'clock and she had several matters that needed attending to. She was auditioning a new oboist at eleven-thirty because the one she had now was going to take the rest of the summer off to have a baby; she had to write up the program for the July Pops concert and send that over to the printer; and there were a few letters that she had to answer. The letters could wait until late afternoon, though, so two o'clock would probably be all right. She was thinking that perhaps she ought to call Bill to confirm the appointment when Harold walked into the office.

"Good morning, Kate," he said. "Did you get the message from Bill Scott?" The gleam in his eyes said, See, I don't forget to give you the important messages.

"Yes, I did, Harold." Kate had forgiven him his oversight regarding the message from Blaine, but she did want to keep a businesslike demeanor. She still felt a little guilty at having treated Blaine so callously. "Thank you."

"I hope I didn't upset anything between you and Blaine," he continued.

"No, everything's fine, Harold." Kate felt that any further discussion about Blaine would destroy the resolve to put him out of her mind.

"I'm certainly glad, Kate. He's really an eligible catch and I'd hate to ruin it for you."

"Don't worry about Blaine and me. We were just going to have a casual dinner. But I'm sure he'll contribute to the orchestra just as generously whether or not he has dinner with me."

"Don't tell me that your concern for the orchestra was the only reason you and Blaine were going out to dinner!" Harold smirked, apparently not noticing Kate's desire to drop the subject.

"If there is any other reason I'm not aware of it," Kate said, a sweet smile on her face but a feeling of irritation beginning to grow.

Harold stepped closer. "Then I wonder why Marissa keeps thinking of you as her rival." He spoke in a low tone, as though he and Kate were conspirators.

Marissa. The name struck at Kate. Why did Harold keep mentioning her name? "I didn't know you and Marissa were so friendly," Kate said, pretending not to notice Harold's conspiratorial tone. "Does Miriam know about this?"

"Why, uh, that's just what I hear around town. You know, at the pub and sometimes when I run into her mother." Harold stepped back now. "Well, I've got to run now. I have a kid coming for a lesson in half an hour and I'll just have time to make it home," he said as he quickly left.

Just thinking about Marissa made Kate angry. She didn't know why that should be because Marissa had a right to date whomever she wished to. As did Blaine, she told herself. But it was upsetting to have Harold keep reminding her of the two of them. She wished he would keep his information to himself. The strength she had felt earlier seemed to have dissipated with her conversation with Harold. She would have to bring it back somehow if she was going to deal with Bill Scott. She took several deep breaths and tried to clear her mind of the morning's conversation.

"Miss Reston?" A young woman carrying an instrument case stood at her door.

It was the oboe replacement. "Come in," Kate said, getting up from her desk and ushering the young woman to a seat. "Let me get some background information from you before we start the audition."

The audition went smoothly and as soon as the oboist left Kate ordered up some lunch. She wanted to be prepared for her argument with Bill Scott.

By the time Bill arrived at her office, Kate had eaten, combed her hair and repaired her makeup and was sitting at her desk writing out the program for the next Pops concert.

"Kate!" he said as he came into the room. "It's great to see you." He walked around to where Kate was sitting, leaned down and kissed her on the cheek.

"It's good to see you again, Bill. How've you been?"

"Fine. We've lined up ten symphony orchestras already and my boss thinks this project is really going to take off and do well."

"If the other symphonies are as good as ours, I have no doubt," Kate said smiling.

"Touché." Bill returned to the side of the desk opposite Kate and sat down in the stuffed chair that faced her. "And today we're going to line up the Whittenburg."

Kate just smiled.

"Aren't we?" Bill pretended to be concerned but Kate could tell from the look in his eye that he had no doubt about the outcome of this meeting.

Kate knew that Bill was aware of how important the record was to Malcolm—indeed to the entire orchestra—but she also knew that she must fight for artistic control. "I certainly hope so," Kate said.

"Well, then, how about going out to dinner to celebrate?" Bill said.

"You clown." Kate began to laugh. "We're here to negotiate. We've got to settle a few things before I sign with you."

"You do want to make this record, right?"

"Right."

"And you do want the record to be as perfect as possible, right?"

"Right."

"Then what's to negotiate? Just sign here"—Bill took a contract out of his jacket pocket and slipped it across the desk—"on this line."

Kate took the contract from him and picked it up. She noticed that Malcolm's signature was already on it, but she began reading it nonetheless.

"Do you think Malcolm would sign a contract that was not in the best interests of the Whittenburg?" Bill asked, watching Kate as she carefully read the contract.

Kate looked up. "As far as the business end of this contract is concerned, I know that Malcolm would be very careful." She stared directly into Bill's eyes and this time she did not smile. "But I'm not certain that Malcolm would know everything about the artistic end."

"Come on, Katie." At this, Kate grimaced. No one had called her Katie since she had been a child. "Malcolm has been with this orchestra for more years than you have. He knows what needs to be done."

Kate put the contract down. She did not like being reminded that she had only recently been put at the helm of this orchestra, because she had been involved with music for most of her life and believed she understood it as well as, or better than, anyone else. "My length of time as director is irrelevant," Kate said, speaking firmly. "My knowledge of music is the only important issue here. And I assure you that in that area I am very knowledgeable."

"Whoa, Kate, I didn't mean it that way," Bill said, putting up the palms of both his hands as though fending off an attack. "I just meant that Malcolm has been keeping this orchestra financially afloat for a long time through periods where no one appreciated the value of a symphony orchestra, and he has an instinct about what is right for it."

Kate calmed down a bit. "I know how efficient Malcolm is, and how wonderful he is with financial matters, Bill. But I think you're missing the point."

"Which is?"

"That while I wouldn't question Malcolm's decision to sign a contract with Maesterling—their reputation is excellent—I do believe that as symphony conductor I should have the last word on the music itself." She paused for a moment. "The music itself, Bill." Kate emphasized the words. "I think that if the strings are too loud, or the brass too soft, or whatever, I should be able to decide not only whether or not changes are to be made but how those changes should be done." Kate sat back, looking directly into Bill's eyes.

"You wouldn't call yourself an unbiased person where the Whittenburg is concerned, would you?" Bill asked.

Kate looked puzzled. She had expected Bill to capitulate after her last little speech. "No, not totally unbiased. What does that have to do with it?"

"Biased people often hear what they want to hear. Wouldn't you agree with that?"

"Sometimes." Kate was not at all certain what Bill was trying to prove.

"Which means you don't always hear the music exactly as it is but as you want it to be."

Kate began to understand Bill's point. "When there is music involved I always hear it as it is. Always!" Kate responded. She waited a moment to calm down. "In fact, if anything, I am too critical."

"That's no good either, Kate. If something is good the way it stands, and you have some fine point—a moment that no one else notices but you —you might change that note and then mess up the rest of the record. Our technicians know when and where to draw the line."

Kate did not respond but just sat there looking at Bill. She hoped that the anger she felt was not apparent in her eyes. But she felt that Bill understood her mood.

"Well," he said somewhat defensively, "they do. I can give you references—"

"I really don't need references. I know the quality of a Maesterling recording or I wouldn't have even entered into negotiations with you. But follow my line of reasoning." Kate leaned forward as though to more carefully impress on Bill what she was about to say. "Composers put their music on a piece of paper, indicating the melody and the tempo. Correct?"

"Yes." Now it was Bill's turn to look puzzled.

"Along comes Isaac Stern. He plays the music and gets a standing ovation. Agreed?"

"Most likely."

"Then along comes a less talented violinist. He plays the same notes at the same tempo. And even if he played on a Stradivarius the performance would not sound the same as Isaac Stern's. Agreed?"

"It boils down to ability."

"Ability—and interpretation." Kate looked triumphant. "How two different musicians interpret a piece makes a great deal of difference in how the piece sounds. And"—Kate paused and then spoke in a quietly controlled voice—"I don't want technicians who have nothing to do with the Whittenburg to make a determination as to interpretation."

"I can see your point, Kate. But I wish you could meet the guys who control the quality at Maesterling. There's a man—"

"I'm sure they're all very well trained musicians and technicians, Bill. As I said, I have a very high regard for Maesterling. But these men, regardless of how well qualified they are, do not determine how the Whittenburg Symphony Orchestra interprets its music."

"Is there room for compromise here?" Bill said. The look on his face told Kate that she had the battle under control.

"That depends on what the compromise is."

"Would you agree to joint artistic control? That way our technicians will have the chance to review the recording and decide what they think needs possible change. And you can have your say. The two of you can then come up with a joint opinion."

"I would prefer that I have final and complete control—"

"There's no way we can allow that, Kate. Remember, we are spending our money to produce this record and we won't get any remuneration on it until the sales start rolling. All you invest in it is time. So we have to have some control over what goes out."

"All right, Bill. I do see your point, and if we can fix the contract to read that there will be joint control over the artistic end of the recording, I'll sign."

Bill looked relieved. "That's great. I'll send this copy of the contract back to my office for the changes and then I'll send it back for you and Malcolm to sign." A sudden gleam came into Bill's eyes. "Unless, of course, you insist that I come back here in person for the signing. I could force myself to do that."

Kate laughed, feeling at ease for the first time that afternoon. "No, I wouldn't want to put you to all that trouble."

"What trouble? You'll cook dinner for me at your place and after dinner we could—"

"Bill! How about taking that contract and going? I have work to do." The smile in Kate's eyes softened her words, but she did mean them.

After the recent fiasco with Blaine she had no desire to get involved with another man just yet.

"Yes, ma'am, Conductor Lady. But this here ain't the last you've heard of me," Bill said, affecting a Western accent.

Kate smiled with affection. "Send me the contract as soon as it's ready."

Bill walked around to Kate's side of the desk, leaned down and gave her a kiss on the cheek. "It's been a pleasure," he said, and then he left.

Kate immediately started on one of the letters that she had to write, but, after holding her pen poised in the air for a few minutes, she put it down. The fact that the record was going to be an actuality excited her. Kate Reston and the Whittenburg Symphony Orchestra. She could see the words on a record jacket. Would the jacket contain a photograph of her alone? Would there be a picture of her conducting the orchestra? She knew nothing of how Maesterling intended to package the series. Would they consult her at all? She doubted it. If they weren't interested in her opinion regarding the music itself, they wouldn't be interested in any of her other opinions.

But packaging didn't interest Kate too much. Just the fact that the music she conducted here in Whittenburg for a relatively small number of people would now be heard nationally was exciting to think about. And as far as promotion went she trusted Maesterling. They had been promoting and selling classical records for many, many years.

Kate picked up her pen again and started once more on the letters that needed to be answered. She took the first one, something from the musicians' union, and started to read it. But a picture of Blaine came into her mind. If she hadn't been so involved with the orchestra would her relationship with Blaine have been any different? Did she want to sacrifice the possibility of a romance for her music? Kate thought back to the hours of lessons, the hours of practice and her dedication to her art. No, she decided, music is my first and only love and if Blaine Eddington gets in the way, he will have to go.

CHAPTER 16

The success of the Hancock Park concert seemed to whet everyone's appetite for the big Independence Day festivities to come. An editorial in the Whittenburg *Clarion* had mentioned Kate, her orchestra, and the dimension it would bring to the holiday. And the chatty radio announcer on whom Kate relied for news and weather urged that those in a mood for an old-fashioned Fourth hie themselves over to Hancock Park next month for food, fireworks and *"The 1812 Overture* complete with church bells, folks!"* But though the Fourth would be the most dramatic of the concerts there were still the regular indoor performances to see to, and Kate devoted her energies to these until, during a rehearsal in late June, she finally turned her attention to the Independence Day bash by saying to the orchestra, "All right, let's try to ignite ourselves for the fireworks special."

With the exception of Gould's *American Salute* this was music the orchestra could do practically blindfolded. Even the difficult string section in the *1812* was rendered without incident on the first try. Kate ran through everything but the Gould selection, her mind wandering freely. She thought again about Bill Scott and Maesterling. Now that the contract problems had been resolved the Whittenburg Orchestra would be recorded. Actually recorded, heard all over the United States and perhaps the world. The thought caused in her the kind of excitement she hadn't experienced since the day she had received her acceptance from the Boston Conservatory. She thought too about Harold, wondering if that small Ohio city would seek him out for an interview, wondering if he and the family would be willing to move. And, hard as Kate tried to resist, she also thought about Blaine, whom she had not seen in more than two weeks, on the night of that first open-air concert when she had told him she felt nothing for him. Harold had since indicated that there had been gossip about Blaine and Marissa. Well, she thought, there was nothing to be done about that, and to continue to dwell upon the situation would be counterproductive.

She had absentmindedly let her right arm fall, causing the flutes to stop playing abruptly. "No!" Kate shouted, shaking her head in confusion. "I didn't mean to halt you. It's fine. You were fine. Let's continue." She raised her baton and the spirited *Stars and Stripes Forever* again engulfed her. A magic tune, she thought. Even now, even after all the times she'd heard, played and conducted it. She grinned, thinking that no one could remain soulful for very long while submerged in the melody of this beloved Sousa. Maybe it ought to be required listening for anyone who was depressed or dispirited.

She heard Sousa again on the radio the next afternoon and for once she did not do a mental critique of the performance. She thought only that marches really did make one feel alive. She was driving southwest in the general direction of the Maryland border. Somewhere along this highway was a gourmet shop, a fantastic place that friends had told her she simply must see. And Kate, partly because the weather was so pleasant, had decided to take a run over. Mile after mile had passed, however, and there was still no hint of the shop. There were, instead, signs proclaiming that Gettysburg National Park was coming up, and she realized that she'd taken a wrong turn somewhere. She was probably a couple of miles south of Gettysburg and nowhere near the shop. Oh, Ellie and her crazy directions! If she'd only given route numbers and street names instead of saying "Take a right at the white house with the green shutters and a left at the big oak tree . . ."

Sighing, Kate pulled over to the side of the narrow two-lane highway and consulted a map. Since there were no route signs visible she still did not know precisely where she was. She did know that this road would eventually lead her to Gettysburg and she could follow the main highway home from there. The gourmet shop would just have to wait for another day.

On the radio a chorus was singing "Rally Round the Flag," a Civil War song. Kate started as she realized that she was now in an area both armies must have streamed through more than a century ago. Come to think of it, it was also late June, the very season in which the daring advance north had taken place. No wonder they were playing the song. Southern Pennsylvania would never forget that tortured June.

Thanks to Blaine and the library visit he had encouraged, Kate knew more about the war now than she'd ever known before. In late June, 1863, when the Confederates had passed into Pennsylvania, the Union Army, which had been protecting Washington, had belatedly begun a furious pursuit. Their aim was to head Lee off before he got to Harrisburg or

Philadelphia. To do this they would have to march quickly. But in which direction? No one had known where the main body of Lee's army actually was.

In time the advance units of the Union column, breathless from their rapid march north, had stumbled into Gettysburg, where they ran into a few Confederates who had come to buy shoes. It was a small town of two thousand people, most of them farmers whose lives would never again be the same.

There was a part in Gould's *American Salute* where the theme—based on "When Johnny Comes Marching Home"—became, briefly, a dirge. It was this section that Kate thought of as she sat in the car south of Gettysburg on this late June afternoon. She imagined that it was the eve of the battle and she could see the infantry making its way up a gravel road. General Meade's mighty army, thousands of men, sweating in the heat, uniforms turning white in the dust, a blue-white snake bulging at intervals with supply wagons and cannon pieces, extending all the way back to where the sky met the crest of the hill.

"No! No!" she screamed in her mind as they approached. "Don't go any farther! There are rebels up in Gettysburg who've come to buy some shoes."

A tired colonel with reddish hair, who looked somehow too young to hold such a high rank, looked down from his mount and smiled. "A couple of rebels won't scare us, miss."

"Sir! Listen to me! This is different! All their army is nearby. And if you go into that town—"

"I have no time to talk, though it was a pleasure to meet you, miss—"

"Reston. Kate Reston."

"It's not often that we meet attractive young ladies. I'm Colonel Josiah Jones." He tipped his hat. "Someday, I trust, we'll meet under more favorable circumstances?"

"Colonel, you mustn't go any farther. There's going to be a terrible battle there."

"Forward, march!" The colonel roared to his men.

"Stop!" She cried again and again but the hulking army rolled past her into a foreordained doom. In that moment she knew Colonel Jones himself would die . . .

Kate was abruptly brought back to the twentieth century by the sound of a car slowing down. She glanced across the road. Whoever it was in that sleek black sports car must assume she had car trouble. She'd better explain that she— Suddenly Kate caught her breath. It was Blaine Eddington stepping out of the car and in a moment he had materialized in the very spot where the imaginary colonel had been talking to her.

"Blaine!"

"Did you run out of gas, Kate?"

"No, I lost my way en route to the new gourmet shop and I— Blaine, did the Union Army ever march along this road?"

"Oh yes. This used to be a dirt road that—" He broke off and smiled. "Learning more about the Civil War, are you?" She nodded but did not smile back. If she were to avoid any more disastrous concerts or rehearsals she would have to stick to her resolve never again to encourage Blaine's friendship.

He said, "I've just been researching the war again too. Or, more specifically, talking to a local farmer who has information on everything from where the armies camped to what they ate for breakfast aside from the ubiquitous hardtack. I wanted to know something about how General Pickett might have spent the days just prior to the battle."

"Oh yes." She remembered that Blaine was preparing some sort of presentation for the Whittenburg Historical Society. But she did not go on to ask what the research had turned up. She must, at all costs, resist any friendly overtures. She could not, however, turn her eyes away at once for today he was wearing a marine-style camouflage T-shirt and well-worn jeans. The shirt emphasized every hard curve in his upper arms and chest and the jeans made his long legs seem endless. She began to smile, thinking that he looked especially appealing when dressed casually. But the smile died on her lips as she forced herself to remember the emotional problems her involvement with him had caused her. She was about to bid him a not-so-fond farewell when he said, "What did you want to know about the Union Army?"

"Only if they'd actually tramped over this terrain." Colonel Jones had seemed so vivid to her that she almost believed he had been real.

"Yes, they marched through here. There was a campsite too, half a mile down the road. There are trees with names and regiment numbers scratched into them."

"Really?"

"If you have a minute I can show you—"

"No, please. I have to get going, Blaine."

"Are you in that much of a rush?"

"A terrible rush," she lied.

He clearly did not believe her. "I thought you said you were lost, but it doesn't seem to be worrying you particularly. There was a dreamy look in your eyes when I came over—"

"I did get lost but I'm not worried. A sign back there said that the next right leads to Gettysburg. From there I can find the highway home."

"Nonsense, that route'll take you ten miles out of your way. I'm heading back to Whittenburg now; why don't you turn around and follow me?"

"All the way to Whittenburg?" She hated following cars. Invariably, at every intersection, someone pulled in ahead of her, obscuring her view of the leading vehicle.

"Not all the way," he said. "A mile or so from here is the main drag into Whittenburg. But between here and there are a few confusing turns."

"How well I know," Kate said, thinking of Ellie's terrible directions.

"All set?" He crossed the narrow road, got into his car, moved ahead and waited for Kate to make her U-turn. They had gone about half a mile, making two right turns and a left, when he signaled to pull over. Thinking that something was wrong with his car, she stopped behind him and got out. It was on her lips to say that things had really come to a sorry pass when the great automobile expert himself had car trouble, but before she could open her mouth he said, "Just a little way in from here is that campsite I was telling you about."

"Blaine, I told you I couldn't—"

"It's just a few paces in from the road. Take you four, five minutes to see it."

"Well, all right." She followed him into the woods, which were dense with thorny bushes. It was a good thing she too was in jeans, Kate thought, and that her shirt, unlike Blaine's, was long-sleeved.

He pointed out inscriptions on assorted trees: the names of men who had paused here for what must have been a very brief rest on the long forced march that had begun in Virginia and ended in Gettysburg. At one tree Kate stopped and drew in her breath sharply.

"What is it, Kate?"

"Josiah Jones." Her voice broke. That had been the name of the colonel she had imagined.

"How do you mean, 'Josiah'?" Blaine asked. "It just says here J. Jones."

She told Blaine the story, tears threatening. He attempted to soothe her by saying, "Kate, Jones is a very common name. The man who carved this was probably a John or a James or a Joseph. And undoubtedly he lived to grow fat and jaded and to make a fortune in the Robber Baron era."

"It was Josiah. And I spoke to him before he died." Kate began to weep. Blaine gathered her into his arms and held her until she was more in control. She stepped back and then, because she was feeling a little weak, sat under a tree, her legs folded under her. "Ghosts," she said. "This whole area is haunted by ghosts, isn't it? Here, and at Gettysburg, even in Whittenburg and on all the roads leading to it. I wonder sometimes if that's why I never wanted to know too much about the war. I remember when I was a little girl my father pointed out some barn where a rebel was supposed to have been shot and I kept imagining I heard the man calling and calling for his mother but that no one could hear him because he was dead."

"Oh, Kate." Blaine sat down beside her and placed an arm on her shoulder.

"But it was wrong of me not to want to know about the war," she went on. "All those Americans, North and South, so many of them died. It's wrong just to forget them. Josiah Jones, for example—he would have been pleased to know that some twentieth-century woman would think about him someday."

"Now you've got *me* believing that you actually met a Civil War officer," Blaine said with a smile.

"What else could he have been? How many modern men do you know who are named Josiah?"

"None." He laughed and kissed her on the cheek. "It does sound like one of those old Calvinist names. Where do you suppose he came from— Massachusetts?"

"Connecticut," she said with conviction. "I see a small town with a big Congregational church at the end of the green. I see a couple of sheep nibbling at the grass. I see—"

"And I see a lovely woman with an incredible imagination," he said in tones so caressing that they immediately sprang Kate from her trance. Good grief, what was she doing here? After all her resolve to have nothing more to do with Blaine Eddington, here she was relaxing in a wood with him and casually accepting his affectionate kisses on the cheek as though she'd known him for years, as though such affection were to be taken for granted, as though—well, almost as though he were her *husband.*

"I have to go, Blaine," she said, rising suddenly and brushing dry leaves from her jeans.

"What? Before we've discovered what kind of house Josiah lived in?"

"I'm late for an appointment."

"All right, but tell me the truth, will you?"

"About what?"

"The incident just before the concert. You were angry at me because you thought I'd stood you up."

"A little," she admitted.

"And you waited the entire evening, didn't you?"

"How did you know— I mean, I—I waited for a while." She was flustered. "I'm in an awful hurry, Blaine."

"You didn't mean it, then, about having no feelings for me?"

"Look, I—"

"You didn't mean it, did you, Kate?"

"No," she whispered.

They were standing face to face. Suddenly, without preamble, he took her into his arms and bent down, his lips hard upon hers. Kate shivered and found herself yielding to sensations she had never before known. His tongue found the space between her lips and gently probed. At the same time his long hard body pressed against Kate's until she was afire. Her arms went up around his neck and she clung to him tightly in part to support her legs, which were no longer firm but as yielding as her lips. Her sense of self had ceased to exist. There was only feeling, a pleasure so intense that it was akin to pain, and a longing for something that she dimly knew was inevitable, beyond her power to halt.

They sank to the ground, both of them groaning, and she closed her eyes as he undid the buttons of her shirt. But as he reached around to unclasp the hooks of her bra, he stopped and murmured, "Kate."

"Yes!" she said breathlessly, thinking that he was tacitly asking her permission to continue. At this point it would not have occurred to her to say anything but yes.

"It's— We're not going to do this," he said.

"What?"

"I didn't mean to take it this far."

Oh, Lord! Couldn't he see that she wanted this as much as he did? Didn't he understand? But how could she make him understand without sounding downright bold? He gently urged her to her feet. "Come on, you're in a hurry." He began to brush dry leaves off her shirt and jeans but then withdrew his hand quickly as though he had touched fire. "Could you—uh—button that shirt yourself? I don't trust myself, Kate."

But why? she wondered. Was it simply that he was too much the
gentleman and thought he might be taking advantage? Didn't he realize
that she was twenty-nine years old and could handle herself? Perhaps not.
Perhaps he thought she'd been too buried in music all her life ever to have
had any experience with the opposite sex. But Kate had a feeling that
something more than gentlemanliness was involved here. Was he afraid of
betraying another woman? Was he afraid to get involved because his work
left him little time for considering long-term commitments? Around and
around her brain spun, seeking answers. She did not look at him as she
quickly buttoned her shirt and brushed off her jeans. But as the two,
without speaking, began to make their way through the undergrowth to
the road, she caught a glimpse of his face. There was a downward tug at
the corner of his mouth and a remote look in his eyes. He looked sad and a
little uncertain, and she had no clue as to why. But as he caught her
glance, the puzzled expression vanished as though a sculptor had
smoothed over fresh clay to start his task from the beginning. Blaine
smiled as he took her by the elbow and maneuvered her away from some
thorny bushes. Kate tried to smile back.

He said as he walked her to his car, which was parked beyond her own,
"Just a half mile or so to the highway."

"Okay."

"Not a long distance to follow a car."

No, she thought. His car was simplicity itself. It was his mind she could
never seem to follow. Suppressing a sigh, she thanked him and got into
her Volvo.

CHAPTER 17

When Blaine called her several days later to ask if she wanted to see Gilbert and Sullivan's *The Pirates of Penzance* with him on the following evening, Kate was confused. At times Blaine seemed to want her but then, when he came close, he pulled away. She was perplexed and a little hurt. Nevertheless, her desire to be with Blaine was strong enough so that she accepted.

"Sorry that I called you at the last minute," Blaine explained when he picked her up at her condo, "but I just received these passes in the mail yesterday morning."

"Passes!" Kate said in mock irritation. "You mean Blaine Eddington gets to see the shows at Whittenburg Hall for nothing while the rest of us mortals have to pay?"

"That's just it, Kate," Blaine said in a serious tone. "If I like what I see, the Whittenburg Foundation would like me to make a nice contribution. You don't think that the price of theater tickets keeps the old hall alive, do you?"

"I guess not," Kate said. "I know that Meade Hall relies on benefactors." She turned and gave Blaine a smile, acknowledging the fact that he was generous in his contributions, "but I didn't think about Whittenburg Hall."

Whittenburg Hall was only a few blocks away from Meade Hall and up until the 1920s had been the only theater in Whittenburg. In fact, when Sloan Eddington was at the height of his career, he had performed in Whittenburg Hall. But then the town and its population grew, knowledge about sound expanded and the town decided to build a larger auditorium. Thus Meade Hall had been born. Since Meade Hall was a larger and more acoustically perfect auditorium than Whittenburg Hall, it became the home of the symphony orchestra. Whittenburg Hall, meanwhile, became home to repertory companies that came to town frequently, exhibiting shows that had been popular on the Broadway stage and operettas like those of Gilbert and Sullivan.

Blaine had to park on the street, since Whittenburg Hall had been built before the days of parking lots. It was a short walk to the theater, but since the evening was crisp and cool, Kate enjoyed it.

Kate had never really decided what she felt about Whittenburg Hall. It had been built during an era when ornamentation and ostentation were considered the epitome of good taste. The outside of the building had elaborate and elegant brickwork and the masks of comedy and tragedy intertwined with the bricks. But it was inside the building where the artisans had outdone themselves. The floor of the outside lobby was made of terrazzo; Italian marble trimmed the upper portion of the walls. The walls themselves were papered with posters of bygone days; a painting of Lillian Russell dominated the area but Sarah Bernhardt, Isadora Duncan, Theda Bara and other personalities who had delighted the world up until the late 1920s could also be found there.

"Good evening, Miss Reston, Mr. Eddington," the ticket taker said as Kate and Blaine walked into the theater proper.

It had been some time since Kate had been to Whittenburg Hall. Not since *West Side Story* had been performed here, she thought, and she looked around to see if the place had changed.

The deep red rug on the floor felt just as plush as she remembered and the gold gingerbread and hanging golden angels looked as though they had just been painted. The panel inserts on the wall were covered with a wallpaper that was basically red but had golden swirls throughout. The fact that someone had modernized the building was apparent in the lighting, however. Recessed lights kept the inside lobby bright but did not intrude on the ambience.

Kate thought that Whittenburg Hall was being wonderfully maintained. She wondered if sending passes to prospective contributors helped to keep the coffers sufficiently full to do all the work required and she wondered if Malcolm practiced this same strategy over at Meade Hall. She made a mental note to speak to him about it the next time she saw him.

"Your seats are right down here in front," the usher said after she had looked at the tickets that Blaine handed her. "Just follow me."

Blaine and Kate walked down the aisle and found themselves seated in the eighth row center.

"Rather an impressive location," Kate said as she sank into the red plush seats.

"I couldn't have chosen better seats if I had gone to the box office to pick them up," Blaine responded.

The two of them had come early and this gave Kate a chance to look around. Most of the people knew who she was and, while she knew many of them, she did not know all who nodded at her. But she returned the smiles of everyone who acknowledged her. She felt as though she were now an important part of Whittenburg.

Blaine also came in for his share of nods and smiles. Though he had few close friends, everyone wanted to say he "knew" the famous Blaine Eddington.

It amused Kate to see how the people who attended this performance were dressed. Most were in rather casual clothes: afternoon dresses and pants suits. Some were even wearing jeans, although these were almost always part of an outfit. She compared the appearance of this audience with that of the patrons who came to Meade Hall. Most of the women attending concerts in Meade Hall wore cocktail dresses and a few, on opening night, had been known to wear gowns. And the men always wore suits and ties. Blaine, she noticed, was dressed that way this evening, but then Blaine seemed to prefer formal fashion most of the time. Kate supposed that people considered the Whittenburg a second-rate concert hall, which was unfortunate because the repertory companies who came here were highly professional troupes.

Blaine and Kate had no time for conversation. The lights had begun to dim and soon the overture was beginning.

The Pirates of Penzance was not Kate's favorite Gilbert and Sullivan. She had always preferred *The Mikado* to everything else the team had written and indeed to all operettas. Nevertheless, it was a fine, rousing show, faultlessly rendered by the Wilhelmsen Repertory. It was hard for Kate to believe masterpieces such as this had been written by two men who had squabbled almost continually. On the other hand, many perfectionists seemed to be hot-tempered, and when two such got together it was very likely that histrionics would be the order of the day. But what did it matter? The feuding had never been reflected in the work, and this was the important thing.

During intermission, Kate and Blaine did not return to the lobby. They remained in their seats humming music from the show. Blaine's uninhibited manner surprised and delighted Kate. It was good to see this light-hearted side of him. He had a deep bass voice that was most respectable-sounding. It turned out that he knew most of the words to the Pirate

King's song and all of the words to the Major General's song. Kate was astonished. She asked him, "How can you remember all that?"

"I've seen this operetta a couple of times."

"Even so."

"The lyrics are so clever that it's pretty hard to forget them. All that nonsense the General spouts about having memorized simple and quadratic equations. Have you ever, in any other song from any country or era, have you ever, no matter how bizarre the song's subject matter, heard references to higher mathematics?"

Kate laughed and shook her head.

"And it's that way with all Gilbert lyrics," he said. "It's not just the bouncy rhythms. It's the social commentary, the topical humor, the unlikely allusions and the irony in phrases like 'many cheerful facts about the square of the hypotenuse.' 'Cheerful,' of all words." He began to laugh helplessly.

"You're really enjoying yourself, aren't you?"

"Hugely." He began to launch into verse two of the Major General's song, and Kate, playing the part of the chorus, sang back at him. In seats around them people smiled and nodded. Some of them timidly joined Kate when it came time for her to do the chorus lines. By the time the second act opened, the audience was buoyant, expectant, so enthusiastic that Kate began to laugh in sheer joy. The evening had an air of unreality about it. It was more than just magical. It was crystalline fun.

The merriment continued long after the closing curtain. Blaine had intended to take Kate on to the Lincoln for drinks but when he parked the car they were laughing so hard that it would have been impossible to make a dignified entrance into the hotel. They were giving contemporary topics the Gilbert and Sullivan treatment, trying to make up tunes about such twentieth-century phenomena as the battle between the colas and the proliferation of answering machines. They were congratulating one another for being astonishingly witty, even though both admitted at one point that few critics would agree with them. And they were having a wonderful time.

During one of the few sober moments Kate experienced that evening she reflected for a while on the nature of good relationships. In most of the poems she'd read and the songs she'd heard, all the attention was given to passion, to longing, to great heights of ecstasy and cavernous depths of despair. And these were all aspects of a relationship, true. But what about fun? What about laughter? Why were they rarely written

about, sung about? She thought for a moment. Was it because most poems and songs were about courtship, and the fun in a courtship was never
completely genuine no matter how much it gave the appearance of being
so? It was a hard thing for Kate to admit, especially on an evening charac-
terized by great hilarity, but it was the truth. To have true no-holds-barred
fun, she thought, one had to be able to let down one's guard completely.
And one could never do that with a love unless there was a commitment.
It wasn't possible to abandon oneself absolutely to mirth or to anything
else that was mindless unless one knew that one could not be attacked
while consumed by the emotion. This meant that a person had to be very
secure with a love, had to know that the beloved could be depended upon
forever and ever, in sickness and in health, until death—

Good heavens, what was she thinking of? The marriage vow?

"You've gotten very quiet." Blaine turned in his seat and touched her
arm lightly. "Aren't we going to finish writing this operetta?"

"Of course we are."

"Or would you rather go in for that drink now?"

"No. I'd rather stay here," she said.

"What were you thinking about, Kate?"

"That it's been a wonderful evening."

"Oh? Then why do you look so solemn?"

"Do I? I'm sorry."

"Was it something I said?" Blaine asked.

"No. It's just that all this libretto-writing got me thinking about music
and the Fourth of July concert coming up."

"Problems?"

"No. Not really." And she thought, Not with music, at any rate. The
problem is with you. She remembered that day in the woods near Gettysburg. Ah, the feel of his lips, the hardness of his body. But he had re-
treated from her, had drawn into himself. He had definitely not wanted a
relationship of any depth, and she must not let herself forget that. What
he'd wanted, perhaps, had been more dates like this one: light and bright
and thoroughly uncomplicated.

"Are you feeling well, Kate?"

"Sometimes when I laugh too hard, I get an upset stomach," she lied.

"I see. Would you like me to take you home?"

"Please."

"Were you thinking of the other day, Kate?"

She did not reply.

He said, his voice hoarse, "I'll explain it eventually. I can't do it now."
Kate nodded, but she wondered if he ever would explain.
"I'll take you home then."
"All right."
And when he said good night this time, he didn't even shake her hand.

CHAPTER 18

On the Fourth of July Kate rose at ten. It would be a very full day and Kate had to be at Hancock Park before noon. She wanted to enjoy the picnic and to help set up in the gazebo for the concert in the evening.

A quick shower forced Kate to come fully awake, and after a small breakfast she was able to organize her schedule. She dressed for the afternoon, selecting a white sharkskin suit that had a short skirt, and a floral halter top to wear under the jacket should the day become extremely warm. A pair of white sandals completed the outfit. Later on she would come back for the navy organdy shirtwaist dress she would wear for this evening's performance. Grabbing her attaché case, which contained her music and the notes she had made to herself regarding her responsibilities for the day, Kate drove to Hancock Park.

When she arrived there she saw few people. There were members of a local political group setting up an ice cream booth and others organizing a fried-chicken stand. The firemen were arranging their fried-dough booth and other groups in town were setting up various booths of their own.

Kate hurried over to the gazebo to see if the chairs and music stands for the evening's concert had been delivered. She knew that chairs were not going to be set up until late in the afternoon, so that the townspeople could use the gazebo during the day, but all the equipment—chairs, stand, podium—was supposed to be behind the gazebo before the big crush of people arrived. Kate looked around back and saw the stage manager standing next to several large boxes.

"Good morning," she called. "Those the things we'll need for tonight?"

"Yes, Miss Reston. We brought them early this morning, when we were sure it wouldn't rain today."

Kate grimaced. She remembered one Fourth when the weather had been threatening and the stagehands had left the chairs packed until very late. When the sun had finally come out, they set up the equipment for the concert, but by the time the musicians had found their seats it was pouring. But today's weather forecast offered no such surprises. The day promised to be fair and pleasant.

Now that Kate was certain that everything was where it should be, she went back to her car. She had brought all her music with her but she wanted to double-check before the picnic started. Malcolm Merriwether had invited her to join his family for the picnic lunch but she wanted to have a little time to study the scores for the evening. She sat in the front seat of the car, her legs touching the ground, as she looked through the pieces of music she had brought with her.

"Good morning, Kate."

The deep bass voice sent a shiver through her and she looked up to see Blaine smiling at her. "Good morning," she responded. Blaine stood there in dark blue linen slacks and a light blue shirt. "Don't tell me you are going to be working all afternoon."

Kate looked puzzled but then followed Blaine's eyes to the music which was all over her lap. "No," she said, laughing. "Even the conductor gets an afternoon off to eat. But I thought that if I had time I could look over this score again."

"And do you think you're all ready for tonight?"

Kate gathered up all the scores and slid them back into her attaché case. "Yes, I do." She looked up at Blaine and smiled.

"Can you spend part of the afternoon in Hancock Park with me?" he said, taking her hand and helping her out of the car. He seemed to want to forget the awkward ending to the Gilbert and Sullivan evening, and she hoped not to think of it either.

"That sounds very nice," Kate said, putting her music on the seat and locking her car door. And then, "Oh, I forgot!" Kate stopped suddenly and clapped her hand to her head. "I promised Malcolm I would have lunch with him and his family."

"Oddly enough, so did I," Blaine said, taking her hand once again. "Maybe he thought we two needed looking after." Blaine's smile seemed to caress her.

"Looking after?"

"Although I grew up here, my roots have been in California for a long time, and I'm kind of a loner here in the East. And you"—Blaine looked at Kate in a way that caused the redness to climb up her cheeks—"everyone wants to share lunch with you, so he's keeping you from being divided into several parts."

Kate laughed. It was so comfortable being with Blaine. "I doubt that.

Some of the members of the orchestra might want to see me in several parts, but not for the reason you think."

Blaine tucked Kate's arm through his. "In that case, I shall be your protector."

Kate laughed again, and the two of them walked to the area where all the picnic tables had been set up.

In the distance they could see Malcolm Merriwether. "I decided to come a few minutes earlier so I could reserve a good table," Malcolm called to them as he walked toward them, "but I see I could have left the job to you two."

Kate blushed. Did Malcolm think that they had planned to come together? "Actually, I met Blaine this morning, while I was checking over the music."

Malcolm patted her arm. "You already have the job, my dear. And you do wonderfully well. You don't have to convince me that you are a hard worker." The twinkle in Malcolm's eye told her that he was teasing.

"It can't hurt, you know," Kate said, responding to Malcolm's mood.

"Ah, here comes the food." Malcolm pointed to his son and son-in-law carrying a large picnic hamper between them. "Put the hamper here," Malcolm said, pointing to a table that was in the center of the picnic area. He turned to Kate and Blaine. "When I sit here I never miss any of the action."

"Mother and the girls will be along in a little while," Malcolm's son said, "but they told us to set up. The tablecloth is inside the hamper"—he retrieved a red-and-white-checkered cloth from the top of the food—"and they told us to put out the plates."

"Why don't I help?" Kate said, taking the plates and arranging them on the cloth. "Everyone should contribute to this picnic, and since I didn't bring any food . . ."

"Did you boys bring the cooler with the wine and beer?" Malcolm said, turning to his children.

"Oh yes," one of them said. "We'll go get that." And they went off to the car.

More and more families were coming to the picnic area and before long the area looked overrun with people. All the Merriwethers had arrived by this time and the group sat down to lunch.

"I have all the traditional Fourth of July food," Mrs. Merriwether said, as she and her daughter and daughter-in-law removed the food from the large cooler, "but I couldn't help but throw in a few family favorites." She put a bowl of pâté on the table along with some crackers. "Just as an appetizer," she said.

Malcolm poured wine for everyone, and, after toasting each other, the group proceeded to devour the food that had been prepared.

"That was a great picnic lunch," Kate said to Malcolm's wife, "and I appreciate your having invited me to share it with you."

"Same for me," Blaine said. "I mean, I'm delighted that you asked Kate and me to join you."

Kate wasn't sure she wanted the rest of the world to know how she felt about Blaine, so she looked down to keep anyone from seeing how red her face had turned.

"We're always happy to have the two of you," Malcolm's wife responded.

"You have enough for another meal," Kate remarked as she helped put the containers of food away.

"We need it," Mrs. Merriwether said. "Malcolm loves to munch while he's listening to the beautiful music of the Whittenburg Symphony Orchestra." She looked fondly at Malcolm. "Actually, we all do. And you're welcome to join us also, Blaine. We have enough for you, too."

"Thank you for inviting me. Perhaps I will. But now"—Blaine looked around the group with a mischievous grin—"how about some ice cream?"

Everyone groaned. "I'm afraid not even I could fit any in at this moment," Malcolm said.

"Oh, what has befallen the spirit of the Fourth of July picnic?" Blaine moaned. "The revelers are not as hearty as they used to be."

"I'd like some," Kate said. "Besides, I want no one to impugn my Fourth of July spirit."

Blaine stood up, a victorious smile on his face. "I knew I could arouse the old-time ability," he said.

Kate and Blaine left the table and made their way to the ice cream booth. "I'm glad no one else wanted to come," Blaine said. "I wanted a chance to have you to myself for a while."

Kate looked around at the huge crowd. "I'm flattered at the thought, but this is hardly 'alone.'"

"I'm sure you're familiar with that old line about being alone in a crowd. Besides, we haven't reached our destination yet."

Kate looked confused. "I thought our destination was the ice cream stand. And we're almost there. And from the look of the line, the only thing that would keep us alone would be for us to become invisible."

"I would never want you to become invisible," Blaine said, clearly relishing her well-proportioned bosom, small waist and rounded hips, especially as they looked in the halter top and short skirt.

"Thank you," Kate said, turning away. She hoped that people would think the crimson in her face was caused by the strong sunshine.

The ice cream line went quickly and Kate and Blaine had their chocolate cones in hand before very long. "And now, I want you to come with me to my special tree."

The look in Kate's eyes was one of puzzlement. There weren't too many trees that she could see and she wondered which one was special to Blaine.

"It's at the other end of the park, the one near all the monuments."

Dimly, Kate could visualize a tree at the end of the park. "Why is that one special? Is it a variety that doesn't usually grow in this part of the country?"

"Oh, it's just an oak tree. And it is venerable with age. But it's special because I spent a lot of my young years under it." He continued in a hoarse voice, "Although I must confess that this will be the first time I've shared it with anyone."

"Then it can be our tree, can't it?"

Blaine stopped walking and turned to face her. "I'd like that very much."

They began walking again, and were almost finished with their cones by the time they got to the monument area. Kate looked at the tree, wondering why Blaine had selected it as his own. It was very old and gnarled with roots. The branches were so full it was almost as though Kate and Blaine were enclosed by the tree. The din of the large crowd in the picnic area of the park was barely audible.

"This is a lovely spot," Kate said. "How did you manage to—I mean, why did you—"

"Why did I come to this particular place?"

"Yes. It seems so open, not at all the kind of secluded spot most kids would look for."

"Actually it's more secluded than you think. The only time anyone comes to this end of the park is Veterans Day and Memorial Day. The rest of the time it's ignored by everyone but the man who mows the lawn. So, as a young boy, I could come here and dream away the afternoons without being disturbed at all."

They had come close to the tree and were standing up against it. Blaine was looking up into the leafy boughs. "Hello, old friend," he said, as though unaware that Kate was standing beside him. This was a side of Blaine that Kate had never seen. In a moment he looked down at her. "It's good to be home again. Would you like to sit down?"

The two of them sat down on the grassy surface beneath the tree, leaning against the old oak.

"What were you like as a little boy, Blaine?" Kate asked.

"Like every other little boy, I suppose."

"But what did you dream about while you were sitting under this tree?"

"Oh, about how I would grow up, meet a wonderful lady . . ." Blaine fell strangely silent. Kate did not want to impose on his mood.

After a while, Blaine spoke. "It's very peaceful sitting here with you, Kate. Almost as though we're protected from all the cares in the world."

Kate looked over at Blaine. His head was back against the old trunk, his eyes closed. "You don't look like a man with too many problems, Blaine," she said. "You have a successful business, you're highly respected in the community and"—a teasing look came into Kate's eyes—"you're not bad-looking, either."

Blaine opened his eyes and looked over at Kate. "You noticed!" he said, laughing. "There's one more tradition you should know about," Blaine said. "Any girl who comes to sit with me has to kiss me." Without waiting he reached over and gave Kate a gentle kiss. It was sweeter than the passionate one in the woods near Gettysburg and somehow this told her more about Blaine than his other kisses had. She felt safe and secure.

"Hey," she said suddenly. "I thought I was the only woman you ever took to this tree!"

"You are."

"Then what's this about the tradition of kissing the females you bring here."

"Oh, that's a tradition that just started with you." He took Kate's arm. "And I hope we can maintain it."

Kate reached up to touch his cheek and caught a glimpse of her watch. "Oh dear, I didn't realize it was so late."

Blaine looked distressed. "Late? You have to leave?"

"The concert! Remember? I have to go home and change and then get back here to get the orchestra organized."

"So soon? I thought we had at least another hour."

Kate stood up, wiping the sand from her skirt. "I wish we did."

Now Blaine stood up, taking Kate in his arms. "Under this tree time stands still. Didn't you know?"

"But near the gazebo time is racing. Why don't you walk me back to my car?"

"All right," Blaine said. "But promise me that we'll come back here sometime soon."

"I promise."

Blaine and Kate walked to her car and though they continued to talk, Kate's mind turned more and more to the concert she was going to give that evening, and to the massive fireworks display that would take place immediately afterward. Somehow it seemed fitting. The day that she and Blaine had come together in spirit was being marked with beautiful music and fireworks.

CHAPTER 19

The Independence Day Pops had always been planned to please as much of the audience as possible. Thus, in addition to standard symphonic and patriotic fare, there was always one sing-along and one rousing dance medley to which people in the park could clap or dance or just jump up and down. Last year's rock medley had inspired several break-dancing exhibits (difficult on grass but managed deftly nevertheless by energetic junior high-schoolers.) This year Malcolm had requested swing—and now it was the grandparents' turn to trip the light fantastic, accompanied by a medley of Benny Goodman, Harry James and Glenn Miller hits, tunes that would have delighted Bill Scott.

In this part of the concert, Kate would have preferred watching to conducting, for, judging by the clamor, everyone down on the green seemed to be having a wonderful time. There was much cheering, singing and shouts of "Hubba, hubba!" and she longed to drop the baton, turn and watch the hijinks. But a relative of Malcolm's was videotaping the best of the dance sequences, and one of these nights he planned to have Kate and other members of the orchestra come to see it.

After the swing segment, the audience, keyed up as it was, took some time getting into the mood for the low-key beginning of the final work of the evening, Tchaikovsky's *1812 Overture*. This was the only piece played every single year, by popular demand. Kate sometimes wondered how many people realized that the *1812* did not commemorate the second American victory over Britain but rather the Russian triumph over France in that same year. But it didn't matter; ever since Arthur Fiedler had popularized this Tchaikovsky favorite in his televised Boston Pops concerts, it had become the most American of works. It was fortunate that three major Whittenburg churches were located close enough to the park for audiences to hear the bells when they clanged joyously at the finale of the piece. This being Whittenburg, there was also a proud Civil War artillery piece to be put into use at the same time. Even more impressive than either the bells or the cannon were the fireworks. The first display was always synchronized with the cannon booms. Then there would be a pause while the orchestra was applauded. And then everyone would move toward the north end of the park, where the fireworks would continue for some time after the concert ended.

The performance received rousing cheers—not surprising, given the fact that the audience was buoyant, as it always was on the Fourth. If they'd missed entire measures or entire sequences only a minority of the listeners would have noticed, Kate thought. This was not Meade Hall, where subscribers were far more critical and particular. If only, on bad days, she could somehow be transported back to Hancock Park on the Fourth.

She was gathering her scores to put them into her attaché case when Blaine came up to the gazebo to congratulate her on a job well done. He was still in the blue linen slacks and the light blue shirt he had worn this afternoon. Since she was in her navy organdy shirtwaist they actually matched, she thought. Like two Union soldiers.

"How was it out there?" she asked.

"In the park? Delirium. St. John's bells came in much too early, so—"

"Yes, I heard them."

"—so the cheers were a bit premature, but it was just as well. By the time the cannon sounded, the crowd was ecstatic." He paused. "Would you like to go over and see the fireworks?"

"I can see them well enough from here." She followed him to the part of the bandstand that faced north. They stood behind several of the other musicians, Harold among them.

"Hello, Blaine," Harold said.

"Harold," Blaine said heartily. "How are you? Been a while since I've seen you."

"Ever since they stopped dynamiting your construction site things've been quieter. There was no reason for me to stop by and complain," Harold said. His eyes moved from Blaine to Kate. She knew that he was thinking, so you're seeing each other again, and she hoped he wouldn't remark on it later. But it was a futile wish. Harold was always commenting on the situation. He was either hinting to her that she and Blaine would be the perfect match or he was reassuring her that the other women in Blaine's life meant nothing. It had been Harold, she remembered, who had first reassured her about the society woman Blaine had brought to the Sloan Eddington Memorial Concert. Kate recalled that night with a shudder. Her anger at thinking that there might be someone else in Blaine's life had so unnerved her as to nearly wreck the performance. It had been almost as bad as the rehearsal following the night Blaine had failed to keep the dinner date. Had she not pulled herself together in time for the concert later that week she would surely have been out of a job then and there. Now she remembered that Harold had been involved in that episode too, though not intentionally. He had simply forgotten to deliver Blaine's message. But it was odd, now that she thought about it, that a man who took such a keen interest in her affairs would forget such a vital message. Could it be that Harold hadn't really wanted her to be involved with Blaine? But if that were true, why was he always encouraging the relationship? Kate shook her head, confused. It was probably just as Harold's wife had said: too many responsibilities, too little money. Kate remembered that the directorship in Ohio had just been officially vacated. As soon as the small city announced that they were interviewing, she must speak to Harold about applying.

". . . and have a drink some night," Blaine was saying to Harold.

"I'd like to," Harold said. "I'll drop by at the site."

Blaine turned to Kate. "Are you through here?"

"Yes. Just about." She picked up her attaché case and began moving toward the bandstand steps.

"Can I help you with that? It looks heavy."

"Thank you."

Blaine took her attaché case and they walked companionably across the grass to the tree-rimmed edge of the park. Here, in a place especially reserved for her, was Kate's car.

"Where's your car?" she asked.

"I left it home."

She knew he lived in Maplecrest, the town's most exclusive district, at least two miles from Hancock Park. "How did you get here?"

"A primitive form of transportation. I walked."

"A sports car manufacturer? Walking?" She laughed.

"Why not? It's a novelty." He opened the door to the passenger's side of the car. "However, the novelty's worn off. I'd appreciate it if you'd drive me home."

Blaine slipped into the car and began examining the dashboard. When she had gotten in on the driver's side he said, "What, no talking ignition?"

"No, and no voice telling me to put on my seat belt. A silent car."

"Amazing," he said. "Of course, my models are silent too, but there's pressure on me to put a nagging voice into the dashboard. I keep telling the department heads that if we keep it out we'll get more customers, may even be able to jack the price higher. People may pay just for silence, I tell them, but nobody listens. Not only do my experts want cars that tell people what to do, they also want voices to remind people to stop at the cleaners', pick up milk, get tickets for the football game. Is it any wonder I left them and moved back East?"

She smiled, started the car and said, "It was awfully good of you to come back to town and build a plant here. The city's been hit terribly by the industrial recession. Hundreds are unemployed and in some cases the insurance has run out. When they heard you were coming back and building a plant—well . . ."

He nodded.

"You just might revitalize Whittenburg," she said.

"I'd like to help."

"Why did you do it?" she asked.

"Select Whittenburg as the site for my eastern plant?"

"Yes. I mean, it's so off the beaten track, far from suppliers and such. And there are few workers experienced in automotive work. So why—"

He shrugged. "The home folk were hurting."

He cared that much, she thought, touched, remembering how he had felt about the sturdy oak in Hancock Park. It was odd, she thought. Some people could not have cared less about the place they had been born in. And others, like Blaine, felt that they owed it to a town to give something back to the land that had nurtured them. It was an intensely gallant attitude that fit in with his overall nature—his devotion to the men who had fought in the nation's wars, his boyhood habit of pondering life under an oak tree, his gentlemanly withdrawal when their kisses became too ardent . . .

But no, the word "gentlemanly" did not strictly apply to that day in the woods. There had been something else holding him back. Something else . . .

". . . and take a right here," he was saying. "There, up on the hill—my house."

As though she didn't know where the Eddingtons lived. It was only the oldest house in the city and the most faithfully preserved. It was not a large or ostentatious manse but a square and dignified Federal that would probably have housed, when it was built in the 1700s, a large family plus a few sets of visiting guests, plus quarters for the servants.

"It seems very quiet," she said as she braked the car.

"Our butler's gone to visit friends in England and our cook's down in Richmond with her new granddaughter."

"And your parents?"

"Touring Europe. I'm alone here, though I come here only to sleep and sometimes not even then. I have a cot at the plant site and another at the house I'm having built for myself on the other side of the hill. It'll probably be ready by Christmas."

She nodded.

"Kate, would you like to come in for a drink?" He grinned. "Don't worry about my ulterior motives."

If she'd ever had any worries, she thought, they'd been put to rest that day in the woods and on the occasions before that when he'd turned away from her suddenly. "Yes, I would like a drink," she said.

He led her into a living room and she had no view of the formal parlor at all aside from the glimpses of gold-framed ancestral portraits she saw as she passed through the imposing front hall. The living room was comfortable and restful to the eyes—pale green chairs and sofas, airy cream-colored curtains, small scatter rugs in green-and-cream floral print, silver-framed family photographs set on tea tables, walls with suspended bookcases, etchings and small paintings, most of them pastoral scenes. There was a cabinet with sliding doors in an unobtrusive corner. Blaine opened it and asked what she would like to drink.

"White wine, if you have it."

"Certainly." He reached down and extracted from the cabinet's lower depths a bottle of Sauvignon Blanc. Expertly he uncorked it and he poured a glass for each of them. "Sit down, please, Kate."

She sat on one of the French Provincial chairs and let her eyes scan the room. "This is so lovely. So light and delicate."

He grinned wryly. "My parents like it, but I—I always have the feeling that if I breathe too hard everything will shatter."

Kate could well understand that. Blaine was made for heavy furnishings, beamed ceilings, leather sofas—a room to accommodate his masculinity and his size.

"Here's your wine," he said, handing her the glass. "Would you like some cheese or— But no, there isn't any here. I haven't eaten here since our cook left and she'd cleaned out the kitchen entirely. If I were home in the mountains I'd have a refrigeratorful of things to offer you, but—"

"Home?"

"I have a house in the Sierras. In California."

"What's it like?"

He described a redwood house of modern design, furnished and decorated in the dark earth tones she had imagined. "Except for what Amanda called her 'sunshine room,' " he said. "It was her study. It overlooked the valley—all flowers and crystal, pastel walls and curtains—and furniture that would break if I laid a hand on it."

"Amanda was your wife?"

He cleared his throat. "Yes." His expression did not change. She had been gone several years now, Kate remembered. She wondered if Blaine had left the room the way it was or if he'd redecorated.

"Anyway," he said, "I have no refrigerated hors d'oeuvre to offer you but perhaps there are crackers or peanuts in the pantry."

"No, thank you. I'm not hungry."

They discussed the concert again. Blaine told her that the sing-along part of the performance had been almost as big a hit as the dance sequence. "Some good choices there," he said. " 'The Band Played On,' 'Sidewalks of New York,' 'After the Ball,' and that Cohan medley. Of course, half the audience didn't know the words but the other half made up for that."

"Do you know the words to those songs?" she asked.

"Every one."

"I figured you'd know them. Just as you knew Gilbert and Sullivan. It fits in with everything else about you. The history, the love of the old hometown, your affection for the tree." She paused. "You're such a contradiction, Blaine. You're the very image of the athlete, the man on the go. And the business you're in—sports cars—is the symbol for the busy, athletic, impatient man. Yet deep down I think what you're looking for is stability, serenity, old traditions and such."

"Yes," he said, and she could tell that he was thinking of something or someone else. He stared at the window on the far wall for a long time.

"Blaine?"

"Um?"

"Do you agree?"

He turned his full attention to her now. "Agree? That I value serenity and tradition? Yes. But . . ." He trailed off. There was something like fear in his face.

"But what, Blaine?"

"I value them," he said shortly, "but I've had to learn not to count on them."

"What do you mean?"

Now his tone was even sharper. "Are we psychoanalyzing Blaine Eddington again?" he muttered.

Kate let a moment pass before carefully setting down her untasted glass of wine. Then she stood and said as levelly as possible, "Good night, Blaine."

He looked startled. "Where are you going?"

"You don't seem in the mood for company tonight."

"What do you mean?"

"Your tone—what you said about not liking psychoanalysis."

"I was harsh. I'm sorry. It wasn't you I was criticizing, just . . ." He let the sentence trail off and Kate filled in for him. Other people must have wondered about some of his cryptic answers to certain questions and other people must have asked him "What do you mean?" Blaine simply did not like talking about his feelings, not even to her.

"Kate, please don't go. You haven't even finished your wine."

"It's late, Blaine, and I'm very tired."

Blaine suddenly seized Kate by the hands and held them hard, his eyes fixed on hers, confused and troubled. Then, as though blotting something from his mind, he pulled her to him. She responded to him in spite of herself, but it was not the same as that day in the woods. Even as her lips parted to admit his plundering tongue she remembered the look in his eyes a moment before and was puzzled by it.

But soon she was again caught up in the moment, the sweet drowning that his kisses invariably caused. She returned his ardor, moaning a little, breathing hard. And when he undid the top buttons of her shirtwaist she did not resist. His hand moved inside the dress, brushed over her breasts, and moved around to the clasps of her lacy bra. Deftly he undid them. He removed the bra and the dress, took her over to his family's French Provincial sofa and eased her down onto it. His lips caressed her. She was panting now, moaning softly.

Kate opened her eyes and saw that Blaine's eyes were glazed. She was reminded again of how his mind had seemed to shut down in the moment he'd reached for her. Though driven by passion now, it was clear that his body had refused to listen to his mind. Deep down Blaine didn't want to do this thing; he feared its consequences. And still she did not understand why.

"Blaine," she whispered as he tugged at her half-slip, "I can't."

"Why?" He drew back suddenly. His voice was hoarse.

"Because you don't want me. Not really."

"But I do want you. I want you more than anything in the world." His hand slid over the top of her hip. "Ah, Kate." He began to moan.

"You don't want this. There's something—maybe even you don't know what it is, Blaine—something preventing you, frightening you, I don't know. But just now, in order to hold me, you had to blot out your reservations. I saw it in your eyes." She rose from the couch, picked up her discarded clothes and hastily put them on. All the while, Blaine stood with his hands on his hips looking more confused than angry. "I have to go now," she finally said. "I'd appreciate it if we didn't see one another again. It's . . ." She let the sentence trail off.

Blaine said nothing.

"Good night," she said.

"I'll see you to your car."

"Please don't."

"I'll see you to your car," he said, his tone firm.

The walk was silent. The only word uttered was her final goodbye. She started up the ignition and drove back to town. It was Independence Day, she remembered. How apt a moment to cut herself off from Blaine.

She raised her chin and drove on.

CHAPTER 20

The day after the Fourth was another perfect day, but Kate could find no beauty in it. Instead, the blackness of her mood colored everything around her. She knew that she had done the right thing in breaking off with Blaine, because their relationship was too difficult for her to handle; however, she felt as though she had lost something very precious, something she had looked for, longed for and might never find again.

Kate wandered around her apartment—sitting in bed and reading a mystery, attempting the *Polonaise* at her Steinway, sitting at her dining table with a cup of coffee—but she did not feel comfortable. She felt the need to get out of the house. Maybe then she could recapture her feelings of freedom and independence.

She showered quickly and slipped into a pair of jeans, something she seldom wore anymore, and put a sleeveless cotton knit shirt over it. She put on her oldest sandals and went down to her car.

For a while, Kate drove aimlessly. The town that she knew so well, that she thought she knew intimately, in fact, somehow looked strange to her. She recognized the buildings but they didn't seem quite the same. She realized that her feelings were affected by her separation from Blaine, but she knew that it would have to be this way. She would have to adjust to living without him.

Without realizing it, though, Kate found herself driving toward Blaine's new plant. She had no intention of getting out of the car once she got there, but she was curious to see how far the construction had progressed on the plant he was building. And, deep down, she hoped that being near to Blaine, or something that belonged to him, might help ease the distress she was feeling.

As Kate drove closer she could see that the shell of the plant was already up. Workmen were hurrying in and out of the building, getting material from trucks that were parked outside. In spite of herself, Kate was impressed with the size of the building and the interesting shape it had. It was so typical of Blaine not to build a "boxy" building.

Out in the back of the building, fenced off at the side adjoining its neighbor's property, was a racetrack. A group of men were standing at the far side and a silver-and-red sleek sports car stood alongside them. Kate drove nearer to the fence to see what was going on. One of the men, dressed in a white jump suit and matching helmet, separated himself from the group and walked toward the race car. As he walked toward the car one of the men from the group came up to him and appeared to be arguing with him. Kate wondered if one of the men standing there was Blaine.

Kate had mixed feelings about seeing Blaine this morning. What could she possibly say to him? It had all been said last night. And would he even want to see her again? Would he ignore her if he happened to see her here? She sat in the car, fascinated by what was going on on the track but worried about what would happen if Blaine should find her hanging around his plant.

The man in the helmet pulled away from the man who had been arguing with him and got into the car. Kate had never seen a race car operate and she looked on, engrossed. The engine started up with a loud "V-r-r-oooom," and the car slid smoothly onto the track. One of the men standing outside the track held a strange-looking gadget. It looked almost like a policeman's radar gun. She wondered what was happening.

The car gradually gathered speed as it ran around the track, and by the time it had gone twice around it almost seemed a blur. Kate held her breath when the car approached the bend in the track. She wasn't sure it could negotiate the turn successfully. The car seemed to glide around the bend and Kate marveled. The man who was driving that car had unflappable nerves. But then she reasoned that it was probably someone who test-drove those cars all the time. Probably he was used to that kind of speed.

As the car continued to round the track its speed seemed to intensify. Kate watched with a fascination she usually reserved for music. She could not help but wonder at how this man managed to defy the laws of nature.

The man with the radarlike instrument came close to the track each time the car whizzed by. She decided he was probably determining the speed of the vehicle. Kate wondered why anyone would even want to drive as fast as the car was going. Surely no one who was untrained could possibly manage that sort of speed safely. But she had to admit that the car's performance had a mesmerizing effect.

Kate got out of her car and walked up to the fence that set the track apart. She wanted to get a good look when the car sped past her. By now she had forgotten that she might run into Blaine, so hypnotized was she by the performance of the speedster. And each time the driver reached a turn she would hold her breath. Would he maneuver the car around safely this time?

The men who were gathered at the opposite end of the field watching the performance seemed just as hypnotized as she. Their eyes seemed riveted to the car as it made its way around and around the track. Kate wondered how long the car would continue to drive. If this were a new model that the company was testing, surely it had proven itself by now. The driver, however, seemed bent on bringing his speed to even greater heights.

Once again the car was approaching the curve in the road and once again Kate held her breath. Then, as though it were happening in slow motion, the car spun out of control. Wheels screeched and metal groaned. The car flipped over on its side and then flipped over again. The sound of metal ripping and bending rent the air.

An ambulance which had been standing on the side of the track raced over to the car, its sirens screaming. The men who were watching the performance also began to run. The car lay on its back like a dead animal, the wheels spinning and going nowhere.

"Blaine, Blaine, get out of there," Kate heard someone yell.

Blaine? Had it been Blaine driving that car? All of a sudden Kate felt her knees buckle. Was Blaine lying dead in that smashed-up piece of metal?

Without thinking, Kate looked around to see how she could get past the fence. She ran around to where the fence ended and started racing across the track toward the car. She felt as though she could not breathe. Her legs seemed to have a mind of their own, moving her steadily toward the car.

As she ran toward the car she could see someone being dragged from the metal. She supposed they were working as quickly as they could but their actions seemed to be in slow motion again. After what seemed like hours, but was probably only seconds, she could see them pull the man with the white jump suit from the car. Two men pulled at him from underneath his shoulders, removing him as far as possible from the car. The man was safe for only a moment when there was a loud explosion. The groaning piece of metal had turned into an inferno, igniting as though it had been hit by a bomb. Kate could see the flames shoot higher and higher, but she was now concentrating on the inert form that lay on the ground several feet away from the burning wreck.

The men from the ambulance had jumped out of the vehicle and were bent over the body. There were all kinds of medical equipment around and the medics were checking out the driver. Was he dead? Kate could not help but think this, since the figure did not move. But if he were dead, wouldn't the medics just leave him alone? As it was, they were working furiously, while the other men who had been on the track this morning were standing around, white-faced.

At last Kate reached the body. She looked down, and there, on the ground, pale-faced but conscious, was Blaine.

"Blaine, oh, Blaine!" she cried. She could feel the pressure of someone's hand on her arm, pulling her away.

"We have to make sure nothing's broken, so please step aside for a minute."

"Let her near." A weak, breathless voice came from Blaine, but he was definitely aware of what was going on.

"Mr. Eddington, we have to—" one of the medics began to say.

"You can do it while she's near me," Blaine whispered. It was an effort for Blaine to speak.

"Just take it easy, will you?" one of the other men said, relieved that Blaine was alert. Nonetheless, the group allowed Kate to come close and kneel down beside him.

"Blaine!"

"I'm okay," Blaine said, a weak smile on his lips.

"Don't talk," Kate said, relieved. Then she realized how she must appear to Blaine, flustered and upset. Kate wanted to present a more cheerful picture. "Of course you're all right."

The medics finished their checkup. "He seems to be all right, but he should go to the hospital for observation."

Blaine was making an effort to sit up. "I don't think I need a hospital."

"Maybe you should. Just to be certain." Kate was emphatic.

Blaine looked at her. "Does it matter so much to you?"

Kate could feel her breathing return to normal. She was suddenly aware of the circumstances under which they had last seen each other and felt somewhat embarrassed. But she wanted Blaine to receive the best medical attention. "Yes," she said, looking at him directly, so there could be no mistaking her meaning.

Blaine smiled and stopped his effort to sit up. "Okay. But you'll have to ride the ambulance with me."

"Why not?" Kate said. "I've never ridden in one of these things. But make sure you tell the driver that we don't need to race."

The two medics pulled out a stretcher and carefully put Blaine on it. Then they put him into the ambulance. "Are you riding to the hospital with us, miss?" one of the medics said.

"Yes," she answered without any hesitation, and climbed into the back.

Color was now coming back into Blaine's face and he seemed to be breathing more easily. At the same time, Kate's legs seemed stronger. Now that she was relatively certain that Blaine was going to be all right she was beginning to feel more normal. And as she began thinking more clearly, she wondered what she was doing there.

After all, she and Blaine were just casual friends now. How could she explain her presence here this afternoon? One of the medics climbed into the back with Blaine and Kate and closed the door to the back of the ambulance. The other medic got into the front seat, turned on the siren and began speeding off to the hospital.

The medic was attaching all sorts of monitors to Blaine, after first removing his helmet and unzipping his jump suit, giving the two of them no opportunity to talk. While this was happening, Kate noticed that Blaine had dozed off. After a few minutes he awoke with a start.

"At first I thought I dreamed you were with me. I'm glad to see it wasn't a dream."

Kate smiled at him, not knowing what to say and unable to get too close to him because of the medic. Then Blaine drifted off to sleep again.

When the ambulance arrived at the hospital, once again Kate was pushed aside as nurses and doctors hovered over Blaine. But by this time he had regained some of his strength and he tried to push them aside. "I'm fine," he kept repeating. "I'm just here for observation."

"Yes, we know, Mr. Eddington, but we do need to check you over."

Blaine submitted to all the fussing, keeping his eye on Kate all the time. "You'll stay for a while, won't you?" he said at one point. Kate agreed.

After a while, Blaine was put into a private room and, having assured themselves that there was nothing untoward about Blaine's health, the doctors and nurses left his room.

"Alone at last," Blaine said, smiling at Kate as the last nurse disappeared.

"Actually, I think you need to be all alone," Kate said, rising from the chair in which she had been sitting. "I think you need the rest."

"No, don't go."

Kate felt some discomfort. She wasn't sure about how to handle Blaine's question about how she happened to be at the plant. "We can talk when you're out of the hospital."

"No," Blaine said, his strength having returned and his voice firm. "I'm too wide awake now to sleep."

"All right," Kate said. "I'll stay for a little while. Tell me," she said, "do you always race your cars around the track?"

"No, actually I seldom get the opportunity to do it. Usually one of my test drivers does it."

"But you did it today?"

"Yes. That was a new model you saw, one that I've had shipped East for the Scarpatti Racing Team. They want a new car to take to the Indy 500 and they commissioned us to develop it. We got the model ready and were testing it this afternoon."

"It looks as though Scarpatti will have to find another car."

"No, we'll build another out in L.A. But I'm afraid this crash was all my fault."

"Your fault?"

"Yes. I was only supposed to take it for a few laps around the track at a mild speed. The car wasn't ready for the high speeds yet."

"Then why did you take the chance?" Kate was puzzled and upset.

"I don't know." Then he said, "It's not as dangerous as it looks. Especially when there's no competition to race against."

Kate just shook her head. She could not trust herself to talk.

Blaine went on. "What I think happened was that one of the gaskets was loose and some oil must have leaked. And after leaking for several laps I went into a skid, and you saw the result."

"Yes. It was terrifying," Kate said, shuddering.

"And how did you happen to be there?" Blaine asked.

"I was just driving around town," Kate stammered, "and found myself at your construction site. And when I saw the car racing around the track I became intrigued."

Another man came barging into the room, shouting as he moved toward Blaine, "What in blazes did you think you were doing out there? Trying to commit suicide? I've seen you angry before, but never like this.

What—" Then he saw Kate and broke off. "Sorry, I didn't know you had a visitor, Blaine."

"Kate, this is Pete Maloney, the man who tried to talk me out of testing the car."

"Only because he was in a foul mood," Peter said, "and I figured he'd do something reckless."

Kate wondered if the foul mood had been caused by her walking out on him the night before. He'd been so angry then.

After Pete had left, Blaine said, "I'm glad that you rode the ambulance with me. And that you're here." The endearing tone of Blaine's voice made Kate look up at him. Did he really mean that? Looking into his eyes she could tell that he did. But Kate did not know how to respond.

Blaine said, "I don't want us to stop seeing each other."

Kate had realized how much Blaine meant to her when she had seen him on the ground, possibly dead, and though she was not sure she should entangle herself with the complicated man, she could not refuse him. "No, we won't stop seeing one another," she said in a low voice.

"Good," Blaine said in a hearty voice. He sounded as though he had recovered completely. "Innkeeper," he shouted.

"Blaine, what are you doing?" Kate said, trying to get him to keep his voice down.

"Innkeeper, a bottle of champagne!" he shouted.

"Mr. Eddington, please." A tall, husky nurse came hurrying into the room. "You'll really have to keep your voice down. You are disturbing the other patients."

"I'm sorry," Blaine said. His voice was contrite but his eyes said that he was having a good time.

"I have to go, Blaine," Kate said. "You need your rest and I need to get a cab to take me to my car."

"I would love to drive you," Blaine said, removing the covers.

"You get back into that bed," Kate said. "And I'll see you tomorrow."

"You can't leave without kissing me good night," Blaine said.

"If you insist," Kate said, planning to give him a peck on the cheek. She leaned over him and without warning he took hold of her with both his arms, holding her in a grip that she hadn't thought he was capable of at this time. His lips found hers and Kate found herself sinking into a delicious oblivion. Kissing Blaine—knowing that he would be holding her again, kissing her again—made Kate feel that the world had righted herself. It was a wonderful day.

But common sense told Kate that she had to leave the hospital. "I really do have to go now, Blaine."

He seemed reluctant to let her out of his arms.

"I could call Florence Nightingale for help, you know," Kate said, grabbing hold of the buzzer that would summon the nurse.

"Not that," Blaine said, pretending misery. He closed both his eyes and then opened one up. "I will see you tomorrow, won't I."

"I can guarantee it," she said.

CHAPTER 21

Two days later Blaine called Kate to thank her for her visits and her concern and to say that he was home and feeling fine. "And I was wondering," he added, "about your rehearsal schedules this week."

"Nothing until Thursday evening," she said.

"Perfect. I mean if you agree."

"About what?"

"You remember I told you that it was a loose gasket on the car that had leaked some oil and caused that skid?"

"Yes."

"Well, I had my mechanics investigate and it was more complicated than that. A possible problem with the design of the engine itself. I won't go into details, but I have to go out to L.A. today and talk to the engineers. And I wondered if you'd like to accompany me."

"You mean to Los Angeles?" Her heart began to race.

"Well, yes. If it's not too inconvenient."

"When would we be leaving?"

"Today at about two."

"Today." She glanced at her calendar. "All right, but I have to be back by Thursday at seven. Could I get a night flight back tomorrow so that—"

"I have my own Lear, Kate."

His own Learjet? Because Blaine was so down-to-earth, it was too easy to forget that he was also very wealthy.

"So there'll be no problem about getting back by Thursday evening," he was saying. "How about it?"

"It sounds good." All she could think of was of being alone with Blaine on a three-thousand-mile trip.

"I'll pick you up at twelve, twelve-thirty. Can you be ready?"

"I— Yes. Of course."

"Great. See you then, Kate."

She had no idea what to bring or even how many bags to pack. She had come far in the world, true, but it was still a very circumscribed world bounded by Meade Hall and her condo. Though she had traveled many times on vacations, she was not accustomed to just dropping everything and jumping aboard a plane. Until now, a trip, for Kate, had meant at least a week's planning, a week's anticipation of the problems and pleasures to come, a week in which to get her hair done, buy some comfortable shoes, assemble a clever wardrobe that could convert from day to nighttime use with but a few changes in accessories. Now, with only hours in which to get ready, she flew from one end of her condo to the other. First she dragged out the suitcase, throwing in essentials like toothpaste, underwear, a nightgown, curling iron, hair spray, makeup. Then she plowed through her closets. What did they wear in L.A.? Whatever, it was bound to be lightweight, now that it was July. She didn't even know where they were going exactly. After considering taking several outfits, she finally pulled out a white linen suit that would cover all contingencies and two blouses to wear with it—one a subdued businesslike blouse to wear under the jacket; the other, a soft plunging pale blue silk that tied at the waist, was suitable for evening and was not meant to wear with a jacket. She selected accessories appropriate to each outfit and packed them. Then she packed shorts and a T-shirt, jeans and a pink ruffled blouse, a pair of pumps for the suit and sandals for the shorts and jeans. For the plane itself she would wear a crisp green-and-white floral-print cotton sundress with a halter top. With it she would wear open-toed white heels.

There; that would cover two days, she thought as she rushed for the shower. And she'd better start getting used to packing. After the record came out it was conceivable that people around the country might start asking her to be guest conductor. She'd better have half-packed luggage in readiness, outfits cleaned and set to go. Scooting from one end of the country to another might soon become as casual a matter as driving over to Meade Hall. She smiled. It was so hard to believe.

In the plane, Kate tried at first to be casual, as though she were accustomed to hopping aboard private Learjets every day. But her act didn't last through takeoff. "My goodness," she heard herself exclaim as she glanced from the leather chairs to the desk, the stereo, the bar, the thick wine carpeting. "It's like a flying living room!"

The ride was smooth. They had to stop for refueling only once, in Denver. There was a steward who served hors d'oeuvre, drinks and dinner but otherwise kept to himself in the galley. The conversation between Kate and Blaine, however, never got so personal that the steward or any-

one else could not have overheard it. They sat facing each other in identi-
cal soft leather chairs talking about the crash, Blaine's hospital stay, the
Independence Day concert, Harold Rawlins, the construction of Blaine's
Whittenburg auto factory, the role of Pickett in the Civil War and Kate's
problems with Maesterling Recordings. They were in the air eight hours,
and never did Kate ask him where he planned to take her once they were
in California. In the back of her mind she had figured it out. They'd land
at LAX, he'd install her in a hotel and then he'd run off to his western
plant to settle the matter of the new Eddington engine's being the possible culprit in Blaine's accident. If the problem was pinpointed quickly, he
would return to the hotel, take her out for a late dinner, and then retire to
his own suite. Tomorrow he'd spend much of his day at the plant, probably taking her with him, and part of it giving her a tour of L.A.—empha-
sizing Hollywood, which she had never seen. Then another dinner, home
to the hotel and back to the airport the next day. She did not overlook the
possibility of something intimate occurring at the hotel but she did not
dwell on the thought. It would be best, she decided, to take things as they
came.

". . . So if the performance meets with your approval," Blaine was
saying, "they're going to package the record of the Whittenburg?"

"That's right."

"That sounds exciting. Any ideas yet on the pieces you'll select?"

"One of them will be your grandfather's favorite, the *Pavane.*"

He nodded. "*Pavane pour une Infante Défunte.* I always thought that a
most peculiar title."

"They say that Ravel originally called it just *Pavane pour une Infante*—
dance for a female child—but decided it didn't sound 'finished' enough.
So he added the *Défunte* for effect."

"Really? He just threw in the French word for 'dead' because it
sounded good?"

"It is crazy, isn't it? That's why some orchestras play the piece as
though it were a dirge."

"You don't play it that way, though."

"No," she said.

"Kate, what will happen if you and Maesterling can't agree on the
quality of the recording?"

"I shudder to think." She shook her head. "If we can't come to terms, I
guess there'll be no recording because they and I share the final word on
what will be pressed and distributed."

The steward moved quietly past them, went through the door to the flight deck and returned in a moment to say, "Will you and your passenger please fasten your seat belts, Mr. Eddington? We'll be landing in a few minutes."

The plane began to descend rapidly. Kate held her breath. This was always, to her, the most nerve-racking moment in a plane trip. But at last the wheels touched down and the craft screeched to a halt. It rolled quietly across the tarmac for what seemed an endless time and finally stopped. After Blaine had a word with the captain, they descended the steep airplane stairs. Someone hurried over to fetch the luggage being handed down by the steward. Kate's heart began to race. And now what? she wondered.

As she had predicted, Blaine had wanted to stop at the plant immediately. They flew into Los Angeles by helicopter and landed on the pad atop the Eddington Motors building. Kate waited in Blaine's luxurious office suite while Blaine conferred with his engineers. He came back in a short time to report that the motor design would be altered slightly to safeguard against oil leaks. Then he said, "All right, skylark, back to the roof."

"Where are we flying to now?" she asked. She hadn't yet set foot on Los Angeles soil.

"To my house. I've called Bromley—"

"Who?"

"Ed Bromley, who takes care of the place. He'll have a light supper waiting." It was now early evening, but by Eastern Time it was well into the night. Though they had eaten a heavy meal on the plane, they were again hungry.

The flight into the mountains was breathtakingly beautiful but frightening too, especially when they were descending. As they set down in a small clearing among towering evergreens Kate closed her eyes and prayed aloud. Blaine said, "Are you afraid of choppers?"

"How did you guess? Blaine, aren't we ever going to *drive* anywhere? I thought California was supposed to be automobile heaven. Here I am with a sports car manufacturer and I have yet to see a single car."

He began to laugh. "I'll drive you back."

"After supper?"

"I hadn't thought it would be that soon," he said, gesturing ahead toward a stunning redwood house in the side of a mountain. "I was hoping you'd spend the night. In a guest room," he added hastily, clearing his throat. "We're fifty miles from a hotel, Kate."

"Fifty miles?" She hadn't been aware of how far the chopper had flown.

"A long drive, too, because of all the hairpin turns on the mountains."

"To me it just looked like bumpy terrain."

"Mountains do look that way from the air." He took her arm as he led her up a walkway. One side was hedged with beds of flowers. The other side was a stone wall overlooking a steep grade. "Here's my place. There's no front entrance per se. The 'front' overlooks the valley."

Kate caught her breath. The house looked like a set of four stairs glued to the side of a mountain. "How does it stay put?" she asked.

He laughed. "I'm not sure I want to know, but the architects gave us their word that it wouldn't fall into the abyss."

While Bromley put the finishing touches on supper, Blaine showed Kate the house, which was in four tiers, each a bit more recessed than the tier beneath so that the terraces on each level were exposed to the sky as well as the mountains. The very top tier, to which he took her by elevator, had a skylight as well as floor-to-ceiling windows. To stand in it was to feel oneself suspended in space. It was, Blaine explained, the place where he usually entertained. Often it had been converted into a ballroom.

Kate, who had had quite enough of heights today, found herself shrinking toward the center of the sparsely furnished room.

He smiled. "Do you have acrophobia?"

"I didn't think so until today."

"Most people are a bit taken aback by this room at first. But they get used to it. And after the sun sets people tend to forget how high up they are. Although one night, when Amanda had invited a number of people out for a dance, a helicopter pilot flew back and forth peering in and doubtless ogling the cleavage on some of our guests. Amanda finally drew the drapes." Blaine chuckled.

The top tier was a single large room, but the three larger tiers underneath it were broken up into rooms of assorted sizes. Levels two and three each contained a parlor overlooking the valley and several bedrooms. The lowest level contained a large kitchen, a dining room, a parlor that looked more like a man's den, a game room, a utility room and the master bedroom. The garages were not attached to the house but were down near the clearing where the helicopter had landed.

Blaine took Kate into the denlike parlor which he said was the room he himself lived in. It had heavy dark red carpeting, a fireplace, several book-cases, leather chairs, an elaborate stereo hookup, two computers, each with many peripherals, a bar and a small television set. Bromley, an aging and formal man, though casually dressed in the Western style, served drinks with Brie and crackers. Kate had Perrier on the rocks. Blaine drank Johnnie Walker with a splash. Shortly afterward, Bromley served dinner in the dining room, which featured a table that looked as though it could accommodate forty guests.

"I have a feeling," she said, "that you don't eat here every day."

He smiled. "No, I eat in the kitchen. I haven't seen this room in quite a while. But you're a special guest, Kate."

She blushed, smiled and began to eat the light seafood salad Bromley had prepared for them. It featured a remarkable herbed mayonnaise that made Kate eager for seconds. A mint dessert and coffee followed the meal and then they returned to Blaine's den, where he put on some music and poured brandy for each of them. They walked over to the picture window that overlooked the valley. This room, unlike the one on the top tier, had three secure-looking walls for Kate to retreat to whenever she felt acropho-bia threatening.

"You can't see much out there now," he said. "It's too dark."

"That's why I feel safer, I guess. I gather you rarely visit the upper tiers."

"They're mostly guest rooms. This house is very remote and when people come out from the city they often stay the night."

"How many guest rooms do you have?"

"Let's see"—he counted to himself—"ten, I think. Bromley's prepared one of them for you, by the way. Your bags are in there. Originally, of course, we thought there'd be a family, which would have meant bed-rooms for the children and for additional servants. But when Amanda died . . ." Blaine trailed off. As Kate looked away, clearing her throat, he recovered a bit and gestured toward the stereo speakers in the ceiling. "There. Just for you. Daniel Barenboim." She remembered that she had once teased Blaine because he'd never heard of this conductor.

"So you've finally discovered him," she said. "Isn't this *La Mer* every-thing I said it was?"

"Yes," Blaine whispered. And then, without prelude, he bent to kiss her. His lips at first were tender. Then they grew more and more demand-ing . . .

Kate responded urgently, then almost wildly, her heart pounding so fiercely that she thought she would explode. In time he gripped one of her hands and gently led her from the parlor into a bedroom through whose ceilings *La Mer* could still be heard. The room, which was dominated by a king-sized bed, also had two heavy bureaus, a large desk and a leather chair. As in the parlor, there was one huge window facing the valley but in this room the drapes, in a bold black-and-brown geometric print, were drawn. Blaine walked her over to the bed.

The music crashed around them until the beautiful and terrible pressure was released. Then they lay in spent abandon on top of the spread, which neither of them had thought to turn down. Their hands moved lazily over one another's sated bodies.

"Oh, this is good," he said.

"Yes," she said, sighing, wondering whether she'd finally found heaven.

Much later, after they'd dozed awhile, she said, "What about Mr. Bromley? What if he finds out I'm in here with you?"

"Do you care?" Blaine asked.

"Of course I care. He'll think me a wanton woman."

"Oh, Kate." He began to laugh helplessly.

"I'd better go up to the guest room. Can you show me how to get there? Is there a staircase—"

Blaine sighed. "All right." He groaned and got out of bed. "Here, I'll get you one of my robes. We can carry your clothes up . . ."

But in the guest bedroom, she did not at once go to sleep. Blaine would not leave until they had made love once more—a gentler act this time; they were able to spend more time savoring one another's bodies. But at the end, during the brief seconds when the acute phase of the pleasure convulsed her body, she cried out his name. A moment later she looked up to find him staring at her oddly, his mouth slack, eyes glazed.

"Blaine, what is it?"

He shook his head.

"Was I too—shameless?"

"Good God, no! No, you were wonderful. You—" He broke off, looking first at her, then at the room and again at her. He stared for a long time at the glass doors which led to a terrace and there was fear in his face—as though he too were wondering just how this house managed to keep from sliding. It was all too confusing to Kate. Before she could reason out his abrupt change of mood, he had kissed her quickly and left the room, saying he'd see her in the morning.

Kate watched him depart, still wondering what had been troubling him.

But she was so exhausted from the day's sustained pleasures that she could not think. She yawned and closed her eyes. Whatever the problem was, they would solve it, she thought. They would have to solve it because he must know as well as she did that they were meant to be together. This glorious night had shown them that.

CHAPTER 22

Tired though she had been the night before, Kate awoke early. Sunlight streamed into her room through drapes that had not been fully drawn. Like most of the rooms in this house, this one had a valley view. Kate opened the drapes and stood for a long moment looking at the surrounding mountains, one with snow still visible on its peak. There was a terrace outside with a white wrought-iron table and matching chairs that reminded her of Whittenburg's favorite ice cream parlor. Kate pulled back the sliding doors, stepped outside and breathed deeply of the brisk mountain air. It was chilly. She tied her flimsy robe a little tighter and sat in one of the chairs, wondering whether Bromley was going to serve her breakfast here, wondering whether or not Blaine would join her.

She remembered last night and felt a flush stealing over her cheeks. They had acted with such abandon, both of them, that she could scarcely believe it had been Kate and Blaine. But it had been glorious, so exquisitely delicious that she knew she would never forget it. The second time, up here in the bedroom, she had cried out his name, she remembered. Now she recalled that a moment later his face had seemed very troubled. He had gazed for a long time at the sliding doors to this terrace and she had imagined that he was thinking the house was going to slide into the valley. Why had she imagined that? What had there been in his expression to indicate that he feared this? Kate shook her head. She did not understand. She wondered if she ever would, for he seemed most reluctant to share his feelings with her, though he had once promised he would.

Kate rose from the terrace table and went back into the guest room, where she showered, applied a light coating of lipstick and put on jeans and the pink ruffled blouse. She ought to have brought a sweater too, she thought, but how could she have anticipated, in steamy Whittenburg, that she would end up in a place where the air was cool even in July? Dressed, she wondered what she ought to do now. Should she go down to the kitchen and look for Bromley? Or should she wait for Bromley or Blaine to knock discreetly on the door?

She decided that for now she would explore the rooms on this second tier, starting with the large one adjacent to the guest room. Kate walked in and saw that it wasn't a bedroom at all but a kind of study with a long glass slab top facing the window. It was used as a desk. The room was all done in pastels, even the bookcases. Flowering plants were everywhere, making the study look like an English garden. Kate knew that this room had been Amanda's, for Blaine had once described it to her. What Kate had been unprepared for was the fact that nothing in the room had been changed. It seemed to have been preserved as a kind of shrine. The books that Amanda, a microbiologist, had once used, were still on the glass slab, still open. A notebook and a pencil lay next to it. There was a Wedgwood cup to the right of the pencil. It was clean, but Kate knew that this had been the last cup Amanda had drunk from. Next to it there was an earring. Amanda had probably removed it absently while puzzling over some problem.

Kate noticed a few photographs at the other end of the desk. She picked up the first one. It was a picture of Blaine and a pretty young woman with short blond hair standing in a clearing near the house. The woman was Amanda, certainly, but why did she look familiar? Kate puzzled over this and then picked up another framed photograph. It was the same woman's face, but here she was in a gown and her hair was much longer. This version of Amanda seemed even more familiar than the other photo. Kate looked at it for a while, wondering why. And then, in a flash, it hit her. Amanda bore a marked resemblance to Kate!

It was odd, she thought, that Blaine had never told her. It was stranger still that Whittenburg people, who had seen Amanda's picture in national magazines, had never remarked on the resemblance either. But then Amanda had been a blonde and the short hair style might have emphasized different features. Kate had always worn her hair long.

Kate took a deep breath, walked over to Amanda's chair, sat down hard and closed her eyes. The story was falling into place now and she could not bear it. She wished she could run from the truth like a colt running down the mountainside. But it had to be faced. She forced herself to remember the day Blaine had first met her on the steps of Meade Hall. How he had stared at her! Stared and stared and then turned abruptly and run from her as though from a ghost.

He had been drawn to her because she'd looked like Amanda. Again and again he had come to her in spite of himself. Again and again he had pulled away at the last moment, doubtless chiding himself, "You fool.

She's not Amanda. She never can *be* Amanda!" Yet still, against all reason, he would return to Kate, seeking what he could never have again. Even last night . . . last night . . . Kate gulped and blinked back tears as she remembered that after the second time they had made love he had left the room, a look of desolation in his eyes. Had the act of love finally convinced him, as nothing else could, that Kate Reston was not and never could be Amanda?

Kate let the tears flow. She knew now that it was over. If Blaine was awake now, would he be realizing this too? What should she do now? Should she stay around and make polite small talk over breakfast? Should she allow him to take her on a tour of the mountains and later Los Angeles? Kate shuddered. To gaze on that dear face, now forever lost to her, would be agony—especially now, after they had finally come together. No, she could not do it! And yet what choice did she have?

Kate glanced at her watch and saw that it was still early, just after seven. Downstairs no one was yet stirring. If both Blaine and Bromley were still asleep, it would be possible to sneak out of here, she thought. But where would she go? She was fifty miles from the nearest town and hadn't the foggiest notion of how to get out of the Sierra Nevada mountains, much less back to an airport. Still, there was a road leading away from this place. She'd call a cab to take her to the nearest airport, but one way or another she would find her way out of here. First, however, she must leave a note for Blaine.

She tore a page out of one of Amanda's notebooks and wrote, "I understand now, Blaine, and I think you do too. I'm sure you'll agree that it would be best if we did not see one another again. Should we meet again in Whittenburg and you be tempted, please try to remember what happened to you last night and cling to that recollection. You've got to make yourself face the truth." She scrawled "Kate" at the bottom of the note, went back to the guest room, made the bed and left the note on top of the tautly drawn bedspread. Then she walked slowly toward the stairs.

She had seen a telephone in the hallway downstairs and she was determined to call a taxi and get away as quickly as possible. Once downstairs she saw the phone and made for it, but, having picked it up, she didn't know what number to dial. What was the phone number of the nearest taxi? Where was the phone book? She thought perhaps she should call information but she didn't know the address—or even the name of the town—in which Blaine's house was located.

"Can I help you, miss?" Bromley was walking toward her.

Kate felt embarrassed. She had wanted to get out of this house without being observed by Blaine or by his servant. But she did need help. "Uh, a sudden emergency just came up and I need to get back to Pennsylvania. Could you give me the telephone number of a taxi? I have to catch the first plane back."

"Let me do that for you, Miss Reston."

Kate handed Bromley the phone. "Thanks. I'd appreciate it."

Kate headed back up the stairs to get her luggage. "I'll be down in a minute," she called to Bromley as she began racing upstairs.

"Up so early?"

Kate turned at the sound of Blaine's voice. Her heart sank. He had a big smile on his face and he was walking toward her. "Yes. I—uh—just remembered an important appointment with—uh—Maesterling, and I have to get back to Whittenburg as soon as possible."

Blaine looked stunned. "Back to Whittenburg? Today?"

"Now," Kate said emphatically and turned to continue up the stairs.

"Wait a minute, Kate." Blaine came running up the stairs after her.

"Excuse me, miss." Bromley stood at the phone. "What time shall I tell the taxi to be here?"

"As soon—" Kate started to say, when Blaine exploded.

"Taxi! Why do you want a taxi?"

"I thought I would—" Kate found it painful to explain all this to Blaine. How she wished she could have gotten out of the house before Blaine awakened. "I need to—" she began again.

"Cancel that, Bromley," Blaine said. "I can take Miss Reston to the airport."

"Yes, sir." Bromley put the phone back in its cradle and discreetly headed for the kitchen door.

"Now, Kate, I want this straightened out." Blaine took hold of Kate's arm and hurried her up the steps. At the top of the steps was a large parlor and Blaine sat her down in an overstuffed blue brocaded chair. He sat down in the companion chair. "Tell me what this is all about." Blaine's face was dark and his eyes barely hid his anger. "Why were you about to sneak out of the house?"

"I wasn't sneaking," Kate said, trying to act as self-righteous as possible. "I realized this morning that I had forgotten about a prerecord conference I had with Maesterling." The excuse sounded weak even to her ears.

"Suddenly? Just this morning?" Blaine's words seemed to be controlled fury.

"I have an appointment. I had hoped to avoid a scene," Kate said, for the first time that morning looking Blaine squarely in the eyes.

"Why should there be a scene?" Blaine said. She had the feeling of an imminent explosion. "What happened between last night and this morning?" He stared at her, his green eyes darkening.

"Last night was—last night." Kate did not know how to tell him that the previous night had been one of the most thrilling, most satisfying ones of her life. That her love for him had reached even greater heights. Nor did she want to say that she now knew that he was involved with her only as a way to bring his dead wife back to life.

"What about last night? I thought the feelings were mutual."

Kate could feel Blaine's anger. "It was, but . . ." How could she tell him that this morning she understood why he had made love to her with such abandon, such passion? And explain further that she wanted to be loved for herself and not as a copy of some dead woman? "Last night was last night," she finally said. "This morning I realize that we have too many problems."

Blaine gave her a hard look. For the first time he seemed to back down. "There is a problem," he admitted. "But I thought I could solve it in time." He visibly slumped in the chair.

Kate said sadly, "Time won't change this." Now that Blaine had spent his anger, Kate seemed to regain some of her composure. And some feelings of sadness for him. How terrible to have to go through life loving someone who could never be there, could never return your love. And yet how wonderful the years of his marriage must have been, loving his wife the way he did. She felt a little envy for his wife, the Amanda she saw in the pictures. "The best thing for us to do," she said softly, "would be to go our separate ways. That way, neither of us will be hurt."

Blaine looked up at Kate, a sadness in his eyes that caused Kate intense pain. She turned her eyes away. "I suppose you're right," he said. "But that's no reason for you to slink away in the wee hours of the morning."

"I thought that it would be easier on both of us this way."

"To leave without an explanation?"

Kate could almost feel Blaine's thoughts about his wife, who had left suddenly, "without an explanation." Her heart felt heavier than she could bear. "I did leave a note on my bed, Blaine. I knew you would see it." She thought suddenly of the bed and of how it had been the place of pleasure last night. Now it would bring her and Blaine only a feeling of emptiness.

Blaine took Kate's hand, holding it between his hands as gently as if it were a flower petal. "I'm glad I had this chance to talk to you, Kate. A note would not have been sufficient." Then he stood up, pulling her up as well. She could feel herself swaying toward him, and knew that if she got close enough to kiss him she would be lost.

"Then will you help me get to the airport?" she said, stepping away from him and walking toward her room.

"Yes, but reluctantly. I'll miss you."

Kate felt that if she said one more word she would burst into tears. She swallowed hard. "Then would you ask Bromley to call the cab for me?"

He shook his head. "I'm responsible for your being here and I'll make certain that you get home safely."

Kate knew nothing of where she was and so she relented. "All right."

Blaine turned and went down the steps. "Bromley will get your bag," he said without looking back.

Kate went into the guest room. At last the mystery had been solved, but in a way she wished it hadn't. She wished that her relationship with Blaine could have gone on just a little while longer, so she could have more memories that she could take out and look at when she got lonely and unhappy. As it was, there had been very few precious moments.

But, Kate consoled herself, if the relationship had gone on much longer, she did not know if she could have walked away from it. Perhaps if it had continued she would have had to content herself with being Amanda's stand-in, just to be near Blaine. Kate was confused, unhappy and uncertain as to whether or not she had done the right thing. A knock at the door interrupted her reverie.

"Come in," she called.

Bromley stood there. "I can take your luggage now, miss."

"Thank you." Kate hoped she didn't look as devastated as she was feeling.

"The helicopter will be taking off in fifteen minutes," Bromley continued. "Mr. Eddington suggested that you meet him downstairs as soon as possible."

"All right. Thank you, Bromley."

Bromley took the suitcase and closed the door behind him.

Kate looked out of the window of her bedroom. The view of the valley juxtaposed against the mountains took her breath away. There was something magical about mountains, the way they joined clouds, earth and sky. She believed she was as close to heaven as anyone could possibly get. Perhaps the beauty of this place would help Blaine to heal eventually, to recover from the death of his wife. And perhaps, if he met someone who did not look as much like Amanda as Kate did, he might have another relationship. But Kate knew that Blaine could never be hers. Not fully. After one last look out of the window she left the room.

Blaine was standing in the entrance foyer, wearing a conservative navy suit. "We had better leave for the helicopter pad," he said. His voice was formal and correct, as though he were talking to one of his business associates.

Kate responded in the same way. "I'm ready. If I've forgotten anything, though, I'd appreciate it if you could send it on to me."

"Certainly."

The two of them walked to the helicopter. Their conversation dealt with the weather, the forthcoming record date and how long it would take for Kate to fly home. But the warmth of the previous day was missing. Kate was now speaking to someone who was no longer part of her life.

CHAPTER 23

On the evening that Maesterling, was to record her, Kate paced up and down the floor of the greenroom. A little bit of nervous anticipation was healthy; her feeling this evening was not. Her break with Blaine Eddington several weeks before had left her with an emotional void that seemed to affect everything she did. And the knowledge that the performance this evening might make her into an international star or leave her in the position of local yokel heightened her nervousness. She hoped that her personal problems would not in any way interfere with the performance.

She tried to focus on the performance this evening. Although she had originally anticipated that Maesterling would record one of the symphony's scheduled concerts, the board of directors had voted against that. Malcolm had explained that by scheduling one additional concert, the orchestra could raise revenue. And so the concert to be recorded live was touted among the members of the Whittenburg Symphony as a once-in-a-lifetime opportunity to be part of a recording session. Ticket sales had gone well and, according to Malcolm, the whole house had been sold out almost as soon as the extra concert had been announced.

Kate wondered if Blaine had bought a ticket. She hoped not. If she were to see him in the orchestra, especially if she were to see him with another woman, she might lose her composure. And too much was riding on this performance, too much for the Whittenburg Symphony Orchestra and for her personally.

"Five minutes, Miss Reston." The call was accompanied by a knock on the door.

"Thanks," Kate called.

Kate looked in the mirror for the twentieth time. Her makeup was as perfect as she could get it. She checked her gown. The navy blue silk clung nicely to her body, the jewel neckline and long sleeves giving it a demure look. She knew that there would be photographers in the audience from Maesterling and some of the photos taken would be used on the record's jacket. The tension Kate felt was even more intense than it had been on the night that she had conducted for the first time. But she knew from experience that once she got involved with the music she would relax. If only Blaine— No, she would have to stop thinking of him. She took a deep breath and walked out of the greenroom.

Around her she could see technicians from Maesterling, young men with earphones and other gadgetry. But she forgot all this as soon as she got to the stage area. She continued walking and as she became visible to the audience applause broke out. Kate continued to take deep breaths and avoided looking at the first few rows. She did not want to know who was sitting there.

The applause continued as Kate climbed up on the podium. She smiled, looking out over the heads of the first few rows and up into the balcony. She bowed and then turned to the orchestra. Lifting her baton she turned toward the French horn player and began Ravel's *Pavane*.

Kate made an effort to concentrate on the music, to eliminate all thoughts of her personal life, and as she was carried into the music the effort became easier and easier. By the time the first selection was over Kate was in full control. The orchestra was at its finest and she was confident that the record would be superb. When she turned to take her first bow, before launching into Tchaikovsky's First, she quickly scanned the first few rows, holding her breath. But Blaine did not appear to be there. Although she did feel some disappointment, she also felt relief. The rest of the concert would go smoothly, she felt.

And it did. By the time the last note had sounded, the crowd was brought to its feet, cheering. Kate took several bows, gesturing for the musicians to rise and join, and then she left the stage.

Once back in the greenroom, Kate succumbed to her feeling of exhaustion. She hadn't realized how tense she had been, how important this evening was to her. And now that it was over, she could finally relax. She wasn't in the greenroom long before members of the audience came swarming in to congratulate her.

"Your best this year . . ."

". . . and I very nearly didn't order tickets!"

"When can we buy the record?"

For almost an hour Kate was busy shaking hands, smiling and accepting praise. At last, only Malcolm and his wife remained.

"You did us proud tonight, Kate. I know you've put the Whittenburg Symphony Orchestra on the map."

"Thanks, Malcolm." Kate sat down in the one stuffed chair in the room. "I really am wiped out."

"You've earned some rest, Kate."

Kate kicked off her shoes. "As soon as I change, I'll be off. And I may sleep for a week."

"Not really, Kate. You have to be in New York day after tomorrow to listen to the tapes. You wanted some artistic input, remember?"

"Oh yes. I forgot how soon it was. That part'll be easy."

"Good night now," Malcolm said as he walked out of the room. "Let me know how things go in New York with Maesterling."

"Will do," Kate said as she moved to close the door behind Malcolm.

The flight to New York was quick and uneventful, but Kate could not help but compare it to the last flight she had experienced, the one in Blaine's Learjet. It wasn't that the seats here were less comfortable; it was that the company then had been so much more exciting. Kate allowed her thoughts to wander to Blaine for a moment. Actually, she admitted to herself, she could not stop them, locked in as she was, unable to do anything physical except open and close her seatbelt. She wondered what he was doing, how he was faring. She thought back to Amanda's room. Did Blaine sit in it often, trying to summon Amanda's presence? Did he go to his California home as one would on a pilgrimage? In any case, she, Kate, was not Amanda, and she did not want to feel as though she were walking in someone else's shoes. Even Blaine had admitted that there was a problem.

When the plane landed at La Guardia Airport Kate got off, feeling a new surge of energy. There was something about New York, something about the people, that made everything move more quickly. It was a city that definitely spelled "life."

The taxi ride to the Maesterling Studio, in Queens and near La Guardia Airport, was short. Once at the studio Kate was greeted by Bill Scott.

"It's great to see you on my turf," Bill announced as he gave her a peck on the cheek. "And here there are any number of wonderful places where we can have dinner. You are staying overnight, aren't you?"

"I hadn't planned to. I thought I would get a flight back tonight."

"But that will still leave us time for dinner."

"If the listening session goes smoothly." Kate was determined not to be overwhelmed by the fact that she was dealing with a national record company. She would listen as though she were in her own living room and be very discriminating about what she heard. It was, after all, her name and her future on the line.

After introducing Kate to several people who were connected with the production of the record, Bill took Kate into the recording studio.

"Turn on the tape," he said. Almost at once the room was flooded with music. Kate leaned back, closed her eyes and listened.

For two hours the music that had filled Meade Hall several days before now reverberated in the small recording studio. Kate marveled at how true the reproduction was. She had been told that the record, when finished, would play for forty minutes, twenty minutes for each side, and Kate would have to select two pieces that would finally appear on the record. Having done that, she would listen to those two selections and make certain that they were the best the Whittenburg could do.

Once the entire tape of the evening was over Bill turned to her. "That was magnificent, Kate. How are you going to make a choice?"

Kate found the choice easy. She would pick the *Pavane* and *La Mer*. There was nothing wrong in selecting the favorite piece of a famous Whittenburg musician and *La Mer* had been the piece she'd heard at Blaine's house. In spite of what had happened, this would always be special to her.

"Play those two selections again. Miss Reston wants to check them out," said Bill.

Once again Kate listened carefully.

When the music ended, Bill sighed. "Those are perfect for the record, Kate. You have a marvelous ear."

Kate smiled. "Marvelous enough to have heard that the flutes sound a little too shrill in the *Pavane.*"

"I didn't think so," Bill said.

"Why don't we listen again?"

"All right." Bill signaled to the technician in the booth to replay the selection.

As the music reached the selection which Kate considered imperfectly done she signaled with her hand.

"Still sounds fine to me, Kate," Bill said when the music had ended.

"But not to me. And according to the contract, I'm the one who has to think so."

Bill signaled the technician in the booth to come into the studio. "This is the guy who makes the decisions for Maesterling. Why don't you discuss it with him?"

"Certainly." Kate outlined the problem she was having with the Ravel.

"I'm not sure I agree with you, Miss Reston, but why don't I try some electronic wizardry? I'll soften the flutes a bit."

He went into the booth and after a few minutes, began playing the music. "Listen to this," he said, his voice coming over the first few notes.

Once again Kate listened. When the imperfect part had finished Kate shook her head. "Not good enough."

"Let me work on it some more."

Once again the technician adjusted the sound and once again Kate listened. "Better, but not quite right," she said.

"But Miss Reston—"

"The contract says I have final say. And I want the Whittenburg to sound perfect."

"Maybe you're hungry," Bill Scott interjected. "It's lunchtime and my stomach is growling."

"Are you implying that I'm not hearing the music properly because I'm hungry?" Kate resented the fact that these two people were questioning her ability to interpret the music.

"Not at all, Kate. But it is lunchtime."

"Very well. But that won't change the quality of the recording."

"I know," Bill said, trying to pacify her. "We'll continue with this after lunch."

Bill led Kate to a nearby restaurant, small and cozy, with wonderful salads.

"Try the shrimp salad plate," Bill suggested. "And how about some white wine to go with it?"

"Trying to make me drunk?" Kate said, amused at Bill's obvious tactic.

"Drunk on a glass of wine? I doubt that," Bill said as he signaled the waiter.

Kate enjoyed the salad and, much to her surprise, felt somewhat more relaxed after the wine. Maybe there was some truth to what Bill had been trying to tell her. Maybe she was determined to find a flaw just to demonstrate her power over the music. No, she said to herself, that couldn't be, but, nonetheless, she decided she would approach her next run-through with an open mind.

Kate and Bill returned to the studio. Once again she listened to the music. The flutes were fine, she thought, but now the French horn sounded too harsh.

"Think you can mute the horns a bit?" she said to the technician.

"We can try."

Once more he adjusted something and once more the music filled every corner of the recording studio.

"How's that?" Bill said as the music ended.

"Perfect," Kate said.

"Oh, good," Bill said, looking at his watch. "There's at least an hour before we can go out for dinner. Would you like to see some of the photographs we took?"

"I'd love to."

Bill led her into his office at the end of the hallway. He took out a folder and there, in glorious color, was Kate, the Whittenburg Symphony Orchestra and candid shots of people who were in the audience. Kate recognized many of the faces.

"They're wonderful. Which ones are you going to use for the jacket?"

Bill looked through them slowly. "We're not absolutely certain, but we're thinking of using these."

Kate looked at a photo showing her back as she directed the orchestra, a view of her from the side, and one shot of the audience, sitting, entranced. "These are nice. I really like them."

"Too bad we couldn't get one of you full face." Bill gave Kate a searching look.

Kate pretended she didn't understand. "Why? It's the music people buy the records for, not a picture of the conductor."

"But this conductor is so attractive."

"Thank you," Kate said. She had long suspected that Bill felt their relationship was more than just a business one, and much as she enjoyed his company, she could never think of him as more than a friend. But she wasn't sure how to let him know without hurting his feelings. In the past she had believed that once the record was done there would be no need for Kate to see Bill again, but she was obviously wrong.

"Can't you stay the night, Kate? We could have a lovely dinner and then—" He broke off, his expression expectant.

"I'm sorry, Bill," Kate said as gently as she could. "I really can't. I have to prepare for our next concert and I want to start early in the morning."

"Then why don't you catch an early flight tomorrow? This has been a long day for you and it would be good for you to relax now."

"That's what I was thinking. But"—Kate took Bill's arm and looked at him as earnestly as she could—"I think I would be much more comfortable in my own home."

"I see." Bill looked solemn. "Is there anyone else?"

Kate could now answer truthfully. "No, there's no one else. If you don't count my job, that is. This is a demanding profession, and I'm just at the beginning. There will probably be time for other people in my life once I've gotten myself organized." She gave him a long look. "But right now, there's no time."

"I'll be passing through Whittenburg soon," Bill said. "Can I call you while I'm there?"

At first Kate was taken aback by Bill's determination. When would this man stop pursuing her? But then she caught herself. Perhaps it would be easier to exorcise Blaine if she were dating someone else. And Bill was a gentle, caring man whose interests were similar to hers.

"Thanks, Bill. You're a wonderful friend." She turned and smiled at him. "I'd like us to continue to be friends."

"That's all I wanted to know."

Within an hour Kate found herself on the return flight to Harrisburg, the nearest town to Whittenburg that had a commuter flight to New York. As the plane roared toward home, Kate found herself wondering. Should she have encouraged a relationship with Bill? She felt again the rightness of her decision. He was a kind, considerate man, obviously in love with her and a person who shared many of her interests. Perhaps, in time, she could grow to love him. Meanwhile, she would have the benefit of a good friendship.

Above all, though, she was Kate Reston, conductor of the Whittenburg. And that was just the start. She would make a niche in the world of music, one that was large enough to fill her entire life. One that would make up for days and nights without Blaine.

CHAPTER 24

It was only a few days later that Kate received a call from Bill. "I'm on my way to Virginia again and my car just happened to stop at Whittenburg," he said when she answered the phone. "And there's a bouillabaisse dinner that I've been wanting to try for a long time. Are you busy tonight?"

Kate hesitated. Intellectually she knew that she should go on with her social life and that Bill Scott was a perfect person with whom to start, what with their common interest in music and his easy manner. But she wasn't sure she wanted to get involved just yet.

"Earth to Kate. Earth to Kate," Bill said into the phone. "Are you there, Kate?"

Kate laughed. How could she turn down a man who was such fun and such good company? "I'm checking my calendar," she lied. "And it looks as though I'm free for dinner."

"Great. I'll pick you up at seven. And this time I'll be on time."

"I'll see you then," Kate said as she hung up the phone. Her hand rested on the phone for a few minutes longer. She hoped that Bill would understand that theirs was a friendship rather than a romance. But somewhere she had read that the most lasting romances were always based on friendship. So perhaps, in time, she might grow to love Bill. There might not be the excitement, the magic, of her love for Blaine. But what good was excitement and magic? she thought bitterly. They burned out much too soon. The less spectacular but more enduring love of a man like Bill would suit her needs much better.

Having decided that, Kate turned to the activities of the day. She was writing out a tentative list of pieces to be performed during the fall season and wanted to go over the list several times before submitting it to the board. The first concert in the fall would have to be impressive and she thought she would start off with a good solid Haydn. She leaned back in her chair and mentally reviewed the various symphonies but soon her mind drifted to thoughts of Blaine. No, she thought firmly, that kind of thinking would have to stop. If she were going to daydream about anyone, it should be Bill Scott. She thought of the evening when she had first had dinner with Bill. The two of them had tried to match music with dinner courses. She laughed to herself and then turned back to her work.

The day passed quickly, although, because it was summertime, there were no sudden crises and no musicians or stage managers with problems. She spent her day trying to contact the agents of guest conductors and soloists who she thought might appear with the Whittenburg during the following season. Things did not go smoothly but there would be plenty of time before final preparations had to be made.

When Kate looked up at the clock she saw that it was past six. With a start, she realized that she would have very little time to prepare for her dinner date with Bill. She put down the paper she had been working on and rushed out to the parking lot. It was only a ten-minute drive to her condo but she did want to shower and change.

Kate would have liked to have time to dwell over her selection of an outfit for dinner, but, in order not to be late, took the first dress she could reach. It was a pale yellow linen sheath and she thought as she slipped into it that it was probably an excellent choice, regardless of the fact that she had given no thought to its selection.

The doorbell rang just as Kate finished brushing her hair and she went to the door. "Hello, Bill. Come on in."

"Hello, Kate. You're looking more beautiful than ever." Bill leaned over and kissed her cheek.

Kate felt uncomfortable, especially as their relationship was now strictly personal. The problem with Maesterling had been solved. Nonetheless, she managed to smile. "Do we have time for some wine?"

"No, much as I would like to linger here for a while. The only reservation I could get at Christopher's is for seven-thirty, so we'd better leave now."

"Fine," Kate said.

The two of them walked down to the parking lot and headed for Bill's Corvette. Looking at the sports car made Kate think about Blaine and his interest in fast-moving cars. Obviously Bill's car was not as expensive or as high-powered as the ones Blaine manufactured, but it did represent Bill's desire to get as good a sports car as he could afford. "What is it about men that make them gravitate toward cars that are capable of great speed?" Kate asked.

"We want to impress the ladies," Bill said, slipping his arm about Kate's waist.

"And you think women are impressed by how fast you can drive a car?" Kate said, her disbelief showing in her voice as she recalled the time Blaine was nearly killed driving around a fast track.

"Why not? We can get you where you want to go more quickly and in greater style than in a plain old sedan."

"Actually, I think men drive sports cars to impress other men," Kate said as Bill helped her into the car.

"Why would we want to impress other men when there are women like you around?" Bill asked, leaning over to speak to her through the open car window. Before Kate could answer, Bill walked around and got into his side of the car.

Kate, although flattered at Bill's compliments, was not comfortable with them. When he got into the car she immediately started a conversation that she hoped would not include comments about her. "Are you going to order something other than steak tonight?"

"Certainly." Bill looked straight ahead but Kate could see the smile on his face. "The food in this restaurant comes highly recommended."

Kate lapsed into silence. It seemed that Bill was determined to flatter Kate regardless of the topic of conversation. Was this going to be how the evening was to be spent? Was Bill going to turn everything into one big Kate-compliment? Kate hoped not, because she found it disconcerting. She much preferred the Bill who made jokes about everything, or even the undisciplined trumpeter.

"How are the records coming along?" Kate asked as they got out of the car and walked toward the restaurant. "Will they be out soon?"

"Probably another month or so," Bill said.

"I can hardly wait to see them."

"They're really beautiful," Bill said. "The designer who created the jacket for the series is terrific. You'll be very pleased."

"Are all the records coming out at once, or is each symphony going to have its record appear separately?"

"We'll probably release them a week or so apart, so that the reviewers will have a chance to discuss each one independently. The public relations office thought that up. Although all of them will be ready at the same time."

"That sounds like a good idea. I'm glad our first record is being produced by Maesterling. It's a good company."

"Not to mention their excellent choice of employees," Bill said, smiling. "Handsome, debonair, charming and able to pick beautiful dinner companions." By this time Kate and Bill were seated at their table and Bill was looking directly at her.

Kate forced herself to smile. "Are you going to order the bouillabaisse or are you going to wimp out and take the steak?"

"I'm a man of my word. The bouillabaisse, of course." Bill gave their order to the waiter and the two of them resumed their conversation.

Bill seemed to take every opportunity to flatter Kate and she was becoming more and more irritated. She wondered if she should mention her feelings to him but decided not to. Perhaps he felt that since he would be gone by morning and would not return for several weeks, he had to let her know how he felt about her. She wished he would not.

After a while Kate could see the waiter coming toward them, but before he had a chance to put the food and wine on the table, Kate's heart stopped. There, walking into the restaurant, was Blaine, along with several other men. She tried to look away, but before she could, their eyes met. Blaine had a surprised look on his face.

Much to Kate's dismay, the maître d' seated Blaine and his party directly in front of Bill and Kate. Whenever Kate looked up, she saw him staring at her. But his look was not one of friendship. Rather, Kate could see subdued anger in his eyes, a mocking smile on his lips.

Although Kate continued in her conversation with Bill, she was no longer fully aware of what was being said. She answered him in a mechanical fashion, more interested in avoiding Blaine than in what she was saying to Bill.

"This food is good," Bill was saying.

"I'm so glad you're enjoying it," Kate said rather stiffly.

"Anything wrong, Kate?"

"Why?"

"All of a sudden you seem terribly nervous. Are you feeling all right?"

"Fine. I guess I'm just a little tired."

"This delicious fish stew will perk you up. Just dig in." Bill ate with obvious relish.

"Yes. Fish stew," Kate repeated unthinkingly as she tried to eat. She was finding it difficult to chew and even more difficult to swallow because even when she avoided looking in Blaine's direction she could feel his eyes on her. If Kate hadn't been fearful of making a scene she would have gotten up immediately and run out of the restaurant. Instead, she managed to finish the food on her plate and was looking forward to the moment when she could leave Christopher's.

Kate looked up to see Bill signaling the waiter. She assumed he was asking for the check but instead he ordered two strawberry parfaits for dessert. "A little sugar is a good pick-me-up," he explained, "and besides, a place that prepares such a marvelous entrée must make an even more marvelous dessert."

Kate started to protest but Bill silenced her. "One doesn't need to be hungry to eat ice cream. It just slides down your throat."

Kate thought back to the time when she had had ice cream with Blaine during the Independence Day festivities. She wasn't sure she could make it through the parfait without breaking down.

Before the dessert came, Bill excused himself. "I'll be right back," he said.

Kate sat alone, looking down at her fingers, breaking up the crumbs on her bread plate into even smaller ones.

"You must have changed your mind," a voice said.

It was Blaine, looking down at her from his standing position. "What do you mean?" she said, a tone of defiance creeping into her voice.

"Considering your protestations about Bill being nothing more than a business companion, I am impressed by this cozy tête-à-tête."

"Everyone has to eat."

"Yes, and eating with attractive companions makes the meal even more exciting."

Kate was ready to tell Blaine the truth, that she was dining with Bill just to get Blaine out of her mind. But she caught herself. She knew that she could never compete with Amanda, and if she couldn't have all of Blaine's heart she would take nothing. It occurred to Kate that it might be for the best if Blaine believed she was having a relationship with Bill. Then he would understand that their romance was finally and irrevocably over.

"What's wrong with attractive companions?" she said in a tone that challenged him.

He did not reply.

Bill came back to the table. "It's been nice seeing you again, Blaine," Kate said as Bill slid back into the seat.

"Right," Blaine said, his voice cold and impersonal. He gave Bill a brief nod and returned to his table.

The waiter brought the parfaits. Bill said, "I guess this is a special place if Blaine Eddington eats here." He put his spoon into the whipped cream that topped the confection.

Kate could not tell if Bill was being sarcastic or if he was just making conversation. But she echoed what she had said earlier. "Everyone has to eat."

Kate ate the parfait in front of her but it was tasteless. She knew she had to pretend to be enjoying the dinner and tried to keep a smile on her face. But if anyone had asked her to recall the conversation she could not have repeated it. All she could think of was that she wanted to leave, wanted never to have to see Blaine Eddington again, knowing that he was the only man she could ever love: a man that she could never completely have.

"Are you ready to leave?" Bill was saying.

"Yes," Kate said, smiling broadly at Bill because she felt Blaine's eyes on her. She hoped that at some time in the future she could be in the same room as Blaine with a certain equanimity, but she certainly hadn't achieved that as yet. She all but ran from the restaurant.

Bill caught up with her outside of Christopher's. "Shall we head back to your place for a nightcap? Or would you care to go to a lounge for a few drinks?"

Kate wasn't sure. Should she continue on with this charade of a relationship with Bill? Then she remembered that it had been Blaine who had made the evening difficult. If he hadn't come into the restaurant, everything would have gone more smoothly. She decided to try once again. "Maybe just a few drinks."

"How about the Lincoln Hotel bar?"

"Sounds good," Kate said with more cheer than she felt.

Bill drove to the hotel and they were soon seated at a table in the dimly lit room, where he had once unburdened himself to her. He hadn't mentioned his trumpet in a long time. She concluded that his attempt to discipline himself had failed.

"A Cherry Heering for me," Kate said as the waitress came to take their orders.

"Drambuie, please," Bill said to the waitress and then turned to Kate. "The bar in this place doesn't come up to the cuisine in Christopher's, but just being here with you makes it all right."

"Bill, I wish you'd stop doing that."

"Doing what?"

"You know. Buttering me up as though I were an ear of corn."

Bill laughed shortly. "You certainly have a way with a phrase."

"You know what I mean."

"Yes, I do," Bill said, confusion showing on his face. "But I want you to know how wonderful I think you are."

Kate felt drained. First the confrontation with Blaine and now she had to handle a situation which called for great tact. For it was becoming clearer and clearer to her that while she might enjoy having Bill as a friend, she could never think of him as anything more. And because Kate was fond of Bill, she wanted to let him know exactly how she felt without hurting him any more than was necessary.

"I appreciate your feelings for me. And I think you're a wonderful person, too," she said.

Bill looked directly into Kate's eyes. He seemed saddened. "Your definition of wonderful isn't the same as mine, is it?"

"Not if you mean that I'm in love with you, Bill. But I do respect you and feel comfortable when I'm with you. We have a lot of mutual interests and we have a good time when we're together."

"But you're not in love with me."

Kate looked down at her hands. She could feel Bill's pain and could empathize. After all, who knew better how it felt to love someone without having that person fully return the love? "No," she said softly. Then she looked up at him. "But I wish I were. You're a terrific guy and you'll make someone a wonderful husband."

Bill reached across the table and took Kate's hands in his. "I think your honesty is one of the things I love best about you, Kate, although I'm sorry that it's brought us to this. But I appreciate your being so direct. Other women might have kept me on a string, but not you. No matter what, I think I'll always love you."

"Oh, Bill." Her voice broke. She was silent for a moment. Then she said hoarsely, "I hope we can always be friends."

"Friends," Bill said, swallowing hard and holding up his glass of Drambuie unsteadily.

"And you will call when you come to town, just to say hello?"

"I don't know, Kate. I think it would be hard. But maybe once in a while."

The two of them finished their drinks in silence.

"Would you like me to take you home now?" Bill said.

"Yes, it's getting late."

Bill and Kate went to the car and he drove her back to the condo. Their talk concerned the forthcoming record and the possibilities for sales. Before long they were at Kate's door.

"Good night, Katie. I wish you a happy life," Bill said as he leaned over and kissed her on the cheek.

There was much that she wanted to say to him. She wanted to tell him to keep playing that trumpet, to practice in spite of himself, to hold on to his dreams because dreams were what kept people fully alive. But he was gone before she could tell him any of these things. She hoped that whenever he thought of her he would remember not a failed romance but a woman who believed that he should strive to be the best he was capable of being.

Kate walked into her house very subdued. She was sorry that she could not love Bill. His warmth, his compassion, made him someone to be desired. But love requires more than appreciation. It requires a special spark. And for her, only Blaine had ever had the magic.

CHAPTER 25

A hot dry August came and it withered the grass, burned up the streams, leached the glow from the faces of people who didn't want to see summer go and yet were almost willing to trade vacation time for a breath of an autumn breeze. The third summer outdoor Pops was a fair success though not as well-attended as the first two had been. Kate guessed that everyone was home in air-conditioned rooms watching movies on their video recorders.

Kate had seen nothing of Blaine in almost a month, though she often read about him in the Whittenburg *Clarion*. Equipment was being shipped into his new plant and it wouldn't be long now before Eddington Motors was operational. Unemployed men and women were excited, and few days went by that the *Clarion* didn't carry a letter to the editor praising Blaine Eddington for doing his part to revitalize Northern industry. There were also many articles with photos showing Blaine and other company officials standing in front of the factory or conferring in an office or talking with a congressman. One of these ran next to a story about the Whittenburg's coming recording. There they were, Kate thought ironically, photos of Kate Reston and Blaine Eddington side by side under unrelated but adjoining headlines. It was as close as they would ever get.

Late in the month, Malcolm came into the office one morning to tell Kate that the small Ohio city that had been looking for a musical director was going to begin holding interviews next month. It was time for someone to suggest to Harold that he apply.

"I know it will be difficult for you to tell him something like, 'Harold, take a few days off and run over to Ohio,'" Malcolm said to Kate. "'Let yourself be interviewed and then hang around in suspense for a month wondering whether or not you'll get the job, and think about moving or staying here.'"

Kate groaned. "I don't relish the prospect, but I do know his wife would like to move. She told me they could get a lot of money for the house if they sold now. Developers want to buy the property in that area for apartments and condos for future Eddington workers.

"I'm glad Miriam is agreeable," Malcolm said, "but what if Ohio doesn't like Harold? Knowing him, he'd be at less than his best being cross-examined."

"I know. He's so . . ." Kate trailed off, thinking. "Unless—" A smile crept over her face. "Malcolm, suppose he was interviewed without ever knowing about it?"

"What?"

"The concert we're doing in mid-September is perfect Harold-bait. Beethoven, Haydn, Mozart—"

Malcolm nodded. "A Teuton Trio."

"Suppose we could lure the retiring Ohio conductor and some of his board members over here. I'd get Harold to conduct that night." She'd been intending to do that anyway.

Malcolm nodded. "Good idea. He'd do a first-rate job too, particularly with the Haydn. And meanwhile I'll get those Ohio people out here to see him. I'll tell them the truth. Patience was never Harold's strong suit. I'll just tell them to come, listen and either make him an outright offer or not. No interviews, no suspense." He paused. "It's playing God, I know. Who can say for sure that Harold would shrink from interviews? But I'd rather do it this way than see him hurt again."

Kate nodded. "I know." Then she smiled. "But don't worry. Harold'll knock 'em dead."

Harold was given charge of the mid-September performance and Kate, who didn't want to be around, influencing him even in spirit, took off for Cape Cod, where an old college chum was staying on until October. "Nothing like the Cape after Labor Day," the friend had gushed, though Kate still longed for the Sierras after the Fourth of July. She was gone from Meade Hall for almost a week, through all the rehearsals. But she was back in time for the concert itself. Malcolm introduced her to the people from Ohio, who Harold still did not know were present. They sat in front-row seats, except for Kate, who found an unobtrusive spot in a corner. If Harold knew she was back and watching he might grow nervous.

But by the time the performance was concluded, it was Kate who was feeling nervous. Harold had conducted so brilliantly that she half expected Malcolm to come over and ask her to resign so Harold could be given the Whittenburg. How had he done it? Kate wondered as she watched Harold smoothly guiding the musicians through some of the most difficult passages ever written. She did know that he was tough and temperamental. This week's rehearsals must have been grueling. But he had produced a performance so perfect that if the Ohio people didn't make him an offer on the spot they would surely live to regret it.

Kate was right on the mark. The Ohio people did not keep anyone waiting with promises of phone calls. They made Harold an offer right there in the greenroom, five minutes after bows had been taken. Harold could only stand there stunned. His wife Miriam began to cry but recovered quickly enough, and before they'd even left the hall she was discussing which movers to hire and wondering aloud what the children's new schools would be like. They celebrated at Tony's Pub with musicians Harold had long been close to. So delighted was Harold with the prospects to come that it was some time before he remembered to ask Kate and Malcolm how the Ohio people had come to be there tonight.

Malcolm told the story of how he and Kate had been singing Harold's praises for months, of how they'd heard of this lucrative Ohio post and had lured key people here without Harold's knowledge so that he'd conduct without having to worry about being judged. Harold listened to all this with an expression Kate could not read. At times, she thought, he looked perilously close to tears. Toward the end of the evening he thanked Kate solemnly but there was a look of shame on his face and Kate thought she understood it. He'd been envious of her and sometimes terribly upset because she'd had the job he had wanted and now that she'd done this thing for him he was regretting every nasty thought he'd had.

To put him at ease, Kate said lightly, "You know what I'm going to do, don't you? I'm going to Ohio and convince the board over there that no concert is complete without a Bartók. *Quid pro quo*, Harold my friend."

Harold smiled, but there was strain in it. It would take some time for the guilt to leave him, she thought. But by the same token her own guilt over having the job he had so desperately had wanted was lifting. At last! For the first time since April she felt completely free to enjoy her post.

It was a moment she wished she could share with Blaine. Such moments came up unexpectedly now and then and she felt a fierce longing that sometimes made her throat hurt. But after a while, if she forced herself to concentrate on something else, the pain would gradually pass. It had been like that after the Maesterling triumph. (The record would be out in a few weeks.) It had been so wonderful knowing that all over the nation music lovers would be listening to her orchestra. She had wanted to be with Blaine, to hug him in her exuberance, to laugh in sheer joy as she had laughed so often with him before. But she had ended up treasuring the triumph alone and she was doing so again tonight. Accepting the glass of scotch Harold was now handing her, she murmured to herself, "To Kate. Good show, kid. You really are the Whittenburg now."

At ten the next morning, a Sunday when Kate ordinarily slept late, the doorbell rang before she had even gotten dressed. She threw a light robe on over her short nightgown and went to the door. It was Harold. Far from looking happy over his prospective new job, he looked terrible. His eyes were red and his face was ashen gray. A hangover from last night, Kate told herself as she sat him down at the kitchen table and went to pour freshly brewed coffee. But there was something else wrong too, she guessed, and thought she knew what it was.

"Kate—" he began.

"If it's that you're sorry for giving me a hard time these past months, I do understand it, Harold. If I'd been in your shoes—if the directorship had gone to you—I wouldn't have been the picture of sweetness and light either. It takes time to get over disappointments."

"It was more complicated than that, Kate."

"I don't understand." She set a cup of coffee before him.

"It was more than simple envy. I—I tried to get you fired."

"What?" She set her own coffee down, her face slowly draining of color.

"You went to Malcolm to complain?"

"No."

"To someone else on the board?"

"No. No."

"Then how—"

"I was more subtle. Machiavelli had nothing on me." He pressed his hands against his cheeks and closed his eyes.

"Go on," Kate said tightly. "The whole story. Out with it, Harold."

"At first I thought it would be so simple. Blaine Eddington was so attracted to you that I felt sure he'd marry you in time and spirit you off to California."

"You felt sure?"

"Kate, you know as well as I do that he was head over heels—"

"Primarily because I looked like his wife." She had not intended to blurt that out.

"Did you? Well, if that was the first reason he was attracted, it certainly wasn't the primary reason."

"You don't know what you're talking about, Harold."

"I do. I've had drinks with the man and I'm fairly certain I know how he feels about you." He sipped from his cup. "Anyway, I thought that if you married Blaine and moved to California the job would be mine. Simple. All I'd have to do would be to subtly encourage the romance. But then I realized he wouldn't be moving back there. If he did marry you, you'd both stay here and they'd keep you on as director. So there'd be no point in my matchmaking."

"Go on."

Harold swallowed hard. "My next idea was to think of something that might affect your stage performance. You know how upset Malcolm gets when a conductor seems nervous or uncertain?"

Kate stared at him, her lips a hard line.

"So—so I thought about the sorts of things that might upset you and again Blaine came to mind. What would disconcert you most, I thought, was being uncertain of his affections. So one day I'd be at pains to tell you how lovely he thought you were and the next day I'd remind you somehow of his other women. This uncertainty would result in at least a few botched performances." His hands were covering his face now. Kate was remembering how Harold had talked about the "gossip" between Blaine and the society woman he'd escorted to the memorial concert. Rage threatened to burst her veins. And now she fairly shouted, "Go on!"

But he could not talk just then.

"All right; then I'll finish for you!" she yelled. "So you'd mention first that he liked me and then you'd mention some other woman and pretend that you were dismayed by the prospect of his caring for anyone else. You were supposedly on my side so that I'd never suspect what was going on. Meanwhile you arranged it so that I nearly wrecked a performance and a rehearsal. Is that how it happened?"

"Yes," he whispered.

"And the night you failed to deliver the message. That was a stroke of good luck you never expected, wasn't it? Getting a message from him to deliver to me? I'll bet you thought I could never perform after that blow."

"I'm going to call Ohio and turn down that post," he said quietly.

"You're what?"

"I don't deserve it, Kate."

She stamped her foot. "Oh no you don't! Oh no! I want you to go. The sooner the better. I want you out of the Whittenburg! I don't want to spend another minute looking at your envious eyes and your unspoken criticisms. Of course you're going to Ohio! You owe it to Miriam if not to yourself." She paced around the kitchen, working her anger out, thinking over the past few months. The man was a diabolical genius, she thought, to have come up with such a clever scheme as this. And so workable too! She'd fallen right into the trap. But why was he telling her about it? He never needed to have told her. He could have just quietly slipped away to Ohio without Kate's ever being the wiser.

"Why have you told me this, Harold? Because you couldn't live with the guilt of treating poor naïve Kate so horribly?"

"That's part of it, of course."

"All right; fine. You've done your confession. Does that make you feel better?"

He sat up straighter. "It is true that I feel guilty, and, yes, confession does make me feel better." He cleared his throat. "It was just that I wanted to try to undo some of the damage."

"What do you mean?"

"I wrecked things so successfully that it's over. I know it is; I never see Blaine around anymore. And I thought it would be only fair to lay the facts before both you and him—"

She shook her head. "It's over, yes, but not because of what you've done."

"I can't believe that."

"Oh, you were successful enough in bringing me perilously close to career disaster, but as far as Blaine is concerned you could never possibly change the situation."

"But if I tell him about the missed message and the—"

She shook her head. "He's in love with someone else."

"He can't be," Harold said. "Or if he is, she must have come into his life very recently. When we used to go pub-crawling together it was you he always talked about."

"Did he?" She was interested in spite of the fact that she was still angry enough at Harold to strike him. Then she asked, "And did he ever talk of her?" Kate was wondering if he'd ever shared memories of Amanda with Harold.

"Talk of who?" Harold said.

"He never mentioned her?"

"Blaine's never mentioned any woman but you."

"We've just established that you're quite a liar, Harold. After that long abject confession I'm surprised you're resorting to lies again so soon, even kind little white ones."

"I'm asking you to believe me now."

She shrugged. "Well, maybe he talked about me because I was the only woman you two knew in common. But I know who he loves and nothing you do or say can possibly persuade me otherwise. So you see? Your little scheme was all in vain. Our relationship ended anyway and yet I've managed the orchestra most capably."

"Yes, you have," he said.

She looked pointedly at the clock.

"All right. I'll be going," he said. "I just wish I could make it up to you."

"My first impulse was to say that too much damage has been done. But if you really want to do penance, do something that would really distress you."

"What?"

"Bartók. Your first performance in Ohio will be Bartók. I may not attend, but I'll be sure to consult the papers to make sure you've done it."

"It's a promise," he said, trying to smile.

She could not bring herself to smile back though. It would be a long time before she could forgive him. But she did say sincerely, "I'm glad Miriam's so happy, anyway."

"Yes." He cleared his throat, thanked her for her part in getting him the new position and left the condo, his shoulders sagging.

She did not watch from the window. She wanted to get the thoughts of his duplicity out of her mind as soon as possible. But she could not erase the words he'd said. These burned in her mind long after Harold had gone: "Blaine's never mentioned any woman but you."

What had that meant? Kate wondered. That she, Kate, was a very adequate substitute for Amanda? Or had it meant something more?

CHAPTER 26

In the days to come Kate thought the matter over very carefully. Perhaps Blaine had enjoyed her company. But the fact that he had never mentioned Amanda to Harold meant very little, for Blaine was not the type to share his deepest feelings with anyone but those who were very close to him.

Much as Kate detested Harold's machinations, however, she would have preferred that they had been the cause of the problem between her and Blaine. The real problem was much more serious. Blaine was still very much in love with Amanda, and it was impossible for Kate to compete with someone who was no longer there. Though Blaine had not admitted that he measured every woman he met against his former wife, he had confessed that there was a problem. Only a blind person could have failed to see what the problem was.

The days seemed bleak without Blaine but Kate was determined to survive. She took care of the needs of the orchestra during the day and scheduled rehearsals for at least two evenings a week. Other evenings she spent studying scores and selecting pieces for future concerts. Kate never went to sleep until she was totally exhausted, for fear that she would have time to think.

The days turned into weeks, and after a while Kate fell into a routine. She worked carefully and conscientiously until she was tired enough to fall into a dreamless sleep. Though her emotions were no longer charged very much, neither was she unhappy. Life settled on an even keel.

As the time drew near for the Maesterling record to be marketed, Kate experienced a degree of elation. She would have enjoyed sharing this accomplishment with Blaine, but even without him, she had to admit that she was excited. One day in October Maesterling at last delivered advance copies of the record to her office. There on the jacket was a picture of the full orchestra with Kate directing. Several inserts showed a side view of her face, and there were pictures of the audience, too. Kate was delighted. This would ensure a good sale in Whittenburg.

On seeing the record Kate found that she was too excited to do any work. She got up and walked around her office for a while and then decided to go down to the record shop. It was one thing to look at this in the privacy of her office, but quite another to see it displayed in a shop for all the world to see.

Kate drove from the hall to a record shop in old Whittenburg. As she entered the shop she could see the clerk putting the last-minute touches on a new display. When he moved away she could see that it was a special rack.

America Plays the Classics, read the top banner on the display. Then, in smaller type, she saw "Live Concert by the Whittenburg Symphony Orchestra." The display was done in varying shades of blue, with the lettering in silver. When Kate moved closer, she could see that though the top pocket contained the record done by the Whittenburg, there were three more pockets containing the records done by other small symphonies, each part of the same series.

Kate was curious as to what selections the other symphonies had chosen. She picked up one of the records in the second pocket and was studying it carefully.

"Has the record of the Whittenburg Symphony Orchestra come in yet?" she heard a man's voice say. She had no need to turn toward the speaker to know that Blaine was in the store inquiring after her record.

Kate's heart began to hammer. She was standing with her back to Blaine, but if she tried to leave the store she would have to turn around and he would see her. She continued to stand with her back to the store's entrance, pretending to be engrossed in the jacket of the record she was holding.

"It's over in that corner, sir," the clerk answered. "It's in a special display case near the classical records."

"Thanks."

In a moment Blaine was standing next to her. Kate's vision blurred and she hoped that the hammering of her heart was audible only to herself. She continued to pretend that the record she was holding was holding her total interest.

"Kate. I'm glad I ran into you."

Kate took a deep breath and turned slowly. "Hello, Blaine," she said as casually as she could. Her throat closed up and she could say nothing more.

He looked at the record Kate was holding. "Oh, I see. You're checking out the competition."

"Yes," she said, glad he had given her something she could discuss without getting tongue-tied. "I wondered what pieces the other orchestras had selected for their debuts."

"And?"

"They're all beautiful. Perhaps they'll give me some ideas for our own concerts." Kate selected another record in addition to the one she was holding. "It's been nice seeing you again, Blaine." She turned to walk away. Kate wasn't sure her legs would move properly but she felt she had to leave before she did something foolish.

"Wait a minute, Kate." She could feel Blaine's hand upon her arm. "We haven't spoken in a long time."

Kate's arm tingled at the point of Blaine's touch. Yes, she thought, it's been a long time. And I'd love to spend a few hours with you. But then the separation would be so painful. Aloud she said, "I'd like to chat. But I have to get back to my office."

Blaine turned to face her. He looked deep into her eyes, his green eyes penetrating hers. "Just because you have a serious relationship with Bill Scott doesn't mean you can't spend a few minutes with a friend."

Kate wanted desperately to be with Blaine. But she knew that the more time she spent with him, the more difficult it would be to leave. She swallowed hard. "Bill and I are no longer seeing each other. It's just that I'm very busy. Maybe some other day," she said, her voice weak.

"Then I insist on walking you to your car," Blaine said. "Here, let me buy your records." He took the albums she held and strode to the cashier.

Kate followed and when the records had been paid for, Blaine said, "I'm glad I ran into you this afternoon, Kate."

"It's nice seeing you again, too, Blaine." Kate felt that the longer she stayed with Blaine, the more likely she was to lose control. She steeled herself. It was just a short walk to her car.

Once they were in the parking lot Blaine stopped walking and turned to face Kate. "I've missed you," he said gruffly, looking into her eyes.

Kate looked away. She did not want to go through the pain of another separation. She would have to speak honestly. "Please don't say that, Blaine. There are too many problems."

"I'll admit there was a problem, but things have changed."

Kate turned and began walking again. "I don't think they could have changed enough," she said. By now they had reached her car. She turned to Blaine. "It's been nice running into you again."

"Just one minute." Blaine's voice was firm. He put the records through her open window onto the seat of the car and then took both her arms. "Isn't our friendship worth a few minutes of conversation?"

Kate could see the anger in his eyes. She didn't know how a brief conversation could change matters but she said, "All right."

Hancock Park was just across the street and Blaine suggested they talk there. It was warm for October, yet the trees were already dressed in their glorious autumnal plumage. Blaine led her to the oak tree he had cherished as a child and motioned her to sit down. Above them the once-green oak was now a striking yellow. He patted the gnarled trunk. "Hello, old friend," he said, and Kate remembered that he had spoken the same words on the Fourth of July.

"I wanted to talk about what happened in California," he said.

There was nothing to talk about, she thought. Although she had never known Amanda, she did know Blaine and understood that the kind of woman who could hold his attention and his love had to have been someone of considerable character. It was understandable that he would cherish her memory.

She said, "I know what you're going to say. That it wasn't fair not telling me from the beginning how you felt."

"I apologize, Kate, but I couldn't foresee then how our relationship would turn out."

She caught a falling leaf and crumpled it in her hand. "You knew when you met me that I looked like Amanda."

"Yes." He knit his brow as though to say, What has this to do with the question?

"And you thought that by being with me, you could somehow be with her again?"

"What?" He shook his head. "What do you mean?" Then he said, "Oh, you mean the time you conducted the Brahms and I didn't stay to listen? Yes, I did think of Amanda then, and I had to walk out. Later, I told you that you were like her and yet quite different. I told you I was talking about my sister, but actually—"

"I know now who you were talking about." She could not hide the bitterness in her voice.

He looked at her, puzzled, and then said in a tone of amazement, "Wait a minute: did you think I wanted you only because you resembled Amanda?"

"Of course that's what I thought. What else could I have—"

"I admit that it's what first attracted me to you, and once in a while I would marvel over the resemblances, but from the beginning you were Kate. Always Kate."

"Then why do you still maintain a shrine to her?" Kate heard herself say.

"A shrine?"

"Amanda's study. The one that has her coffee cup and earring still on the glass slab overlooking the valley."

"Coffee cup and— Oh, that. That was Bromley's idea."

"What?"

"Bromley worked for Amanda's parents before he worked for us. He'd known her since she was a baby. When Amanda died so suddenly, he couldn't bring himself to put her things away. He liked to imagine that she was still there. I allowed it because I spent so little time in the house. And now that I'm building this plant in Whittenburg, I'll be there even less often. So—"

"So it wasn't you who preserved that room?"

"Of course not." He thought for a moment. "Though I can understand why you might have thought so."

"That morning I got up early and didn't think anyone was awake, so I decided to explore the house and—"

Blaine nodded. "That's why you left so quickly."

"Yes."

"But the note said that you understood."

"I thought I understood. About Amanda."

He shook his head as though to clear it. "But I thought you meant—" He cleared his throat. "I thought you meant that you knew what it was that kept me—"

"Kept you away from me," she said. "Caused you to shrink from me, turn away as though—" She swallowed hard and continued. "If it wasn't memories of Amanda, then what was it?"

He looked down at the dried leaves as he murmured, "I didn't want to risk it again."

"Risk what?" she said. "Loving?"

He nodded. "It seemed better not to be involved at all."

So that was it, she thought. He'd been afraid of risking love and losing it again. Now she remembered that he had said that he could never count on serenity and stability. She remembered too that he had once gazed at his redwood home with fear in his eyes—as though it were going to disappear. So it hadn't been Amanda herself who had held him back. It had been the fear of another loss. He had tried and tried again to overcome his problem. And almost always, when they grew close, he had pulled away. Except for that last night in the Sierras. Then he had allowed closeness at last. But afterward he had again been gripped with uncertainty.

His loss had been overwhelming, she realized. But at the same time she knew that there was nothing much she could do about it. He would have to face up to these fears, cope with them somehow and make a decision either to commit himself to another woman or to live in eternal wariness.

She stood up. "I'm glad you told me what the real problem was. You're afraid to care too much. I can understand that."

"Where are you going, Kate?"

She shook her head. She did not know where she was going.

He stood and took her hand. Then, looking away, he said gruffly, "These past few weeks without you have been difficult for me. But I had to learn to face certain facts."

She said nothing.

"The fact that living means taking risks." His hand gripped hers tightly.

She nodded.

"So, if you'll have me . . ." He swallowed hard. "Kate, I want to marry you." His eyes were steady on hers. No longer was there fear in them.

"Kate?"

"Marry you?" Then louder, joyously, "Yes!"

He took her hand, pulled her down beside him and absently patted the old tree as though to say, Some things do last. You did, old friend.

Then he kissed Kate while the tree shed its leaves like a blessing.